PEACE STICK
STEPHEN JOHNSON

First published by Stephen Johnson in 2022

Copyright © Stephen Johnson 2022

This is a work of fiction.

All rights reserved. No Part of this book may be reproduced or transmitted in any form or by any means, including internet search engines and retailers, electronic or mechanical, photocopying, recording or by any information storage and retrieval system, without prior permission in writing from the publisher.

ISBN: 978-0-473-63801-6 (paperback)

ISBN: 978-0-473-63804-7 (eBook)

Cover Design © Willsin Rowe

Printed in New Zealand: www.yourbooks.co.nz

www.stephenjohnsonauthor.com

Peace Stick was inspired by Ulrike Fischer, a schoolgirl who sought a symbol of hope to cope with the most serious nuclear threat since World War II – the Cuban Missile Crisis.

The book is dedicated to the kinder of the world who suffer the consequences of political folly.

Glossary

a
Altstadt old town

b
Bettdecke duvet
Butterkuchen butter cake

d
Dübel dowel

f
Flutgraben flood canal
Frühschoppen early pint

g
Gefreiter private (rank)
Gildehaus guildhall
Glücks lucky
Glücksbringer lucky charm
Glücksklee lucky clover
Glücksschwein lucky pig

h
Hakenkreuz swastika
Hauptbahnhof central station
Hauptpost main post office
Hoheitsabzeichen national emblem
Hufeisen horseshoe

i
inoffizieller Mitarbeiter unofficial employee
Jugendweihe youth consecration

k
Kachelofen tiled stove
Kaffeeklatsch coffee gossip
Kinder children
Kinderwagen stroller
Krämerbrücke Merchant's Bridge

l
Lazarett military hospital

m
Marienkäfer ladybug
Martinshörnchen Martin Croissant
Maschinenfabrik machine factory
Mittagessen lunch

Mutti mama
Mütze beanie
Mosaik East German comic magazine

O

Oberleutnant first lieutenant
Oberschule high school
Oma granny
Onkel uncle
Opa grandpa

r

Rathaus City Hall
Republikflucht republic escape (defection)

s

Scharaden charade
Schornsteinfeger chimney sweeper
Schrankwand closet
Schrebergarten allotment garden
Schulranzen school satchel
schwarz black
Schweinohr pig's ear
Spitzel spy
Stampfer tamper
Stasi State Security
Stielhandgranate stick grenade

Strandkorb beach chair

t

Tante aunt

V

Vati dad
Volksarmee People's Army
VoPo People's Police

W

Weltkrieg world war
Westpaket gift parcel
Westpakete gift parcels

Z

Zuckertüte cone of treats
Zuckerwatte cotton candy
zum Wohl Cheers (toast)

Tuesday, November 8, 2016

Erfurt, GERMANY

INGRID RICHTER SHIVERED; IT WAS COLD IN THE MEDIEVAL VAULTED archway beneath St Ägidien's Church at the eastern entrance to the Krämerbrücke. It had been five years since she had felt the frosty wind that funnelled through that side of Erfurt's famous thoroughfare. Ingrid adjusted her merino scarf, an airport indulgence as she had left New Zealand three days ago. Its warmth would have been welcome during her school days almost 60 years earlier.

Cobblestones reflected lights from the three-storey half-timbered shops and homes that lined the narrow bridge. Ingrid watched a group of Americans dawdle past window displays of wines, cheeses, paintings and antiques. She wondered if the tourists understood that many were luxury items when the city was behind the Iron Curtain.

The visitors blocked her exit from the archway as their guide started a spiel. Ingrid was too polite to push through. She listened as the city's Cold War history was ignored in favour of an architectural monologue about the bridge's construction – date, width, length and number of homes atop the shops – before segueing into a folk tale.

Ingrid knew it all by heart, plus a few stories that were never shared with tourists. They were the creations of her childhood friend, Sylvie Witzenhause. The Krämerbrücke had been Sylvie's favourite part of the Altstadt.

The overhanging houses inspired Sylvie to create fairy tales about heroes saving beautiful maidens from horrible witches or goblins. Ingrid had laughed with every new creation; the characters changed but not the theme of a happy ending.

Sylvie vowed that the Merchants' Bridge would one day be a permanent part of her life, declaring she would only marry a man who could buy her a home on the Krämerbrücke. Sylvie wanted to be the matriarch upstairs while her husband operated a successful shop below.

The sweet reminiscence was suddenly swamped by guilt: Ingrid didn't know if her friend's dream had ever come true. It was a regret that niggled on each trip home, the years making it harder to inquire.

The street cleared as the Americans filed down a narrow passage between the first two shops. Ingrid's heart fluttered. It did every time she saw the ancient access to the river arches; the steps prompted a flashback to a real-life drama involving the despised Stasi. The secret police force had been disbanded in 1990, yet the fear its agents and network of informers generated still caused distress. Ingrid loosened the woollen scarf; the heat flush would pass, but the memory of Pedro's run in 1962 would never fade.

A bell tower in the distance struck the hour, an indication that Ingrid was late for dinner. The Italian restaurant within the Gildehaus on Fischmarkt was a mere 200 metres away. She smirked; her companions would chide her for picking up *bad* habits in the South Pacific.

Ingrid admired the décor of the historic building a few minutes later as she shed the scarf and coat. She had never been inside the Guildehaus. Had the timber panels, lights and curved ceilings looked so ornate during four decades under the Socialist Unity Party? She doubted it. The elegant gabled façade had required repairs during her school days that the State could not afford. The priority was to build schools and homes and create jobs, and to control the population.

Belly laughs echoed around the restaurant. The five elderly friends – three men, two women – were seated at a semi-circular maroon banquette. Smudges of sauce on their plates were the only remains of their macaroni, tortellini, and gnocchi dinners.

Two millennial couples at a nearby table briefly lifted eyes from mobile phones where fingers communicated with the world or their dining companions. The digital conversations resumed as the chuckles faded.

The merriment was caused by recollections about arriving for their first school day in September 1956 with the traditional zuckertüte.

'Gerard stole the best candy from my cone,' said Kurt Neubert.

Ingrid giggled. She remembered Oma and Opa arrived early to help Mutti and Vati ensure she had the best treats. 'I saw Oma smack Gerard's hand away.'

Gerard Mueller shrugged, then smiled. 'Ingrid had formidable family defences. Kurt's and Thorsten's parents were lazy. I got their best westpaket chocolates.'

Thorsten Koehler snorted into his red wine.

Ingrid poked her friend's protruding belly. 'Looks like you haven't lost your sweet tooth. Do you leave candy in your dentist surgery to create more business?'

'No,' said Kurt. 'They're not tax deductible.'

Ingrid joined the new round of laughter; Kurt smacked the table a little too vigorously, Thorsten steadied the wine bottle. She was pleased the friends had re-established a rapport after years of separation. Her returns had been infrequent following the deaths of her parents. She had seen more of Gerard because their mothers had been lifelong friends. Kurt, a university professor, and Thortsen, a commercial pilot, would occasionally join them depending on their schedules. The wait for a dinner with Petra Stelzer had been much longer: the Berlin Wall was still standing the last time they were together.

'I was so pleased when Gerard said you were in town, Petra.' She gestured at the men. 'I've seen these rogues over the years, but that's because they never left Erfurt.' She smiled at the slender, ash-blonde lawyer. 'I understand you rarely get the chance to visit from Göttingen. Are you here to see your family?'

Petra dabbed her lips with a napkin. 'No. They all moved to Lower Saxony to join me after the wall came down. My company sends me here when it has corporate work in Thuringia.'

Ingrid grimaced. It was an unintended tweak of the emotions; German life could do that with a few words about the past. It was no secret among Petra's friends that she had hated the socialist regime and the Stasi. She tried to escape with a false passport via Budapest. Hungarian police were told to look for Petra's red suitcase that had *thoughtfully* been provided by a friend. Her punishment for republikflucht was a year in jail. Petra was expelled to West Germany upon her release, just a few months before the Berlin Wall tumbled.

'I'm sorry I never had the chance to say goodbye.'

Petra waved off the apology. The men busied themselves with refilling wine glasses to cover the awkward moment. Ingrid knew Kurt didn't share the same critical view of the former GDR. The other two were ambivalent. Their careers had flourished during and after the regime.

A waitress arrived to remove the plates, then returned with dessert menus. The distraction gave Ingrid a few moments to recall her attitudes to life in East Germany. She had despised the insidious nature of the Stasi and had been uneasy about aspects of her regimented life. However, she hadn't shared Petra's desperation to flee. Her departure was caused by love after meeting a New Zealander working in Berlin; the authorities had granted an exit permit when they married. Brent had been left at home this time as Ingrid was on a business trip.

Petra brought the conversation back to safer territory. 'Tell me about your job, Ingrid. I hear you are on a recruitment mission. Why would German students go to the bottom of the world to learn English? It would be much quicker to cross the English Channel.'

'It's the environmental and lifestyle appeal. Parents believe New Zealand is cleaner and safer, and they don't mind paying large fees for the opportunity. Many high schools want a share of that market.'

Petra nodded. 'I can understand the fascination, if not the need to pay a fortune for an education.' She twirled her empty wine glass for a moment. 'I wonder what our lives might have been like if we had grown up there.'

'No different, I'm sure.' Kurt splashed wine as he pointed around the table. 'Those two would be still chasing flight attendants and pulling rotten teeth, you would still be a lawyer, and I would still be lecturing bored physics students. The State gave us the opportunities to pursue the careers *we* wanted.'

Petra's lips tightened. Would their pleasant reunion descend into a debate about the rights and wrongs of their former rulers? Ingrid was grateful when Petra broke eye contact with Kurt. Acrimony had been averted, for the moment.

Gerard picked up the menu. 'Help me select a dessert, Ingrid. Should it be tiramisu or panna cotta? Maybe both – and a large bowl of ice-cream. What about you?'

Ingrid laughed. 'I'm not used to such rich cuisine – a herbal tea will be enough.'

Petra made the same selection, then unexpectedly tapped a new vein of guilt for Ingrid.

'I thought Sylvie Witzenhause might have been here. You two were such close friends during school. What happened – did you have an argument?'

Ingrid shook her head. 'We drifted apart when I moved to Berlin in 1972 and she went to teachers' college. My job as a court recorder left little time – or money – to travel home. I deeply regret losing contact. We lived next to each other for so long that we never developed the habit of writing letters. Communications … just stopped.'

Petra offered a reassuring hand. 'She had such a fearless approach to life. I can still recall Sylvie asking Herr Schumann to explain the craziness of the Cuban Missile Crisis to a class of 13-year-olds. Do you remember that?'

'Yes. Sylvie asked him, "Why do the Americans want to drop a nuclear bomb on us because of Cuba?" I'll never forget that.'

Gerard grunted. 'Wasn't that a shocking day?'

Ingrid felt it was more like a terrifying week. For the others, she expected the biggest shock was their teacher declaring that World War III could be upon them within a few hours.

Thorsten brushed a lock of artificially dark hair from his forehead. 'It was so unexpected. The Soviets developing nuclear bombs was supposed to counteract the American threat, not end the world.'

Kurt Neubert nodded, scratched his grey beard. The pot belly, threadbare jacket and wild mane completed the stereotypical ensemble of a professor.

'The American generals were like rabid dogs, desperate to launch their warheads. They wanted to attack the Soviets and their allies – *us* – before the missiles were set up in Cuba. It was *right* that the Russians wanted bases in the Caribbean. The Americans had missile sites in Turkey and Italy. They always had a squadron of nuclear-armed B-52 bombers in the air. The Russians needed to balance that threat. We had good reason to be terrified in 1962.'

Silence descended. Ingrid looked around the table, assuming her friends were thinking about President Kennedy's television address that revealed that fingers were on the nuclear triggers. The Russians were told to remove the missiles and dismantle the launchers or face the consequences.

That ultimatum was not relayed via the East German media; it was shared by their teacher who risked the wrath of the Stasi to do so. He told his students that fate gave them no voice in the conflict, yet they were the innocents who might die if the nukes were unleashed. Along with tens of millions around the world.

The current tension was eased by the arrival of the desserts. The men eagerly spooned their sugary treats. Ingrid felt pious, but slightly envious, as she sipped her peppermint tea. Petra once again turned the conversation to a safer topic.

'You lost contact with Sylvie – why would you stay in touch with this old man?' She indicated Gerard.

'Because Mutti kept telling me about Gerard's *wealth*, hoping to lure me home. But then I found out how many hearts he was breaking!'

That brought more raucous laughter that was missed by the millennials; they had departed, and the restaurant was barely quarter full.

Thorsten paused between mouthfuls. 'How many divorces is it now, Gerard?'

Two fingers were raised between scoops of tiramisu. 'I can't afford the brides like you pilots.'

Ingrid was surprised. 'You and Steffi have separated, Thorsten? She's a lovely woman.'

'Just a trial separation, Ingrid.'

Kurt snorted. 'Yes. While you trial wife number three!'

Ingrid and Petra shook their heads; the men sniggered. 'Nothing has changed. You two always had an eye for the girls. I thought both of you fancied Sylvie.'

Thorsten's lips pursed, Gerard's eyes sought the Pavarotti portrait on the wall, Kurt sipped his wine. Petra laughed.

Ingrid could not suppress a giggle. 'Oh no. Not all three of you – I hope it wasn't at the same time.'

'The glamour fly boy stole her from me in '73.' Gerard's eyes twinkled. 'Luckily, I had a spare girlfriend.'

Thorsten pushed his empty dessert bowl to the middle. 'Sylvie and I had a pleasant summer; we parted as friends. Plus, I knew that Kurt had been secretly lusting after her for years.'

Ingrid looked at the professor; he showed no sign of joining the banter. She thought it wiser to steer the Romeos out of dangerous waters. 'You boys must have led the Stasi a merry dance.'

'They followed Sylvie and me to my parents' Schrebergarten once,' said Gerard. 'The cabin window had a thick curtain; they could only guess what we were doing.'

'Sorry to burst your ego, Gerard.' Petra replaced her teacup. 'They probably bugged the cabin after the first visit. Better check your Stasi file; you might find some *interesting* audio tapes!'

Gerard paled as his friends laughed. It was a rare occasion to find humour in the Ministry for State Security.

'So, what happened to Sylvie?' Ingrid raised a stern eyebrow. 'Did she flee Erfurt in tears after you brutes broke her heart?'

Kurt answered quietly. 'She married a doctor.'

'She's actually a patient of mine,' said Gerard. 'Healthy set of teeth, although it's been about 12 months since I last saw her. She was living on the bridge.'

Ingrid was stunned – her friend's Krämerbrücke dream had come true. She felt the conflicting emotions of delight and guilt.

'I walked past her home tonight without realising. Do you know which house is hers, Gerard?'

The dentist shrugged. 'There are only 32; you could start at this end and door knock your way across and back.'

'I don't have the time. This is my only free evening – I have appointments at four schools over the next two days.'

Gerard retrieved his mobile phone from his jacket. 'I'll call my receptionist. She can access the office files from her home computer.' He walked towards an empty area of the restaurant.

'Maybe Sylvie can join us for a coffee?' Petra said. 'I haven't seen her for … goodness, it must be almost 40 years. I would love to hear about her life.'

Thorsten nodded; Kurt was less enthusiastic. Ingrid wondered if he still carried a torch for Sylvie. His own marriage had lasted five years and there had never been a second trip to the registry office.

Thorsten poured more red wine for himself, Kurt and Gerard, then waved the empty bottle at the waitress. 'Sylvie was always garrulous. She often opened her mouth without thinking of the consequences. Like that day when Herr Schumann announced the end of the world.'

Petra tsk-tsked. 'I prefer to think she had an inquiring mind. Sylvie asked the questions that we wanted to know but were too afraid to voice.'

Thorsten turned to their international guest. 'Was she merely gabby, or truly curious about what brought the world to the edge of destruction that week?'

Ingrid poured tea from her pot as she weighed an answer. 'I think she was a mixture of both. I often had to hush her in public when she was too loud. Queues outside fruit shops could be risky. She would be saying, "Why doesn't the Party ensure there are enough fresh bananas and pineapples for everyone? The Party wants us to be healthy socialists." If something puzzled Sylvie, she wanted answers.

'The same with the Cuban Missile Crisis. It didn't make sense that a war between the United States and the Soviet Union over Cuba should involve East Germany. Particularly, why it should threaten us in Erfurt. She didn't appreciate the risk Herr Schumann took to reveal the danger.'

Gerard returned to the table.

'Good news. I tracked down Sylvie's phone number and called her. She's still living on the river!' He smiled. 'She will be here in a few minutes.' Gerard looked at the empty wine bottle. 'I hope another Italian red is on the way.'

Thorsten waved acknowledgement of his duty. 'You have been away so long, Ingrid, yet those school memories are still vivid. Especially Schumann's bombshell. It was … October … 23, 1962? Was it a Monday or Tuesday?'

Ingrid shivered. 'You have the right date, and it was a Tuesday. But that horrible week started a day earlier for me. Can any of you remember what we did on the Monday?'

Four blank faces provided her answer.

'We went to Buchenwald. It was our third visit to the concentration camp.'

Four heads slowly nodded.

'I have tried to forget those visits,' said Petra. 'We were so young to be subjected to that evil.'

The men reached for their wine glasses.

'I could not erase the memories,' said Ingrid. 'The ovens, the inhumane conditions, the hair and teeth the Nazis collected from their victims. Those sights and the shame – Erfurt's shame for building the crematoria. The guilt stayed with me all the way to New Zealand.

'I found peace in Auckland. But the nightmares of Buchenwald and World War II were fresh in my mind when Herr Schumann walked into the class the day after our visit. It was the longest week of my life. And Sylvie shared much of that anxiety.'

Ingrid looked at the grim faces around the table and was annoyed with herself. Reunions were meant to be fun, chatty – focused on the good times. She had dampened spirits by dredging up dark days. Cuba had been a shock awakening to the realities of the world.

Had Western children endured the same traumas during that worrying week in October? Did they sit in school in America, England, France, India, Japan, New Zealand, ears open for the shriek of the missiles? Did they lie exhausted in their beds at night wondering if they would awaken in the morning?

Or did they have their own childish rituals, like Ingrid and Sylvie, to give them hope of living another day? A chance to become adults, to bear their own children who would grow up to end the threat of nuclear destruction. Ingrid thought of their solution to the madness engulfing the world.

'You talk of difficult times, Ingrid,' said Gerard, 'yet now you are smiling. What has New Zealand done to your mind?'

Ingrid saw the twinkle in Gerard's eye. He was always the cheekiest. 'Kiwis have a quirky sense of humour, but I was thinking about what Sylvie and I did to get us through the crisis.'

Gerard held up his wine glass. 'We were too young to drink, so what was your solution?'

'A glücksbringer to save us – and the world.'

Tuesday, October 23, 1962

Erfurt, EAST GERMANY

INGRID BUTTED AGAINST THE OVEN DOOR. IT WOULD NOT YIELD. SHE WAS trapped, tangled, unable to free her arms. It was stifling; soon the flames would lick at her feet, her nightdress. Ingrid did not want to burn alive. She was a Thälmann Pioneer, respectful to her parents and loyal to the Party. The Nazis had no right to incinerate an East German schoolgirl in Buchenwald.

A distant voice called: 'Ingrid!' It sounded like Mutti.

Ingrid wanted to reply, 'I'm here inside the Nazi oven. Save me, Mutti!'

The plea would not escape her lips. She pushed again with her knees and shoulders, her face rubbing against the metal plate. She felt the raised metal of the horrific words emblazoned there. Her eyes were closed, but she knew what they said:

Maschinenfabrik

J.A. Topf & Söhne

Erfurt

Ingrid was being burned alive in a crematorium furnace made at the factory a 15 minute-walk from her family's apartment in Friedrich-List Strasse. How cruel was that?

'Ingrid! Hurry up!'

Mutti was close.

'Save me, Mutti! Save me!'

Was her scream contained in the claustrophobic chamber, or were the words barely a whisper because of the lack of oxygen? Mutti would never know her only child was inside the death oven. Her strength was fading; the wriggling and squirming could not open the oven door. The flames would engulf her any second.

Light! Freedom! Coldness!

Exasperation.

'Wake up, child! You will be late for school, and I need to get to the shops. I promised your father soljanka for mittagessen.'

Eyes opened to find Mutti nursing the feather bettdecke, the cold spreading through Ingrid a motivation to obey. There was no heating in the mornings, and the single-glaze windows were unable to deflect the autumn chill.

It had been a nightmare; a reaction after a school trip to one of the horrors of Hitler's Third Reich.

The palpitations slowly subsided as Ingrid watched Mutti fold the thick comforter. The sheets were straightened while she gathered warm school clothes: cardigan, white blouse, pleated skirt. Should she tell Mutti about her terrible dream and what she had learned at Buchenwald yesterday?

'Wash yourself and have breakfast. I've sliced and buttered your bread; there is marmalade or honey. The milk has been poured.'

Mutti swept through the curtain wall of Ingrid's bedroom, officially called the middle room. It connected to the master bedroom on one side, the lounge on the other. There was no cause for complaints about lack of privacy. The Party had treated them well: the apartment was big for two adults and a child. They also had a kitchen, bathroom and a little room that frequently was rented to people in need. The housing shortage in East Germany created by air raids during the war was taking a long time to resolve.

Vati had already left for work at the tailor's shop and Mutti was too busy tidying the apartment to talk about childish dreams. Ingrid resumed her morning routine, suppressing the terrors the compulsory concentration camp visit had unleashed. Ingrid wondered if any of her friends had experienced a similar night.

'Sylvie was shocked. Maybe she had bad dreams too?'

The question was rhetorical as Mutti was in the master bedroom with the sweeper. Ingrid could hear it clatter over the timber floor, then go quieter as it rolled over a carpet. Talking aloud as a single child was acceptable, according to Oma. Her grandmother said it was good to share thoughts with the universe; sometimes it provided solutions to life's mysteries.

At least Sylvie would listen as they walked to school. The wall clock told her she had five minutes to finish her meal, brush her teeth, pack her leather schulranzen and meet Sylvie next door outside Number 11. Any longer and her friend's lips would be turning blue from the cold.

Sylvie's winter jacket was not as warm as Ingrid's. Mutti was a gifted seamstress; she had cleverly fashioned many warm winter clothes from westpakete. The regular care packages from Mutti's family in West Germany had been their only access to luxury items since the Berlin Wall completed the Iron Curtain just over a year ago.

Ingrid looked at her breakfast. Usually she would have gobbled it down, but today her stomach was churning after the dream. Yet she could not throw the food away. What would the captives at Buchenwald think of this meal? Was it more than they were given to eat in a day? A week? She could not imagine trying to survive on stale bread, watery soup and scraps.

Ingrid ate quickly, thinking her Pioneer leaders would be proud of her. She was a good young citizen. However, a wrinkle in that relationship had surfaced at Buchenwald. The Party was lying to Ingrid and her school friends.

She had not been able to tell Sylvie about that revelation yesterday on the journey back to the 31st Oberschule. It was about 20 kilometres from Weimar back to Erfurt, plenty of time to share reactions to what they had seen, felt and smelled. Ingrid was sure the odour from the ovens lingered still, 17 years after the last fires had been extinguished. She could almost taste the ash on her tongue.

But nobody had spoken from the time the class exited the camp gates until they separated at school. Not even a whisper between best friends. Herr Schumann had sat alone at the front near the driver. Ingrid noted his gaze never left the road ahead, no glance in her direction, seated next to Sylvie; nothing to indicate the horrific moment they had shared in front of the crematorium.

It was the third time they had seen the horrors of the camps. The shame that had been carefully nurtured by the State was overwhelming. Silence was a temporary balm, even on the walk home from school. But Ingrid knew she must tell Sylvie what she had learned.

The Monday musings swirled through Ingrid's mind as she completed the school preparations. Mutti had made a gherkin sandwich for the long break, enough to sustain her through to the soljanka at lunch. Ingrid pulled her thick coat from the stand and buttoned it to her neck. It reached her bare knees; it was chilly outside, although not yet time for tights. They had to be used sparingly as Mutti preferred to create lovely fashion rather than spend all night darning rips from outdoor adventures. A cloth beanie matching her coat covered her blonde bob. The satchel, with homework and sandwich, was slung on her back.

The sweeper paused momentarily as it moved from the middle room to the lounge.

'Bye, Mutti.'

'Have a good day, Ingrid. Study hard.'

The sweeping resumed as Ingrid ran along the tiled hallway and burst from their ground-floor flat. She never had to look for vehicles in the driveway; none of the six families in the apartment building owned a car. Vati said the waiting time for a Trabant was several years. Besides, most of the important places in Erfurt were within walking distance. There were regular trams for visits to their Schrebergarten, or the leafy Steigerwald, and her grandparents' home in the northern suburbs.

The school was 15 to 30 minutes away, depending on their chatter and the temptations. There were three bakeries between home and the classroom; fresh bread smells were often hard to ignore.

There was no time to dawdle today. The kitchen clock had shown 7.10am as she'd left, and first bell was always punctual at 7.30. Failure to make the class line in the courtyard would result in detention.

Tomas Schumann

It was chilly in the second-floor apartment in Anger on the edge of Erfurt's Altstadt. Heat from the ceramic kachelofen in the living room had died about an hour before midnight. Tomas Schumann considered the morning air bearable enough to avoid wasting precious briquettes until he returned from school. He had endured colder conditions in Belgium during the Weltkrieg.

Schumann took his breakfast bowl and coffee mug through to the kitchen. He was a man of routine; wash, drain, dry, listen to the news report on the bakelite radio. It was tuned to West Germany, as usual. The *enemy* could be relied upon to provide a wider perspective of world politics and events. It was illegal to listen to Western broadcasts in the German Democratic Republic. The Ministry for State Security would never know if he kept the volume low – unless they had microphones in the wall.

He rinsed the dregs of his oats – then dropped the bowl onto the sink. It didn't shatter, but Schumann felt the world was about to fracture. The broadcaster announced that the Soviet Union and the United States were on the verge of nuclear war. The simmering Cold War was about to boil over – in Cuba, of all places.

He pulled a pine chair from the table closer to the radio and listened. President Kennedy told his nation the previous night that the United States had evidence the Soviets were building missile sites in Cuba. Schumann understood the implications: Soviet nuclear warheads could reach every major American city within minutes.

'You old fox.'

Nikita Khrushchev had sneaked a nuclear arsenal into America's backyard – but it could blow up the world.

'You silly old fox.'

The radio volume was increased. Why worry about the Stasi when Armageddon could be mere hours away? Schumann was not normally inclined to morose thoughts about mortality. He had been a soldier in two world wars; the first out of patriotism, the Nazis gave him no choice the second time. Schumann survived both conflicts and the current dictatorship by being adaptable: keep your head down, don't be a target, follow the rules. They were simple tactics, yet enough to keep him alive in the muddy trenches of Flanders, the dying days of the Third Reich and the police state Erfurt found itself inside after the Soviets *liberated* them from the Nazis.

The radio announcer revealed President Kennedy's first response to the Soviet expansion: a maritime and air blockade of Cuba.

'Khrushchev won't accept that.'

The announcer would never hear the rising anger in the rattled teacher.

'The idiots.'

Schumann listened to more extracts of Kennedy's speech.

'This urgent transformation of Cuba into an important strategic base by the presence of these large, long-range and clearly offensive weapons of sudden mass destruction constitutes an explicit threat to the peace and security of all the Americas.'

English was not taught in his school, but the teacher had secretly sustained his language skills via the US Forces radio and a stash of Western thrillers. He noted a more belligerent tone in Kennedy's address, a contrast to the humiliation dished upon the new president after the Bay of Pigs invasion and the closing of the Iron Curtain.

'You've pushed Kennedy too far, Mr Khrushchev.'

His shoulders sagged. For so long the Cold War focus had been Europe. Berlin had been a canker on the Soviet's bum since the Nazis defeat in 1945 led to the joint occupation. The recently built wall was the flashpoint where bullets were already being fired, mostly at East Germans trying to escape to the West. How long would the world tolerate that open slaughter? Schumann and his closest friend, Jürgen, often debated when retaliation would escalate from rifles to rockets, sucking a war-ravaged continent into another maelstrom. And yet it's Cuba where political folly has pushed us to the edge of the abyss.

Schumann rose slowly from the seat as the bulletin ended. He switched the radio off, but it did nothing to quell the fear.

'What about the kinder?'

His students, the dozens of young teens who were his primary responsibility in life, and his greatest joy. President Kennedy indicated he was prepared to use military action to remove the Soviets. He was setting everyone on the path to World War III. That could be minutes, hours or days away. One nuclear superpower had thrown down a gauntlet to the other – who would pull the trigger first?

It was with a heavy heart that Schumann packed his satchel for the day's lessons. 7A was his first class – would they know anything about this threat? Should they know?

Ingrid Richter

'Hello, Ingrid!'

Sylvie was waiting across the driveway. She was the same age – 13 – and roughly the same height as Ingrid, although they were never mistaken for sisters. Her wavy blonde hair was shoulder length, neatly capped by a mütze similar to Ingrid's. Fingers were tucked into armpits, her feet dancing a jig to keep her warm. Sylvie's grey jacket was thinner and older, made in East Germany. Her family had neither relatives in West Germany to send westpakete nor a clever seamstress to shape any traded Western cast-offs into practical fashion for a growing daughter.

'Morning, Sylvie.'

They fell into step, crossed tree-lined Friedrich-List Strasse, ignored the first bakery across the road – it was too close to home – and were immediately at the first turn onto Bodelschwinghstrasse.

There were few cars; pedestrians and children were hustling to beat deadlines. The sky wore its familiar October grey blanket. There would be occasional sunny days in the months ahead but little warmth until spring. The first snow was a few weeks away.

The smell from the brewery near the Stadtpark, two blocks north, was normally welcome. Ingrid loved the aroma of the hops, malt and yeast they used to make beer, but not today, the morning after visiting Buchenwald. Her stomach roiled again.

They walked close, thumbs and fingers wrapped around the straps of their ranzen, occasionally bumping shoulders. 'How did you sleep last night, Sylvie?'

'I was okay.' Sylvie sucked on a strand of hair, an annoying habit that highlighted its length. Her mother allowed Sylvie to grow it longer than most girls in middle school. 'I was upset – like you – by the concentration camp. But I tried to distract myself by reading a story from *Struwwelpeter*.'

Ingrid knew the classic children's collection well. Heinrich Hoffmann's book may have been more than 100 years old, but its stories were still entertaining.

'I read 'The Story of Flying Robert'.'

'You wanted to forget the horrors we saw? By flying away in a storm with Robert's umbrella?'

Sylvie nodded. 'It was a nice thought. I imagined myself being blown south, all the way to the Pacific Ocean. It's hot and sunny all year round in Fiji. The temperature is always 30 degrees.' She pulled her coat tighter. 'I would never have to be cold again. Coconuts fall from the trees. I could eat pineapples and bananas every day, not have to queue at the fruit shop when they receive a shipment. Did you know Germany used to have a colony in Samoa?'

Ingrid shook her head. They reached the intersection with Tschaikowskistrasse. That would take them left, closer to school, if they walked past one of their favourite bakeries.

'Do we have time for a schweineohr?' Sylvie jiggled a few pfennigs. 'I don't have enough for an éclair today.'

Ingrid preferred the chocolate and cream treat over the pig's ear-shaped pastry, but neither appealed.

'We don't have time. Maybe after school. My tummy is feeling a bit strange.'

Sylvie slipped the coins into a pocket and crossed the road, Ingrid in step.

'You were very pale after our school trip yesterday, Ingrid. Did you dream about the concentration camp?'

Ingrid looked around. The street was quiet, just a few men gathered around the entrance of the third bakery at the next intersection. That was unusual at this time of the morning. Normally, the men would buy bread rolls and hurry to work.

A schoolgirl conversation should not be of interest to adult factory workers. Yet, every child had been drilled about the need for discretion with public chatter. The secret police had ears everywhere; anti-social comments or criticisms of the Party would be reported to the Stasi regional headquarters on Andreasstrasse. Ingrid was always anxious when the apartment block's doorbell rang at night. The fear probably stemmed from watching movies about the raids of the Gestapo. She would hold her breath until a friendly voice was heard.

Ingrid's reply to Sylvie was barely more than a whisper. 'I had a nightmare about the ovens at Buchenwald. I was trapped inside – the flames were burning my feet and I could not escape. I was pushing the metal door, but it wouldn't open. I was so panicky – why would the Nazis want to burn me alive?'

Sylvie stopped, placed a hand on her friend's arm. 'That's awful. How did it finish?'

'Mutti pulled the bed cover off – that woke me up.'

Sylvie grimaced and resumed walking. 'I understand we need to learn the history of the camps. Germans will carry that guilt forever. But I don't think it's right to show those awful places to children. We might all have nightmares, and not everyone has an umbrella like Robert!'

The image of a generation of East German kinder flying to the Pacific made Ingrid snicker. She should really tell Sylvie about the most shocking discoveries – that the ovens for burning humans had been designed and built just a few streets away, and that the State had lied about their Russian liberators. The mood of the men at the bakery kept her lips closed.

There were three factory workers – judging by their cloth caps, dark jackets, and trousers – at the entrance to Herr Wenkell's shop. The large baker was standing with them, a smattering of flour on his arms and hands. That was strange; Ingrid had rarely seen him outside the bakery. And he was not smiling. Every customer, whether adult or child, was treated to a hearty greeting by Herr Wenkell. Not that morning. The four men spoke quietly, concern on their faces as the schoolgirls walked past unnoticed. Their low volume was an indication the topic was sensitive.

'Something is wrong.' Sylvie waited until they had rounded the curve into Häslerstrasse to break the silence. That was a rare show of discretion from her friend. Another day she might have blurted her statement within earshot of the men, any one of whom could have been a Stasi informant. 'Herr Wenkell looked worried – they all did.'

Ingrid glanced over her shoulder. The group had broken up, the workers scurrying towards the Stadtpark, most likely to jobs at the brewery. Herr Wenkell had not moved. He stood with hands on his hips, looking at the sky.

'Perhaps someone has died?' Sylvie wrapped her fingers back around the ranzen straps. First bell was close. 'Maybe it was a work friend?'

That was a logical explanation, Ingrid thought. Although, the baker's change of routine was puzzling. It was cold, and Herr Wenkell had a short-sleeve shirt under his apron. Yet he was still on the pavement staring at the clouds.

Within a few metres, the curving street obscured the bakery. Ingrid was about to return to her crematorium experience when Sylvie changed tack.

'You should dream about Pedro tonight. That's more pleasant than concentration camps.'

That suggestion caused a flutter within Ingrid's chest. It happened every time she thought of Pedro or heard his name mentioned. Only two other companions knew that the Cuban had stolen her heart. Sylvie had never met him; Renate Heyn and Katja Reigel had been at the summer camp on the Baltic Sea where the handsome Pedro Barios and his companions had charmed the young allies.

'Perhaps we should go for a walk in the Altstadt after school? We might see him at a café on the Domplatz.'

'Don't be silly, Sylvie.' Ingrid hastened the pace. Am Schwemmbach was a few metres away, the school entrance not far along the main thoroughfare. 'Pedro will be too busy with his studies to sit around drinking bad coffee.'

Ingrid's cheeks flushed, although not from the walking. Everything about Pedro was so exotic: his Latin heritage, caramel skin, the silky accent. She had been captivated from the moment the Erfurt trio encountered the Cubans at the coastal campsite in Glowe.

There was no need for Sylvie to know about her two fruitless visits to Erfurt's main plaza to find Pedro before classes had resumed. Pedro lived and studied at the Pedagogical Institute north of the Altstadt, where teachers were trained. Pedro was 20. He was a true gentleman who would one day return to his homeland to teach young socialists. That was his destiny. She would always respect Pedro Barios and never forget him.

Soon the girls were surrounded by other students ranging from six years of age to their mid-teens, all hurrying to stand in line before the bell. A low brick retaining wall to their right marked the school boundary; a walkway under the first-floor classrooms would usher them to their destination.

Ingrid paused to look at the façade. The 31st Oberschule was barely half a dozen years old, but there was nothing to admire in the concrete building. It was squat, grey and functional. Large windows allowed plenty of light; students would swelter on hot days; the radiators worked extra hard in winter to keep the rooms warm.

There was nothing unusual about the courtyard mood. Pockets of conversation and laughter were stifled when the bell rang and the students proceeded in orderly lines to their classes. 7A, with Herr Schumann, was on the ground floor.

Their teacher was not waiting for them. They were responsible for unpacking books and pens, assuming their regular seats and preparing for the second bell. Herr Schumann would then stride in and take charge.

Gunther Kist

THE MINISTRY FOR STATE SECURITY REGIONAL HEADQUARTERS ON Andreasstrasse was buzzing as Gunther Kist entered. Pockets of agents and support staff gathered around desks, talking animatedly: arms waving, heads shaking, feet shuffling. Kist had not seen that level of excitement since August the previous year when the Berlin Wall went up. That had been a wonderful time. They could finally put the squeeze on the Western ghetto in their midst. It was only a matter of time before the GDR took full control of the old capital.

Kist headed for his desk near the window. Few colleagues bothered to break their conversations to acknowledge or greet him. He knew many considered him surly and single-minded. That never bothered Kist; he was a proud sword and shield of the Party; he had no time for frippery. The chameleon skills of a veteran agent had been carefully honed; he was able to blend in anywhere with a few subtle wardrobe changes. His job was to watch and listen, not be gabby. That was the way to weed out enemies.

One constant through all the office conversations he passed was the word 'Cuba'. Kist knew about the recent revolutionaries living close to the United States. He might struggle to point to Fidel's socialist paradise on a map, but he was aware of its strategic location. Cuba was a communist irritant up the Americans' bum, much like West Berlin was to the GDR and the Kremlin. What was happening in Cuba? Kist had not listened to the radio before leaving the apartment. Had he missed an important Party announcement?

'Gunther!' Carsten Hartwig, his immediate superior, gestured towards an empty chair at his desk. 'Have you heard about the situation in Cuba?'

It was an awkward moment. Kist worried he might be seen as lazy, not keeping up with important events. Bluffing was not in his nature.

'No. I heard comrades discussing Cuba on the way in.' He waved an arm at the room behind. 'But I have not seen anything official.' That was a safe reply. Kist was waiting for a superior to brief him.

'Our Soviet allies have been caught out. They have been stealthily setting up missile bases in Cuba and the Americans have just spotted them.'

Kist reeled. 'That … is surprising.'

Hartwig laughed at the agent's reaction. 'You must be the only one who doesn't listen to West German radio broadcasts.'

'They are a corrupting influence. I know as a Stasi agent I can listen, but I dare not expose my family to such treason.'

His superior dismissed the comment with a wave. 'Yes, that is understandable. But if you don't know what the enemy is talking about, how will you know where to look for threats to the Party?'

Kist squared his shoulders, sat straighter. 'Corruption lurks everywhere. We do not have to look far for traitors, black marketeers and Western liberals.'

Hartwig shrugged and shuffled a page on his desk. 'Okay. Well, the gist of what is happening is this – the United States is about to blockade Cuba. They are threatening to search every Soviet vessel that approaches the island.'

'That's piracy!'

'A little more serious than that, Gunther. The Americans want any missiles already in Cuba removed and the launch sites dismantled. If Khrushchev refuses or retaliates to US naval intervention, we could be, to paraphrase President Kennedy, on the edge of a nuclear abyss.'

Kist was stunned. A nuclear firestorm initiated by the Cuban situation. Surely it would never come to that. He understood that launching a nuclear weapon could push over the first domino and the rest would follow in order, leaving a smoking planet. He struggled to accept that the Soviet or American leaders wanted that to happen.

'Anyway, those decisions are above our pay grade. We deal with what our officers require.' He handed a typed document to Kist. It had three names. 'You know we have several Cuban students at the Pedagogical Institute?'

Kist nodded. 'I followed them for a few days when they arrived. They were good students, loyal socialists.'

'The Colonel wants to make sure that is still the case. The Party doesn't want them to think they have a better chance of survival in a West German shelter.'

Ingrid Richter

INGRID AND SYLVIE SAT SIDE-BY-SIDE AT A TABLE IN THE SECOND ROW. There were 28 in the class; a glance confirmed all were present, and none showed signs of suffering side-effects from their Buchenwald visit. *Was I the only one to have a nightmare?*

The tall figure of Herr Schumann appeared in the archway. He stopped. Normally he arrived with an air of authority and marched to the front of the room, ready to launch into the first 45-minute lesson. Not today.

He wore the familiar buttoned, single-breasted grey jacket and trousers, tailored by Ingrid's father from a westpaket in April. The black shoes were polished, although the white hair was untidy. There was no wind outside; the locks looked as if fingers had been raking the thinning locks.

Student eyes looked in all directions, seeking guidance from confused classmates. Should they stand or wait for Herr Schumann to move to the front of the class to initiate the morning ritual? Ingrid looked to their Thälmann Pioneer leader in his blue neckerchief. Hans Rathmann was half out of his seat, unsure about a break in the routine established from their first week at school.

Herr Schumann was old, at least 63. Ingrid had heard him talk about retirement in two years when Vati did the measurements for his suit at their apartment. He wanted to play more chess and devote time to his stamp collection. Mutti and the teacher occasionally traded special stamps. His hobbies were frequently disrupted by the demands of school life: essay marking, outings and State-initiated campaigns to prepare loyal young citizens.

The teacher ended the dilemma for his students by walking slowly to his table. They all snapped to attention.

Hans Rathmann was able to address his classmates. 'Be ready!'

'Always ready!'

The reply came with less than the usual gusto.

Hans turned to their teacher. 'I report that 7A is ready for the classes.' He saluted and resumed his seat.

Herr Schumann nodded. He stood with hands clasped behind his back. That was standard, although Ingrid noticed the shoulders lacked their usual military bearing. He had been in both wars; he told them before the Buchenwald visit that a wound from the first had restricted his service in the second until the final desperate months.

It looked as if Herr Schumann had received bad news, like the men outside the bakery. Ingrid thought back to Buchenwald and the private revelations that had shocked and caused her nightmare.

Had revealing those secrets affected her teacher? It was a risk to share knowledge contrary to the doctrine of the Party. Was Herr Schumann worried that Ingrid would be indiscreet or, worse, that she might report him to the Stasi?

She sought his eyes. They were directed at a spot on the wall behind them. He stood silently, as if trying to form words to start the lesson. No, Ingrid did not believe it was the camp that had spooked their teacher. Herr Schumann had visited many times with different classes. He had experienced the horrors of war. There was something else on his mind.

Ingrid glanced to her right. Gerard Mueller was at the next table with Kurt Neubert. They looked bewildered by Herr Schumann's hesitant start, yet neither would question their pedagogue. Probably the only student who would do that was Sylvie. Ingrid placed a hand on her friend's arm as she sensed that was about to happen. No need to make eye contact, the message was clear: let Herr Schumann talk when he was ready.

The teacher moved to the front of his table.

'Class, I have some news to share. I'm sad to say you will find it shocking.'

Several students gasped.

Herr Schumann swallowed.

Ingrid willed him to continue. What was so bad that it rattled their normally calm, confident figurehead? He had survived two world wars – what could be worse than that?

'I have been wrestling with my conscience about whether to share this information.' He placed his hands inside his trouser pockets, an informality never witnessed in the classroom. 'What I have to say affects you – indeed everyone inside and outside of the German

Democratic Republic. You have a right to know the truth. Your lives depend on it.'

More gasps. Sylvie gripped Ingrid's hand.

'I am afraid to say we are on the brink of World War III. We are facing a thermonuclear onslaught from the imperialist aggressors, the United States, directed at our Soviet … allies.'

Howls of surprise rippled around the room. Ingrid wondered about the pause between 'Soviet' and 'allies.' She had witnessed a fracture in Herr Schumann's party loyalty at Buchenwald. Was it now a chasm?

Crying could be heard from a table nearby.

'Hush now, please.'

The room went silent. Respect for their teacher and elders was instinctive.

'I must explain the background. Cuba is a socialist ally in the Caribbean. It is about 150 kilometres from the American coast. Since Fidel Castro led the glorious revolution three years ago, the Americans have been trying to overthrow his legitimate government. An invasion was crushed, attempts to assassinate the brave leader have failed.

'To stop the aggressors, the Russians are building missile bases in Cuba. They are necessary for defence. However, a few hours ago, the American President went on television to declare he will attack the Soviets and Cubans unless the missiles are removed.

'The consequences of that threat are so serious I felt that you deserved to know. The world as we know it could change – or end – in the next few days.'

The news was a hammer blow. Ingrid had not endured the terror of warfare, but she, like many in her class, was attuned to the damaging impact. Now their teacher was saying that World War III was going to be worse than the first two.

Herr Schumann was taking an incredible risk. The Party controlled the information flow to its citizens. Most secretly watched or listened to West German broadcasts; the border was barely 100 kilometres from Erfurt. Curtains would be drawn, the volume set on low, children repeatedly warned never to reveal the family's viewing habits for fear of a visit by the Stasi. Some families even silenced their televisions during commercials lest children were caught humming catchy Western commercial jingles at school.

Ingrid had heard nothing about a crisis on the State-run radio while eating breakfast. It had been mostly music and a few Party messages that Ingrid ignored. Herr Schumann was listening to Western propaganda – would someone in the class betray him to the Stasi?

Ingrid snorted. That issue paled against the danger of a world war. She knew a little about the Americans' atomic bombs. They had destroyed the Japanese cities of Hiroshima and Nagasaki in the blink of an eye. Since then, the Americans had built a massive arsenal to control the world. The Soviet Union had stood firm, challenging the aggressor and trying to preserve peace. But how could they stop American nuclear weapons?

There was also the question of geography. Erfurt was in Europe; the Caribbean was thousands of kilometres away. Why the conflict in the Caribbean should threaten them was suddenly a grey area.

It was Sylvie who went to the heart of the matter. She raised her right arm.

'Yes, Sylvie?'

'Why do the Americans want to drop a nuclear bomb on us because of Cuba?'

There was a sharp intake of breath from half the class. Sylvie's tone was not challenging, but the question was as shocking as Herr Schumann's declaration of war. Ingrid was sure every student was struggling with the same issue.

Their teacher nodded, straightened, and removed his hands from his pockets to resume his usual formal pose.

'You need to think of it in terms of connections, Sylvie. The State provides well for us. We have free education, cheap housing, good medical care, jobs for life and no unemployment. None of the social problems that afflict the West. But we all know about the *connections* we need to help supply some of the little extras in life. For example, some of your parents have Schrebergartens.'

Ingrid nodded, along with a dozen other children.

'They are wonderful communities where you gather socially and to grow vegetables and fruit. Ingrid's family plants cabbages and carrots. More than they need, so her mother might trade some for apples or potatoes from Gerard's mother. No food is wasted because we look after our friends. It builds connections.'

Herr Schumann's voice sounded stronger, more confident.

'Socialist countries must form friendships to stop the threat from the capitalists. They want to control our countries. So, our governments form alliances – what we might call connections.

'Cuba is a young socialist government; it needs help and protection. The Soviets stand shoulder to shoulder with the Cubans in troubled times, as does our German Democratic Republic.'

Ingrid wanted to feel reassured by the familiar spiel that world socialists would unite against the aggressors. But the Americans had nuclear missiles and planes loaded with bombs – how could anyone stop them?

Sylvie's hand shot into the air again.

Herr Schumann nodded.

'How can the Russians compete against nuclear weapons?'

Herr Schumann grimaced, then replied. 'With their own nuclear missiles.'

Another bombshell. Ingrid had not known the Soviet Union had its own nuclear arsenal. Had she been living in a fairy tale land? Was she the only student unaware that their friends to the east were just as powerful? She looked around the classroom; many shared the same shocked expressions.

Sylvie was not finished with her questions.

'Then ... if the Americans attack with their nuclear weapons, the Soviets will fire their missiles back.'

'Yes, Sylvie.'

'And how long will that go on?'

Herr Schumann blinked. 'Until they run out of missiles and bombs.'

'How many do the Americans and Soviets have?'

'Enough to destroy our planet several times.'

Fresh cries erupted from the class. Ingrid realised she was squeezing both of Sylvie's hands.

'Class, I am sorry to cause you this distress. You are young and have much to achieve – if given the chance. I felt I must share what I know. It is my duty to prepare you for what lies ahead.

'There will be more news over the coming hours and days. We can only hope the leaders – Nikita Khrushchev and John Kennedy – can reach a compromise to prevent a war that could destroy our world.

'That threat of mutually assured destruction since the Soviets developed their own atomic bomb has kept the Americans at bay. Now, a madness has gripped President Kennedy. He is willing to risk countless lives to pursue his capitalist agenda – unless Khrushchev can force Kennedy to step back from the cliff.'

Ingrid felt as if the air had been sucked from the room. Nearby, she heard Daniela Ruffer sniffling. Herr Schumann folded his arms. Another hand rose tentatively in the front row.

'Yes, Hans.'

'Should we dig trenches, Herr Schumann? Would there be time to make a proper air raid shelter?'

'You are a practical young leader, Hans. However, nuclear weapons are more powerful than anything used in the last two wars, even the atomic bombs dropped in Japan. The Americans have spent years building more-destructive bombs. I am afraid you could not dig a trench deep enough to save us, Hans. Then there is the problem of radioactive fallout – it poisons the air and land for years.'

Another hand, this time from Thorsten Koehler. He looked fierce.

'The Soviet Union liberated Erfurt from the Nazis and prevented our city becoming part of the puppet capitalist state. They can beat the Yankees!'

The defiance brought murmurs of approval, mostly from the boys. Ingrid could imagine them building barricades at the school gate. She wondered whether to correct Thorsten about their *liberators*.

Herr Schumann briefly looked at Ingrid before replying.

'We have much to thank the Soviets for. They have been our bulwark against the aggressors since they liberated Erfurt and rescued the internees at Buchenwald. We can only hope the wisdom and courage of their leader will save the world.'

Ingrid felt her jaw sag as Herr Schumann avoided further questions by turning to pick up a lesson book. He had just lied to the class!

Matthias Kist

MATTHIAS KIST WAS NEITHER TALL NOR SHORT, NOT FAT, NOT THIN. He was dressed in polyester clothes like many of his 8th Class colleagues. There were no bright colours or fancy styles to indicate they were westpaket hand-me-downs. His hair was cut short in the usual fashion, the original blond locks slowly being overtaken by his father's darker shades. That made him look like most other GDR students, which made Matthias happy.

Few students were content to be average. Only Matthias understood what an asset it could be for his chosen profession. He wanted to follow in his father's footsteps at the Stasi headquarters. It was an inspiration every morning to watch Gunther Kist adopt a new personality before walking out the door. A beard, moustache, thick glasses, hats and jackets transformed him. Matthias always knew it was his father, but the enemies of the Party would never see the Stasi man on their tail.

A younger student bumped Matthias with his ranzen as he loitered in the corridor between classes. Matthias clipped the lad over the ear.

'Yow!' The boy was most likely a fifth grader. He had been reading a *Mosaik* as he walked.

'Comics are not to be read between classes. Put it away or I'll confiscate it and make sure you get a detention.'

The boy stuffed the prized new edition into his satchel and scurried away with a reddening ear.

Matthias had no authority to take the comic or punish the boy, but discreet bullying of a fifth grader was never going to be reported. He enjoyed moments like that. The younger classes needed to know the pecking order. It would prepare them for the real world. Outside of school, the Stasi wielded the most power – more than the VoPos or the Volksarmee. Everyone feared the Stasi, even the politicians.

Joining the Stasi had been a shared ambition for father and son since 1st Class. Gunther said he could prepare Matthias to fly through the system. He expected his son to be a senior officer in Berlin by the time he was 40. That would be a magnificent and achievable goal.

Consequently, that meant there was little time for childish entertainment. Attributes of a good Stasi agent had to be refined. They had to watch, listen, and blend in. Dig out corruption, expose traitors. Gunther explained these traits could be honed while at school. Father and son set training regimes. Matthias would be assigned a student or teacher to follow. At the end of the week, they would analyse the data gathered. There were several occasions where suspect behaviour by teachers had been taken into headquarters for further examination. That made father and son extremely proud.

The mission that week, to observe Frau Lange, who taught Russian, did not pack the same excitement. She was a boring old spinster, at least 40. She rarely smiled or talked to anyone outside of class. It was impossible to check her desk as she rarely left the room, even during the long break. Some students joked that Frau Lange slept in the cupboards at night. Matthias did not have any damaging information to share with his father. He wished something more exciting would come along.

Ingrid Richter

THE FIRST TWO CLASSES – MATHEMATICS AND GERMAN LITERATURE – WERE a blur. The third – Russian – was in another room. Frau Lange never said anything about a threatened nuclear attack or reacted to the subdued nature of her students. Ingrid stumbled over familiar phrases through lack of concentration. She welcomed the long break even if it meant half an hour in the breezy courtyard.

She paused momentarily in the wide corridor before exiting, distracted by a series of photos on the wall. They had always been there, part of the furnishings, never making an impression. There was Walter Ulbricht, the republic's head of state and First Secretary of the Socialist Unity Party. Alongside him were the communist heroes Karl Marx and Vladimir Lenin. Then there was the First Secretary of the Communist Party of the Soviet Union, Nikita Khrushchev. He was the man locked in the nuclear standoff with President Kennedy.

Ingrid stared at the bald, grandfatherly figure. The Soviet premier was so different from the handsome, younger American president. She had seen glimpses of Kennedy on West German television. Her future, and that of her family and friends, rested in his hands. Kennedy could order a nuclear strike at any time. The Soviet retaliation would be righteous. But, Ingrid wondered, would it be the right decision?

The sandwich remained in its pack in her ranzen. She noticed few of her 7A classmates were eating; most were already doing slow circuits on the concrete as mandated by the school: students were not to sit idle. Teachers ensured they walked in an orderly fashion.

The courtyard noise level was the same as always; there was no restriction on chatter. It surprised Ingrid as she waited for Sylvie to tighten her jacket. Was Herr Schumann the only teacher brave enough to share news about the end of the world? It would seem so, as boys from the upper and lower classes played silly games, unaware of the approaching danger. Ingrid raised her eyes: were American bombers already overhead, their bellies full of nuclear bombs?

'Looking for B-52s?' Sylvie walked beside her.

'Yes. That's what Herr Wenkell the baker must have been doing.'

Ingrid stumbled as an older boy brushed past. He apologised with a wave and smile but kept moving.

'Did you know the Soviets had nuclear missiles?'

'No. I never think about bombs or missiles. The Soviets have been our friends since the end of the war. I know the Americans have powerful weapons, but there was no reason for them to attack us. That is business for adults to worry about, not children.'

Ingrid looked around. Everyone was walking clockwise. In front of them were Gerard, Kurt and Thorsten, their conversation so low it could not be heard. Occasionally their heads tilted upwards, searching the skies. Behind, two girls from the 3rd Class nattered happily.

'I must share something with you. I meant to do it on the way to school, but I was distracted by the nightmare.'

Sylvie lowered her voice to match her friend. 'Was it something from Buchenwald?'

'Yes — and today.'

They slowed; the younger students walked around them. They had a buffer of several metres.

'Herr Schumann lied to the class today.'

Sylvie stalled. 'Was he lying about the nuclear war?'

Ingrid grabbed her arm. 'I don't think so. He looked upset — as scared as we were. No, he lied about the Soviets being our liberators.'

'What do you mean? Everyone knows the Soviet Union ended the Third Reich's evil reign and freed the camps. We have been taught that since before we started school.'

'No. It was the Americans.'

Sylvie stopped and stared. 'How can you say that? Who told you?'

Ingrid nudged her friends back to continue their circuit. No student or teacher appeared to have witnessed her shocked response.

'Herr Schumann. At Buchenwald.'

'I never heard him say that. We were all together when he gave his lesson about the camp.'

'That was when we arrived. He told me later, when it was just the two of us standing near the horrible ovens.'

Sylvie nodded. 'You disappeared for a few minutes before we caught the bus. I thought you found a toilet.'

'No. I wanted to go check a plate on the ovens. When I got there, Herr Schumann was staring at it, like he was lost in thought.'

The conversation paused as they passed the two supervising teachers huddled near the entrance.

'Herr Schumann saw me, then looked back at the plate.'

'What was on the plate?'

'It said the engineering work was done by J.A. Topf and Söhne – from Erfurt!'

Sylvie stopped, clasped Ingrid's arm. 'You mean the ovens to burn the prisoners were made in our city?'

'Yes. Not far from where we live. Herr Schumann said the company changed its name after the war. Very few know what they did.'

Ingrid looped her arm through Sylvie's to resume their walk.

'How did Herr Schumann find out their secret?'

'From the *Americans* – after they liberated Buchenwald *and* captured Erfurt.'

Sylvie's jaw dropped, although her pace did not falter.

'But we were told the Russians saved us. That Americans are bullies – like their President Kennedy. Are you sure Herr Schumann was telling the truth?'

'I think so. He said the Americans forced him to visit the concentration camp a few days after the Nazis ran away. The American generals were so angry, they marched hundreds of people from the closest town, Weimar, to witness the Nazi atrocities.'

'That would have been terrible. But why did they let the Soviet Union take over the camp?'

'Herr Schumann said the Soviets arrived in the first week of July. Their leaders made a deal during the war on how to divide Hitler's Germany. We were to be in the Soviet zone.'

'So … if the Americans had refused to leave Erfurt and Buchenwald, we would be part of West Germany?'

'Probably.'

'I wonder how different life would be.'

Ingrid thought for a moment. 'Nicer clothes, better coffee and chocolate, fancy soaps, exotic perfumes, kitchen appliances, exciting music – the lovely stuff we get in westpakete from Mutti's family in Schleswig-Holstein.'

'But what about the rampant crime, homelessness and unemployment our teachers are always talking about? Is that real or exaggerations?'

Ingrid shrugged. She knew that many East Germans had run for the West despite those problems. It had become harder to leave, yet families were willing to risk minefields and barbed wire fences. The threat of soldiers with machine guns did not stop them. There were whispered stories about Berliners tunnelling under the wall to reach the West.

They walked in silence. Ahead, the trio of Gerard, Kurt and Thorsten fragmented, joining those loitering near the entrance. Soon they would be summoned back inside for the final three lessons. Sylvie was intent on another circuit.

'Why did Herr Schumann tell you about the Americans yesterday but insist today that the Soviets were our saviours?'

'Because it was only Herr Schumann and me – no adults to hear him. Today he was in front of a class. Someone would tell their parents. Eventually that would reach the Stasi. He would be in trouble. He was telling the Party truth today.'

'What would happen if you said Herr Schumann was lying about the Soviets being our liberators?'

'I might be in danger – and my parents. I don't want to see Vati and Mutti dragged off to prison. I must stay silent. So must you, Sylvie. Please!'

Ingrid received a reassuring pat on the arm. It was only as she voiced those thoughts that she realised the trouble she had created for her family. Herr Schumann had taken a risk by revealing the crisis in Cuba, but that news would soon spread through Erfurt after people watched the West German television news. But contradicting the Party about their allies could be fatal for a talkative elderly schoolteacher – and the student who listened to him.

The courtyard was emptying. Could Ingrid focus on her lessons until the end of the school day at 1.30pm? Was it worthwhile? Sylvie, Gerard, Kurt, Thorsten, Petra and the rest of the class would be diligent, yet a mad American president could press a button and all their dreams for the future would be gone.

Would there be pain? Or would death be instantaneous? Ingrid had seen photos of the mushroom clouds, the flattened Japanese cities, children with radiation burns. They were in books in the library, ones that were rarely touched. What would have happened if the Japanese had not surrendered – would the Americans have kept bombing until every city was destroyed? That thought made Ingrid shiver. How bloodthirsty were the Americans?

Ingrid looked at the sky a final time before joining the crowded shuffle along the utilitarian corridor. There was no drone of bombers or scream of missiles. There was much she did not know about their enemies and their weapons. Was it worthwhile visiting the library to learn more? Or was that a waste of time? President Kennedy would not care about children in the 31st Oberschule in Erfurt when he ordered the bombs to drop. Ingrid felt so powerless; was there anything she could do to save herself, her family – and the world?

Tomas Schumann

Tomas Schumann washed his cup, dried it and placed it in the cupboard. He was the last to leave the teachers' room. It had been an emotional day; every one of his 63 years weighed heavily on his shoulders. Retirement had been a beacon, edging closer every day, until the morning broadcast on his radio. The Americans and the Soviets were a hair's breadth from nuclear destruction. *Have we learned nothing after two world wars?*

The topic had never surfaced among the teachers during the break. The room was quieter than normal; Schumann sensed that his colleagues preferred discretion rather than putting their heads above the parapet.

There had been no Party announcement about the Kennedy ultimatum before he left his Anger apartment for school. The President's television address was at 7pm in Washington, after midnight in the GDR. The Party's response required debate and consultation. To acknowledge the impending Armageddon with colleagues would be an admission that his home radio was tuned to illegal broadcasts. Probably all had listened, but nobody wanted to give the Stasi an invitation to haul them away for interrogation. There were at least three known informants on the staff, probably another six who were more cunning.

Schumann had shared one brief verbal exchange: making a drink appointment with Jürgen Grau, a fellow teacher. Any spitzel who overheard the arrangement would not consider it suspicious enough to inform their handler. Grau was a regular chess opponent for Schumann; their discussions in the staffroom were legendary and boring. Stasi informants usually left the old comrades alone.

The friendship had been forged in the trenches of Flanders: two lowly soldiers praying to see the next dawn. A mutual passion for chess provided a distraction and comfort between bombardments and assaults. Publicly they appeared to spend hours discussing the board game. Privately, their talks ranged across political minefields.

Schumann knew his friend always listened to the morning news from the West. Grau understood what was at stake for the GDR and the world. He nodded when a beer and game were suggested for that evening. A Tuesday match was unusual, a drink even more so. Grau's choice of Zum Goldenen Schwan was good. Michaelisstrasse was the heart of the pub district, the inn unlikely to attract Party loyalists.

The friends had enjoyed many beers, games and discussions since surviving their first contact with the American military at the Battle of Lys in April 1918. Both had been 19-year-old gefreiters. Was it luck or good skills that saw them avoid bullets, grenades, mortars, artillery shells, and strafing by the nascent air forces? Both had been in hand-to-hand combat and still carried the scars. They had looked out for each other, developing an instinct when a back needed protecting in the trenches.

That had been 44 years ago, a different era. Warfare was brutal but contained. In Europe, the trenches stretched from the English Channel to Switzerland. Other theatres consumed the Balkans, Turkey and the Middle East. Enough nations were involved to merit calling it a world war, yet it never threatened to destroy the planet, like America's latest gambit. Civilisation was always destined to continue. Could the same be said tonight, tomorrow or next week if either of the two leaders unleashed their arsenals? Both understood there would be no winners in a thermonuclear war.

Schumann straightened his shoulders as he marched down the corridor to the next class. Had 7A spent the break gazing at the sky for American bombers? Possibly. Would they have shared his revelation about being on the brink of World War III? Probably. Could he expect a visit from a Stasi agent in the next week? Most likely – if the planet was still spinning.

Ingrid Richter

'Do you mind waiting a little longer, Ingrid?' Sylvie said as she caught up with her after school. 'I have to return a book to my cousin. I missed him at his classroom. He should be here any minute.'

Ingrid was leaning against the nondescript brick retaining wall at the school entrance. It was about five metres long and a metre high.

'That's alright. I was thinking.'

Students streamed past, the chatter more subdued than at the start of the day.

Sylvie raised a hand to shield her mouth. 'Do you think they have heard about the threat of war?'

'Yes. I hope other teachers shared the news like Herr Schumann. We have a right to know if there is not going to be a tomorrow.'

Sylvie paled. 'I never thought of it like that.' She rested against the wall. 'Saying there is going to be a nuclear war is one thing, but my mind cannot understand what that would mean.' Sylvie looked at the clouds, then at the departing students. 'We might never see our friends again.'

'No. Or our grandparents. No more pastries on the way home from school.' Ingrid gestured towards the Steigerwald a few blocks away. 'We had so much fun last winter, building igloos and having snowball fights. Dragging sleds along the trails, coming home for hot milk.'

'Yes. I never thought that freezing noses, fingers and toes would sound so good.' Sylvie shook her head.

'Remember those winters we spent looking for fairies during New Year? Opa reminded me every Christmas that the fairies could not fly when it snowed on the first day of the year. If we could catch one, she would have to grant us a wish.'

Sylvie's laugh made several senior students look. 'We spent hours on their trail. I was sure there were tiny footprints. I was so blue when I got home. Luckily, it was bath night – I was second into the tub. My mother had to haul me out to give my brother his turn.'

There was one advantage in being a single child; Ingrid was always first to use the hot bathwater. None of the boilers in the apartments could heat more than one bath per family.

'I used to tell Opa that we saw tiny footsteps but no fairies. He would say, "Don't forget the ritual. Do it correctly and the forest will support your quest."'

Sylvie scuffed a shoe against the wall. 'I would love to catch a fairy right now.'

'What would you ask her to do?'

'Stop the Americans from sending nuclear missiles to kill us in our sleep.'

The departing students had dwindled to a trickle. Most were eager to get home for their warm meal. Would it be their last semolina, goulash or soljanka?

Ingrid suddenly felt irritated. That was gloomy thinking.

'We must do something, Sylvie! We can't sit and wait for the bombs to fall.'

Her friend shrugged, kicked at a stick on the ground. 'We need a glücksbringer.'

That made sense to Ingrid: a lucky charm, like a four-leaf clover, was just what they needed.

'Opa said glücksklee grow everywhere in Steigerwald, but I've never seen one,' Ingrid said. 'Do you have any at home?

'No. My Oma swears by the hufeisen that hangs over her kitchen door at the farm.' Horseshoes were a popular charm; they had to point towards the sky to catch good luck. 'But my father calls it silly superstition.' Sylvie kicked at the stick again.

'I had two marienkäfer land on me at the Schrebergarten during summer.'

Everyone knew that being chosen by a ladybug brought good fortune.

'Did you count the black spots on their red wings? Seven is extra lucky.'

Ingrid nodded. 'One had seven.' She waved at the grey skies. 'Not much chance of another landing today.'

Sylvie rolled the stick again. 'What about a schornsteinfeger ornament? Are they as lucky as meeting a real one?'

Chimney sweepers in their black uniform, top hat and brushes had been symbols of good luck, wealth and happiness since medieval times. They prevented thousands of fires with their annual visits to clear soot and debris. To meet a chimney sweeper was always considered lucky; there were even better tidings for shaking his hand or touching his jacket button.

'We don't have any ornaments at home, and I haven't seen a schornsteinfeger in our district since February.'

Ingrid considered other possible lucky charms that might be in either home as Sylvie continued to toy with the stick on the ground. Her Opa had a glücks cent. It was a copper coin he found on his first day at school in 1900. Opa always said he could never part with it – that would break the lucky charm.

There were glücksschwein symbols in most homes. Pigs represented wealth and prosperity. The Richters, like many families on both sides of the border, always ate marzipan glücksschwein at New Year, but Mutti never fancied glass or porcelain pigs as part of her interior décor.

'Do you have any glücksschwein ornaments, Sylvie?'

'We had a pretty pink one until my brother smashed it with the football.'

'That is annoying. We need a new lucky charm. Something special to give us hope.'

Her eyes kept going back to the stick beneath Sylvie's foot. It was about 15 centimetres, straight and relatively fresh. The two ends appeared to have been snipped. It could not have been clipped from the grassy area behind the wall; there were no trees or shrubs. She picked up the stick.

'Sylvie, where do you think this came from?'

'I don't know and I don't care – it's just a stick.'

'Is it?'

Ingrid did not get a chance to explain the feeling that was building. Bernd arrived to receive his book. The cousins chatted about family matters, leaving Ingrid time to consider the stick in her hand.

There was no obvious tree or bush from which it had been recently trimmed. Yet here it was, fresh and healthy. There were even small buds, despite Sylvie's footwork on the concrete. That was unusual for the season. It was separated from the soil but still thriving. She had no idea what variety it was. It did not matter – the stick was a survivor.

Bernd walked away, tucking the book in his ranzen. Sylvie was ready for home and her lunch. Ingrid's soljanka could wait a few moments. She held up the stick.

'Sylvie. I think this is special.'

Her friend viewed the twig sceptically.

'Look around – there are no trees. How did it get here?' Ingrid displayed the fresh cut ends. 'The snips are recent. No gardener is in sight. There is no reason for it to be here.' Ingrid passed it to her friend. 'I think this stick is here for a purpose: to show us how to survive.'

'That's silly.'

'It might sound irrational, but the stick has found a way to continue growing. Look at the buds. Has it created its own luck?'

Sylvie's feet shuffled; she tugged her coat tighter. The afternoon chill was setting in.

'Maybe.' She returned the stick.

'I think this should be our symbol, Sylvie. The longer it survives, the better our chances of living. Nature can be our guardian.'

Sylvie's head bobbled. Ingrid could tell she was not convinced by the stick's special qualities, but she sensed that her friend wanted hope for a future, just like her. There would be no harm in trying. If they kept the evolving plan a secret, who would ever know if it turned out to be a foolish idea?

'Come on. We need to create a ritual to make it a proper glücksbringer. Just like Opa told us to do in the forest.'

Sylvie snorted. 'You want the stick to attract fairies? We catch one and she will grant us a wish for peace?'

'No.' Ingrid held it aloft. 'We let it create its own luck. We make it a peace stick.'

Ingrid looked at the wall, a wasted support for a non-existent garden. Could it become greater than that? A shrine? She knew little about religion despite the city's annual festival to honour Martin Luther, the Father of the Reformation.

The Altstadt skyline was filled with ancient churches, the most prominent being St Marien Cathedral and Severikirche overlooking the Domplatz. She saw worshippers risk the Party's anger to honour their god every weekend. Their faces were always peaceful after the services. There must be something in that faith. They believed and were rewarded.

There was a small hole in the mortar between two bricks near the top of the wall. It was round and deep, almost as if it had been drilled. Ingrid put the stick at the edge and pushed. It went all the way. She retrieved it with her fingernails.

'Look, Sylvie. That fits perfectly. It's another sign.'

'Should we say something?'

'Yes. Any suggestions?'

'I think you should make it up. It's your inspiration. You summon the magic – if you can.' Sylvie looked at the sky, then back to the stick. She placed two fingers on it. 'I'll give you whatever support I can.'

Ingrid felt goosebumps. Her friend wanted it to work. They both did – something to give them hope for another day. It was a mad idea. But was it any different than the Christians kneeling in the cathedral, praying to their god?

'Okay.' Ingrid bowed her head, thinking hard for the right words. She wanted the chance to enjoy life: simple things like growing her hair past her shoulders, getting a puppy, seeing Pedro again. She placed one end at the hole and slid her fingers along the stick, ensuring Sylvie still held a section.

'We believe this peace stick can protect the world. If our new glücksbringer stays in place, we will survive.'

Ingrid slid the stick into the hole. It sat almost flush.

'So, if the stick is not removed, you think we'll be safe?'

'Yes. If the stick is there each morning when we come to school, we will be okay for another day.'

Sylvie smiled. 'I like that. I won't have to keep looking for bombers or missiles.'

'It gives President Kennedy another chance to think how many lives and countries they would destroy. Every day will be important.'

'Hey!'

Gerard Mueller approached, bouncing a football.

'What are you two doing?'

Ingrid turned towards the wall. 'Don't say anything about the peace stick.'

Sylvie distracted Gerard. 'Where are you playing football?'

Ingrid was pleased. Secrecy was an instinctive reaction when they were challenged; they had found something that might protect them in the crisis. It was natural to protect the glücksbringer.

'I'm meeting Kurt, Thorsten and a few others at the park after lunch.'

'Can we play?' Sylvie asked.

Gerard screwed up his face. 'Girls don't play football. You can watch if you want.'

Ingrid used the typical snub to exit. 'If we can't play, who wants to stand in a cold park? Goodbye, Gerard.'

Gerard shrugged, dropped the ball to his feet and dribbled it in the wake of Ingrid and Sylvie as they marched home.

Gunther Kitz

THE STASI AGENT HAD NO EXPECTATIONS OF MAKING ARRESTS WHEN HE arrived at the Pedagogical Institute on Nordhauser Strasse. Pedro Barios, Hector Delgado, Ermano Garcia were model students, according to the files he checked before leaving the office.

They were sons of prominent Cuban communists, although too young to fight in the revolution alongside Fidel Castro and Che Guevara. The new leader decided education was the future for socialist nations; teachers had an important role in shaping Party loyalty. The GDR was happy to play a role.

The allies had performed well in their studies despite the language and cultural differences. They were considered faithful socialists, although Kist had grimaced when the Stasi files revealed the handsome Cubans were popular with women. They had local girlfriends; Hector and Ermano had several. Kist didn't approve, but apart from that the trio had not aroused any suspicion of disloyalty. Until a break in their routine.

Pedro, Hector and Ermano returned to their dormitories after morning classes, as usual, but exited a few minutes later without their books. They all wore jackets. He followed them to the tram stop and boarded discreetly, staying out of their line of sight until they exited at the Domplatz. That made his pursuit interesting.

The ancient square was the most challenging location in Erfurt for a one-man surveillance operation. The Domplatz spread more than three hectares, overshadowed by the cathedral, Severikirche and Petersberg Citadel. There were no market stalls, buyers or much else to hide 35-year-old Gunther Kitz. Trees guarded the boundary, although too slender and distant from the targets to help. There were more leaves on the ground than on the branches.

The Erthal Obelisk and the Minerva Fountain were two options for semi-covert duties. They stood about 30 metres apart in front of the churches. They were crumbling reminders of the city's bourgeois past, for one of the earliest recruits to the Ministry for State Security. Kitz would not shed a tear if they were struck by lightning or toppled in a storm; the rubble of the 18-metre granite pillar could be hauled away to build a worker's house.

The fountain had served a practical purpose many years ago when it was part of the city's water supply. It was merely a showpiece now, sandstone topped by the Roman goddess Minerva in a helmet with a shield and spear. It was a folly. Protection of the Party and its citizens rested in Germanic hands – loyalists like Kitz.

The monuments stood prominently in the square; anyone lingering would be a giveaway that the Stasi were on a mission. Sometimes that did not matter to the agents when they wanted targets to be intimidated – often, that made them panic and make mistakes.

Kist's concerns about an observation post were dismissed as the Cubans marched across the square without a backward glance. They swiftly ascended the vast stairway between the churches and found the entrance to the St Marien Cathedral.

That was a surprise. A church visit had not been noted before. Sundays usually found the Cubans in the arms of their girlfriends. The Stasi had the audio tapes. Kitz was familiar with the cathedral but had not been inside since before the war. He was hesitant to break that record. The religion held no fears; the Gothic building was the problem. There should be few people willing to pray, given the party's low tolerance for Christianity. The agent would be too obvious. There was a chance they were meeting someone; the 23-year stand-off with God would have to end for Kitz. Even a brief peep inside the cathedral was risky. Two rows of massive columns down the middle would be the only cover. It depended on where the Cubans were standing, kneeling, or praying.

The aroma of incense greeted Kitz at the door, the Latin cadence evoked memories of his days as an altar boy. He stifled the instinct to respond. The Cubans were with four elderly women in the front pews, a priest faced the altar. They were praying for peace. Duty compelled Kitz to identify the women and attach notes to their Stasi records. Discretion convinced him to retreat quietly to the Domplatz and wait.

The inscription on the obelisk provided a convenient prop for Kist when the student teachers emerged from their soul-cleansing 20 minutes later. They wouldn't know the stone text was virtually unreadable, eroded by the elements since it was carved in 1777.

Had the students had time for confession inside the church? Maybe a visit to the priest would be required after Kist followed the Cubans back to their dormitories. Extracting that information could be difficult, sometimes fun, but was never impossible.

Kitz was about to drop in behind the Cubans as they walked towards Marktstrasse when Pedro Barios halted the group to greet a schoolgirl. She looked familiar, probably a kinder from Kitz's neighbourhood. Most likely she went to the 31st Oberschule with his son.

Why would a schoolgirl know the Cubans? Perhaps Matthias should check on her; Matthias was already showing great promise. Perhaps he would set him a new task.

Ingrid Richter

'Ingrid!'

The voice came as a shock, a dazzling and welcome greeting when she recognised it was Pedro Barios on the fringe of the Domplatz. Ingrid had been so focused on reaching the city library, she had noticed little on the walk from Friedrich-List Strasse. Suddenly, there was Pedro – with Hector and Ermano – at the tram junction with Marktstrasse. She had dreamed of a moment like this for weeks. The reality almost left her speechless.

'Oh – Pedro!

She had practised a special greeting for this moment. The chance to impress was gone. The trio of Latinos were even more handsome than she remembered from their days at the beach, especially Pedro. His broad smile made her heart flutter.

'My young friend, it is nice to see you. How are Renate and Katja?'

There was a pang of jealousy when Pedro remembered their names. They had competed for his attention during their eight weeks at the camp in Glowe. The result had been a draw.

'They are good. I don't see them often as they are in another class.'

'I am sure they are studying well, like you.' He turned to his companions, who were lighting cigarettes. 'You remember my friends?'

Here was Ingrid's moment. 'Si, Pedro. Hola, Hector; hola, Ermano. Cómo estás?'

Three pairs of Cuban eyes widened with delight.

'We are good, thank you, Ingrid,' said Hector. 'We are impressed – you remembered your Spanish lessons from the beach.'

'Si. But there has been no chance to learn more Spanish. Our library has no books and Russian is compulsory in our class.'

'Stay patient, Ingrid. Perhaps I can send you a phrase book from Cuba?'

Ingrid brightened at that possibility – long-term contact with Pedro! But then clouds dimmed the sparkle.

'You are going home to Cuba? The Americans may drop nuclear bombs at any minute. You won't be safe.'

The trio's smiles evaporated. They glanced nervously around the empty plaza. Concern for Pedro had made Ingrid careless. Few people in the GDR should know about the crisis developing in the Caribbean – only those illegally listening to West German or American broadcasts. Fortunately, there was only a worker studying the inscription on the obelisk.

Pedro lowered his voice. 'How do you know about the American threats against Cuba?'

'Our teacher told us this morning. He said President Kennedy wants to destroy Cuba unless the Russians remove their missiles. That isn't fair – you have the right to defend yourselves.'

The Cubans shuffled their feet. Ingrid sensed it was not a safe conversation even in an empty plaza.

Ingrid looked at her three friends. 'Herr Schumann said it is a dangerous time for all the world. If the Americans attack with nuclear bombs, the Russians must retaliate.' She swallowed. 'He said the leaders could soon lose control and that puts everyone at risk. Herr Schumann said we had the right to know.'

Hector nodded. 'Your teacher is a brave man. I hope he does not suffer for doing his duty to his students. Protect him, Ingrid.'

Pedro placed a hand gently on her shoulder. 'Now you understand why we must return to Cuba. It is our obligation. We must be with our families and defend our homeland.'

Pedro looked over his shoulder. 'We have been inside the cathedral – the first time in any church since before the revolution. Our fathers are Marxists; they never approved.'

Ermano joined in with a smile. 'But our mothers always kept their Catholic faith and made sure we did. Prayers have helped clear our minds. We accept our responsibilities.'

Hector nodded. 'We are not angels, but we know about loyalty. Our place is with our people in Cuba, standing against the Yankee aggressors.'

The cigarette butts were dropped and ground into the stone.

'We must make arrangements and say farewell to friends.' Hector offered a one-finger salute. 'Stay safe and study hard, Ingrid. I hope you can visit our beautiful island one day when the world is over this madness.'

Ingrid gulped. They were leaving; Pedro was leaving. Should she tell them about the peace stick, that her glücksbringer might stop the bombs?

Hector and Ermano dashed for an approaching northern tram; there was no chance to break the secret pact with Sylvie.

'You are not joining them, Pedro?' There was a flicker of hope.

'Not on the tram. But I will be returning to Cuba. It will be a long journey across Europe to the sea, then we have to find a boat. If the American navy does not sink us.' He raised his eyes to the grey clouds. 'We have been praying that our homes will be there when we arrive.'

Pedro's gaze returned to Ingrid. 'We have enjoyed our time in Erfurt. Your citizens have treated us well. Perhaps we might be able to return to complete our studies. Adios, Ingrid.' He waved and waited for a tram to turn left into Marktstrasse before crossing the road.

An emptiness filled Ingrid as she watched the most beautiful man in the world walk out of her life. It was silly to have such feelings for Pedro. He was a Cuban man; she was a schoolgirl. But her heart did not understand that logic.

Ingrid looked around the empty Domplatz. The worker by the obelisk was finally moving. He glanced at her, then back to Pedro as he disappeared down the road towards the Rathaus. *Stasi!*

It was instinctive. She had never consciously seen a Stasi agent in the field. Hundreds might have passed her by during trips around Erfurt and the Altstadt. They were part of the fabric of the city, no concern to her. Until one set his gaze upon Pedro. Why?

The man was average: mid-30s, his body stocky, his hair dark. His clothes were typical of other workmen. His cap was not distinctive either. He should have been in a factory, not hiding behind an obelisk. Who else but a Stasi agent would be watching Pedro – and now he was following him!

The city library no longer held interest. The trip had been a spur-of-the-moment decision after she had eaten her soljanka and completed her cleaning duties at home. Vati had returned to his work at the tailor shop; Mutti was sewing dresses for her special client. It was the most important connection the Richter family could make in Erfurt: Mutti stitching together lovely fashion for Helga, the Stasi colonel's wife. They usually spent hours surrounded by fabric, patterns and gossip.

Herr Schumann had been too distracted to set homework; Ingrid was too upset to watch the afternoon fairy tale on television. She wanted more information about the threat facing them, especially the radiation. Sylvie had raised an interesting point on their walk home from school. They might survive the bombs, missiles and burning skin, but what would radiation do to the crops? If the fallout could kill people long after the bombs had detonated, what would it do to their Schrebergarten? Could they still grow potatoes, carrots and cabbages? Would the apple tree sprout fruit next year? What use would it be to survive President Kennedy's bombers only to starve to death?

Curiosity had encouraged her to make the long walk to the Altstadt. There were answers inside the library, although they were going to have to wait. Pedro was in trouble with the Stasi. The agent was following him down Marktstrasse. It was obvious to her if nobody else. The man was hiding behind the monument one minute, the next he almost ran into a rattling tram to keep Pedro in sight. She had to warn Pedro the Stasi was following.

It was only 200 metres to the Fischmarkt, the traditional heart of Erfurt. Pedro was halfway there, the Stasi agent 50 metres behind. He seemed to have lost interest in Ingrid. She needed to catch up but not alert either man. Pedro might stop to ask why Ingrid was following him; that could be bad for both of them under the eyes of a Stasi agent.

Pedro was striding easily, a purpose to his walk from what Ingrid could see. Was his destination the Rathaus? Perhaps town hall officials had to approve his travel papers. Ingrid had no idea about leaving the GDR, apart from knowing it had been impossible to visit Mutti's parents in the West since the Berlin Wall went up. Mutti was sad about that.

The agent kept pace with Pedro. Ingrid hugged the walls. There were shops along the way; the window displays were ignored. She scanned for an alcove or doorway to dart inside if the agent should turn his head.

Pedro stayed left at Fischmarkt, passing the gabled Gildehaus and ignoring the Rathaus across the square. The lane took him towards the Krämerbrücke. Maybe Pedro was taking a last tourist view of the city. The cobbled street and buildings were showing their age, needing paint and repairs. The Altstadt was not a priority for the State. It was still a magical place to Ingrid, especially the puppet shop. She loved looking through the window as the craftsman worked on new creations for lucky children.

There was enough foot traffic for Ingrid and the Stasi agent to look like innocent pedestrians. He was a worker at the end of his shift; she was a schoolgirl on her way home. Ingrid was grateful Pedro was intent on his destination. There was a kink to the right in the bridge, about 20 metres from the start. Pedro appeared to hasten his steps a few moments before he was lost from view. She watched the Stasi man rush to close the gap; the cobbled street was only 120 metres long with a warren of narrow streets on the other side. She scurried forward.

The arch below St Ägidien's was the portal at the eastern end of the bridge. Pedro should have been close by the time Ingrid rounded the bend. Instead, it was a confused Stasi agent under the brickwork, checking doorways on either side. Pedro had vanished.

There were four doors to check, then the Wenigemarkt beyond. Ingrid wondered if she should turn back. There were few shops of interest to a schoolgirl on the bridge, no convenient escapes if the agent backtracked. She was shielded by two Frauen and their shopping bags. There was a passage to the river between the last houses on the left. Everyone in Erfurt knew about them. Ingrid reasoned the Stasi man had seen no sign of Pedro in the tiny lane and had rushed towards the arch and square.

Was Pedro running alongside the river to escape the Stasi?

It was only a few seconds to the gap. Ingrid darted around the elderly women and down the lane. She scampered down the steps to the plaza that afforded a picturesque view of the bridge and its medieval homes. She heard feet running on cobbles, briefly saw a dark jacket before it disappeared down a narrow road to the right. Pedro? Ingrid did not know these back streets; was it wise to continue? Pedro had evaded the Stasi; he was safe for the moment.

Did he know that he was a target? Pedro might have been late for his appointment and ran to make up time, not knowing he was under surveillance. Ingrid should tell him – if she could find him. That was what a friend would do.

Ingrid ran through the plaza. There was no sign of Pedro or anyone in the street where he had disappeared. She ran to the next fork, her heart racing. She turned left and the noble pursuit ended at the walls of the Augustinerkloster. The beating in her chest took her breath away – this was an area that carried its own terrors.

The world knew it as the monastery where Martin Luther had taken his vows. Some of the ideas that initiated the schism at the Diet of Worms had probably germinated in Luther's monastic cell. It started as an important church in the 13th Century; currently it was a Lutheran seminary. For Ingrid, the Augustinerkloster represented death. She always begged Vati to avoid it on their city walks.

Ingrid turned, seeking the quickest way back to the Domplatz. Pedro was gone, the library could wait; she wanted the sanctuary of home.

A hand clasped her jacket.

'What are you doing here?'

It was the Stasi agent. He had backtracked and followed the same route by the river. Ingrid's face flushed. Pedro had escaped the Stasi, and she had almost put them back on his trail.

The hand roughly shook her shoulder.

'Answer me. What are you doing here? You spoke to the Cuban in the Domplatz – where is he?'

'I don't know where he is.'

'How do you know him? And his friends? You spoke to all of them. Tell me or I will have to take you to Andreasstrasse.'

A chill ran through Ingrid. She had not heard of children being interrogated in the prison. Was the Stasi allowed to do that? She was not sure and did not want to find out. But she could not betray Pedro.

'I met the Cuban teachers at a summer camp.'

'Where?'

'Glowe, on the Baltic Sea. My mother was working as a cook for the teachers. She helped run the kitchen with an aunty and some friends. They were allowed to take their children for a free holiday'

The grip on her jacket loosened.

'What did the Cubans say to you in the Domplatz?'

'They asked how my studies are going. I practised some of the Spanish they taught us at camp. It was the first time I have seen them since we returned to Erfurt in August.'

The hand fell away from her shoulder. Ingrid felt hope build. Telling the truth was working. Maybe not all the truth – especially the part about the Cubans wanting to go home to fight the Americans. That was their business, not the Stasi's.

The agent looked up and down the street. There were no pedestrians or vanishing Cubans. He waved at the walls of the Augustinerkloster.

'What are you doing here? I know where you live – this is a long way from home.'

Another chill rolled through Ingrid; did the Stasi know everything?

'I was about to pay a tribute to a special woman. My middle name is Katharina. She was killed in the Augustinerkloster in 1945 during a bombing raid.'

The agent nodded. 'I remember that – hundreds died.'

'Today is Katharina's birthday. Vati and Mutti said I'm mature enough to come alone to honour Katharina.'

'Are you going to pray for her?'

'No. We are loyal to the Party.'

The agent grunted. 'Who was Katharina to your family?'

'A close friend.' Ingrid swallowed, hoping she did not have to share the full story. Katharina was Dutch, her father's fiancée during the war. Before he met Angela, her Mutti. Katharina was granted permission to visit Erfurt, which had not been heavily bombed like most German cities. Until the last months of the war. The church basement was a public air raid shelter. It could not withstand the British attack on February 25 – Katharina was one of the 267 who died not far from where Ingrid stood. The Augustinerkloster spooked her every time she saw it. Another shiver rippled through her.

The agent saw the shudder and backed off.

'Make your peace then.'

He turned back towards the Krämerbrücke.

Pedro would be safe.

The truth had worked again. Well, most of it. Ingrid did not know Katharina's birthday. It was a small fib, not like the big lie about the Soviets saving Erfurt and liberating Buchenwald.

She felt drained after the confrontation with the Stasi. Goodness. What would she tell Sylvie in the morning? She had finally seen Pedro again, he was going home to fight the Americans, he had run away from a Stasi agent – and Ingrid had been questioned. Would Sylvie believe anything? More importantly, would Sylvie be waiting as usual tomorrow?

Herr Schumann

SCHUMANN SWUNG HIS WORK SATCHEL CASUALLY; A RATTLING COULD BE heard with every forward swing of his arm as he crossed the Krämerbrücke. He did not expect the small timber chess pieces to line up for battle that evening; there was much for him and his old friend to discuss.

The teacher had not diverted to his four-room apartment in Anger after school. There was nobody waiting at home to share supper. Schumann had been a widower since the first British air raids on Berlin. He had never forgiven Reichsmarschall Hermann Göring for his boast that no enemy bombers could reach the Ruhr.

The World War I veteran had returned to his birthplace in Erfurt after losing Claudia. At 41, he had expected the bayonet wounds in his side and the shrapnel in his left leg would exclude him from further service for the Fatherland. Schools were still open, students needed educating; he reasoned that his birthplace in Thuringia in the middle of Germany would be safer than most towns. It had been until the final months of World War II.

Schumann usually enjoyed crossing the Krämerbrücke, often humming Johann Pachelbel's Canon in D. The composer spent 12 years as an organist and teacher at the nearby Predigerkirche. Impending nuclear disaster doused any joy to be taken from the ancient façades. The State had done some restoration work on the half-timber buildings but not enough to guarantee their long-term survival.

Schumann had always studied the history of his city: Martin Luther was an icon, the medieval Altstadt was a treasure under threat from negligence, the Dom and Severikirche were permanent links to the past. Erfurt had been a crossroad for pilgrims on the Camino to Santiago de Compostela when Christians were welcomed in Thuringia.

Faith in an all-powerful divinity lapsed for Schumann after November 11, 1918. He had survived the Great War. But, safe from the trenches, Schumann's rational mind wanted to know why God could allow that carnage on the Somme, Flanders and every other battlefield.

There had been no reason to pray again until Thuringia was caught in a military sandwich between the Americans and Russians in 1945. Schumann was given a ragtag uniform and a rifle, sent to Weimar and told 'the Führer must be protected'.

No prayers were offered for the lunatic who had led Germany into the maelstrom. There was not a hint of hypocrisy in the prayers Schumann muttered as artillery shells fell upon the final meagre defences. He begged God for his own survival and that he could surrender to the Americans and not the Russians.

Schumann arrived at Zum Goldenen Schwan. The inn had seen better days, but the local beers were worth the walk. So was the schweinsteak with Thuringia dumplings; lunch had been bread and sausage. He looked at the darkening sky. Would this be his last supper?

'Ach! You are a grumpy old man.'

A large hand slapped Schumann on the shoulder.

'You have always been grumpy, Tomas.'

It was Jürgen Grau.

'Come inside, let a beer and schnapps lift some of your woes.'

It was too cold for the biergarten, which would not reopen until spring. Dark ceiling beams and supports set the tone for the interior. The lighting was sparse; coal fires glowed dimly against the walls. None of the five patrons hugging their drinks had removed their jackets. They showed no interest in the old teachers who settled in a corner far from everyone.

The toast was spoken in unison. 'Prost!'

They drank, the glasses were returned to a scarred table that might contain carvings from Martin Luther when he was a student at the university.

Schumann took a moment to study his friend. Grau was the same age but looked five years younger. He was tall, trim despite the beers and dumplings they regularly consumed. Grau's weekend walks through the Steigerwald must be the difference between their elderly frames.

Grau had never married, vowing as they marched despondently home from France in 1918 that Germany was not a fit place to raise kinder. Ironically, he was allocated a place at teacher training college a week after Schumann in 1922. The pair wanted to help the young shape a better world.

Schumann snorted at the long-ago idealism. Their work in educating malleable minds had not prevented World War II or, it would seem, World War III. He sipped more beer without offering their second traditional toast to good health. 'Zum wohl' would have been wasted words.

Grau knuckled the table. 'Come on, Tomas, the bombs are not falling yet. There is time for more beer. Maybe even time to find a lovely Frau and a night of fun?'

His friend had always had a cruder streak, which had to be kept in check at school.

'I am a respectable teacher, Jürgen.' A smile creased Schumann's face. 'I will not be found dead in the arms of a widow after an American attack. Especially one of your castoffs.'

The table rocked from a fierce slap; laughter roused three of the other drinkers to briefly raise their heads from their beers.

'That's better, Tomas. We should laugh at what fate dishes out. Besides, what is wrong with my former lovers?'

'There are too many, for a start.'

Schumann quelled his laughter and drank more beer. Grau could snap him out of the glummest moods. He was able to live more for the moment, a trait that escaped the practical Schumann. Secretly, he had envied Grau's success with women. There were many who had lost husbands during the war. They sought companionship without commitment, such as Grau offered. Not Schumann: he could never replace his soul-mate, Claudia. It was almost a blessing she had died quickly in the 1940 raid. She had had enough Jewish blood for the Gestapo to condemn her to a concentration camp.

Schumann lowered his voice. 'I have not been home yet. Is there any news about the naval blockade around Cuba? Have they sunk any Russians ships?'

'Not that I have heard.' Grau twirled his glass. 'I think the blockade – or quarantine, as the Americans call it – does not start until tomorrow afternoon our time.'

'Maybe the British and French can talk sense into their NATO ally. If Kennedy goes to war against the Russians, they all get dragged into the conflict. They have nuclear weapons as well.'

Grau spread his arms in exasperation. 'We could have missiles and bombers flying in all directions. Just like when Hitler was in charge. Do you remember the skies filled with planes?'

Schumann nodded. 'Then the bombs fell.'

The beer was their refuge from those memories.

'It should not happen again.' Grau slapped the table. 'We fought two wars to make the world safer. Now a few generals can end it in minutes.'

Schumann smiled. 'Careful, Jürgen. You are starting to sound like me – a grumpy old man.'

'I have been trying to avoid thinking about the danger. It is frustrating when we have no control. At least we had guns and grenades in the trenches. The threat was 80 metres away across the mud. If the French, British or Americans slithered across no man's land, we could stab them with bayonets or shoot them. I had to bash one Tommy with a stielhandgranate.'

'I remember. I stopped you after the fourth blow when you split his skull. I thought one more hit would blow us all to hell.'

'They were brutal times. But we had a duty to defend the Fatherland.' Grau gestured at the ceiling. 'What can we do against B-52s loaded with nuclear weapons? They don't target combatants – they kill everyone. The old, the young, women, children. Innocents. The ones who have no say and who probably have no idea of the threat hanging over them tonight.'

Schumann's lips pursed, but he didn't raise the glass. 'My class understands.'

Grau replaced his beer without drinking. 'You told your class about the American threat?'

'Yes.'

'How much?'

'As much as I knew this morning. That President Kennedy said he had evidence the Russians were building missile sites in Cuba. They will be capable of hitting every American city with nuclear warheads. He wants the missiles removed and will impose a blockade around Cuba to stop more missiles reaching the sites.'

'That was a huge risk, Tomas. How did they react?'

'They were shocked, which is natural. But they are also mature. We have raised our kinder to be more aware. They know about the socialist-capitalist divide. American children chew gum and play baseball. Our students know about the threat to daily lives from the West. I was proud of how they coped with the news.'

'That Kennedy could start a nuclear domino that could end their world?'

'Yes. I felt they had a right to know.'

Glasses rattled as a barman cleaned them in a sink behind the counter. The aroma of cooking pork drifted from the kitchen. Schumann was surprised that his saliva glands activated. Old soldiers knew when to eat a hot meal; you never knew if there would be another.

Grau caught the barman's eye and waved for two refills.

'You know most of the class will tell their parents this evening.'

'I am sure they will.'

Grau snorted. 'Are you going to wear your best suit to class tomorrow? You want to look good when the Stasi haul you away for interrogation.'

Schumann grasped the lapels of his jacket. 'But this is my best. Hand-made by Dieter Richter.'

The gallows humour waned as Schumann thought about Ingrid and their discussion at Buchenwald the day before.

'Everyone in Erfurt will know about the Cuban crisis by morning. Everyone watches the television news from West Germany. My revelations will be quickly forgotten. However, I did take another risk.'

Grau groaned. 'You are getting sillier every day, Tomas.' The rebuke was tongue in cheek. 'What else have you done?'

'Class 7A went to Buchenwald yesterday.'

Grau took a swallow from a fresh beer. 'It's always a horrible experience for kinder to see what the Nazis did. What happened?'

'I always find myself drawn to the crematorium. Thousands of bodies were destroyed there, in ovens made by Topf & Söhne. That Erfurt connection to the Holocaust always upsets me. My Claudia could have ended up there for having a Jewish grandmother.'

'Few of my classes ever notice that plate,' said Grau. 'They always walk quickly through the camp, eager to get on the bus and back to school.'

'It is usually the same with my students. Except for Ingrid.' He tapped his lapel. 'Dieter's daughter. She saw the Topf nameplate and returned to question me. I told her what I knew: that the company designed and installed the ovens at Buchenwald. I have heard they also made ovens for Auschwitz and other camps. Not that I shared that information. Ingrid was horrified to know the ovens were manufactured a few streets from her home.'

Grau wiped droplets from his glass. 'The Stasi will say you were indiscreet but might let you off with a warning and a broken arm – or two.'

The pair chuckled. Dark jokes had always been a default setting since the trenches.

'The brutes in Andreasstrasse might still get a chance to grind my bones for their bread. I told Ingrid that Buchenwald and Erfurt were liberated by the Americans, not the Russians.'

Grau's beer spilled onto the table.

'That was silly, my old friend. I would joke about the Stasi shooting you for treason if I wasn't worried they might do it. Will she tell her friends?'

Schumann made calming gestures with his hands. Grau's agitation had aroused the attention of a new drinker at a table close to the bar. A spitzel? Stool pigeons were everywhere.

'I was caught up in a moment of honesty – about Buchenwald, about Erfurt and what happened in 1945. But I'm safe.'

'How can you say that?'

'I had a chance to reconfirm for the class that the Soviets were our liberators from the Nazis. If Ingrid should ever repeat our Buchenwald conversation, it would be her word against mine.'

Grau sighed, then drank deeply. Two beers were normally their limit, carefully nursed throughout a chess game or dinner to enable them to walk home sober. Schumann thought his friend might want to break that habit.

'You know truth would be no defence for treason if the Stasi put you in front of a firing squad. Every adult who was in Erfurt that day the 80th Infantry Division rolled into town knows to keep their mouths shut. The Socialist Unity Party dictates what is truth – not dumb teachers like Tomas Schumann.'

Schumann shrugged. Ingrid knew he had lied to the class today. She should be smart enough to know it was necessary. They drank in silence for a few minutes. Thoughts ranged from the personal quandary he had initiated at the concentration camp to the existential crisis for the world in Cuba. It suddenly struck him that both might have been avoided if he had sacrificed himself 17 years ago.

'Jürgen. I probably could have prevented this drama during the last war.'

'How? You weren't on the Russian front; you couldn't shoot Khrushchev. We had no troops in the Pacific, so you could not shoot Kennedy. Shooting one of those roosters might have saved the world.'

'But I could have shot Eisenhower.'

Grau's jaw dropped. 'At Buchenwald? How? There were too many American soldiers. They would have riddled you with bullets before you got close to a gun.'

'I had my own.'

'The Luger? You took the pistol to Buchenwald to shoot the Supreme Commander of the Allied Forces in Europe?'

Schumann almost laughed at his friend's incredulity. It was one of the rare secrets he had kept from his comrade.

They had stripped off their threadbare Wehrmacht uniforms and blended into the Weimar community before the American military arrived. They had never been Nazis; the community was willing to protect enforced recruits when the war was lost. Schumann and Grau were incorporated into the staff of the makeshift schools.

Their teacher status could not prevent them being caught in a round-up of military-age men after General Patton discovered evidence of the Holocaust in Buchenwald. They were among the hundreds from Weimar who were marched to the camp by American soldiers to witness the horror.

Schumann had no idea what danger they faced. The Americans were angry. The camps were a dirty secret that was too risky to acknowledge. Were the losers about to be confined in the same barbaric conditions, or would the Americans want revenge? Schumann had not survived two wars to march silently to his death.

The Americans had not searched anyone before ordering them along the road to the camp. The Luger – taken from a dead commander in Belgium – rested in a makeshift holster in his jacket.

Grau found his voice again. 'I remember Eisenhower walking near the truck loaded with bodies … the disgust on his face …' Grau shook his head. 'We were only a dozen metres away.'

'Yes. Technically we were still at war. We had not surrendered. We were probably not even officially part of the Wehrmacht. We were given a gun like thousands of young kids and old men, told to shoot Russians and Americans. I could have shot Eisenhower and then surrendered.'

Grau's laugh lifted heads all around the Goldenen Schwan. 'If you had done that, there would have been no chance to surrender. You would have been shredded by a hundred Tommy guns in seconds. Me too – I was standing beside you. And what would you have achieved?'

'Prevented the nuclear arms race. Eisenhower went home a hero to win the presidency in 1952. He walked into the White House with the backing from capitalists and the military to build the world's biggest nuclear arsenal.' Schumann waved a finger at the smoke-stained ceiling. 'Eisenhower is the reason we are living in fear tonight. He escalated the global arms race and left a young idiot in charge.'

Grau stared at his beer, dabbed a finger in the moisture gathered on the table. 'Maybe you are not so silly, Tomas. But you think of the wrong leader at the wrong time.'

Schumann puzzled over that conundrum for a minute. Then he made the connection.

'Hitler. Here in Erfurt in 1933.'

A nod. 'There were several opportunities: signing Erfurt's golden book as the chancellor, the photos on the Domplatz, the rally at the stadium.'

'It might have been easier the year before at Gera. He was mobbed by everyone.'

Grau leaned on the table and rubbed his brow. 'We were believers in '32. We wanted someone to drag us out of poverty and starvation, give us back our dignity.'

Schumann nodded at the memory of what had happened in the following 12 months.

'Then Claudia made us read *Mein Kampf*. We saw the real monster.'

They witnessed the growth of the public fervour for Hitler, supported by his thugs. Their private dread grew through the rearmament and expansion of the Third Reich: the unchallenged return to the Rhineland, the Anschluss in Austria, the marches into the Sudetenland and Czechoslovakia.

They were appalled, but not surprised, by the treatment of Jews. It was all signposted in Hitler's book. The Führer committed them to another confrontation with France and Britain when troops invaded Poland. By then it was too late. Hitler was untouchable.

Gunther Kitz

The paperwork on the Cuban teacher trainees took longer to complete than Gunther Kitz would have expected. It was supposed to have been a routine day. Their agitation at the Pedagogical Institute, the tram ride to the Domplatz, the prayers inside the cathedral, the meeting with the schoolgirl, the split and the deliberate evasion by Pedro Barios all had to be explained. With copies. The report delayed his final mission of the day: a visit to Friedrich-List Strasse to check on the Richter family. What were their loyalties to the Party?

Kitz was dedicated, and angry the Cuban had sneaked away at the Krämerbrücke. His report did not detail the Cuban's cleverness; it highlighted a guilty dash through the narrow streets and lanes, assisted by traitors who would be identified. He had submitted a request to the commander to order a sweep through the river-side district the following day. Kitz would plot the likely escape route.

The other two Cubans had returned to the dormitory and shown no sign of following their friend. If anything, they appeared calmer than they had during the morning classes. The supervisor decided not to *invite* them into Stasi headquarters until the senior officers checked with Berlin. The Cubans were allies, their homeland in danger of being obliterated by the United States. The Colonel advised his agents to be diplomatic. They could harass Erfurt citizens; Kitz would have to wait to find out why Pedro Barios was on the run.

The delay meant Kitz did not reach Friedrich-List Strasse 10 until after eight o'clock. It was a four-level apartment block of golden brick. A small lawn with a spiked-iron fence provided a secure area for children to play. Kitz decided they must have good connections.

Every curtain in the block was closed, not surprising as it was dark and cold. Inside, he expected the families were enjoying the warmth of a kachelofen. The neighbourhood had recently received its winter supply of coal. Kist saw the stain on the grass from where the briquettes had been dumped; all hands in the apartments would have been enlisted to shift them to the cellars.

Most likely the Richters were watching the West German television news. He could disrupt their evening: ring the bell, demand to know why their daughter was wandering the Altstadt by herself. Kitz knew he would not catch them breaking the law; one parent would have returned the television to a GDR broadcast while the other *slowly* answered the door.

Scaring the Richters would be fun, but maybe it could wait until he had compiled more background information. The Stasi's inoffizieller mitarbeiter in the block was in hospital for a gall bladder operation. There was nothing to stop Kist from visiting the informant on security business at any hour, but it had been a long day; he did not want the extra travel.

There was another collaborator on the second floor at Number 11; he had a view over both properties and should know some of the gossip on Dieter and Angela: who visited them, what they discussed in the communal courtyards. That was the informant's duty to the Party – to keep an eye on everyone in the neighbourhood.

Digging for more information might explain the daughter's strange behaviour. She had spoken to the Cuban before he ran. Then she was found close to where Pedro Barios vanished. Her explanation about the tribute to a family friend was plausible. Should he inquire further?

The Richter file revealed they had a spare room that was frequently made available to needy boarders. The most recent had been a Polish mother and daughter. The bedroom was empty now; perhaps the Stasi should encourage one of their informants, or even an agent, to take up residence for a few weeks

One more item to check and file. No detail was too inconsequential for a good agent. It was like putting together a jigsaw; piece by piece the Stasi built a picture of each citizen and their loyalty to the Party.

He would talk to the informant at Number 11, then walk home to consider his next move. He lived 700 metres away; his own connections ensured an equally nice apartment and suburb. He would brief his son about surveillance on Ingrid. Matthias would enjoy following a suspicious student – good training for the future. Kitz looked forward to Matthias being the second generation to join the Ministry for State Security.

Ingrid Richter

INGRID HAD NEVER EXPERIENCED SUCH A FEARFUL DAY; SHIVERS HAD swirled through her body almost hourly. The cause of the latest shudder was a loud bell at the entrance to the apartment block. It was distant, thankfully not theirs. Maybe the next floor up. The timing was scary: mid-evening on a Tuesday during the West German television news: not a traditional time for visitors. That would not be good for the family upstairs.

She gently parted the curtain to the lounge. Heat from the ceramic lime-green tiles of the kachelofen was welcome. Ingrid thought of the winter days when she and Vati waited for apples to bake on a tray inside. Would they get to enjoy that simple treat again?

Mutti had ushered her to bed early, saying Ingrid looked exhausted. Ingrid did not object, but when sleep refused to ease her troubles, she slipped out of bed in time for the news. There was so much at stake; her mind could not rest.

Her shoulder, hip and thigh rested against the arched doorway as she avoided the squeaky floorboard in the middle. She could see the backs of her parents' armchairs. They had been moved to sit side-by-side, close to the screen so the volume could stay low. The gap was wide enough for Ingrid to watch and just hear the latest news on Cuba.

There were pictures of President Kennedy and Comrade Khrushchev. They were smiling and waving one minute, the next they were serious and surrounded by stern men. Then came the shocking images: nuclear explosions, the mushroom cloud over Hiroshima, devastated Nagasaki. Next were close-ups of homes, trees and trucks being destroyed in an instant – examples of how nuclear weapons were getting more powerful with every test.

Ingrid kept a clenched hand over her mouth to prevent her from crying at the horrible images. She occasionally watched the broadcast with her parents. That evening, she suspected Vati and Mutti were trying to shield her. Then came a moment of tenderness and love: her father reached out a hand to her mother. She heard a sniffle; Mutti was crying. Yet they could not take their eyes off the television. The hunger for news of their fate was reflected in the daughter who hid behind the curtain.

The only new information since Herr Schumann's morning report was that the United States Navy would blockade Cuba the next day. Any Soviet ships that tried to break through would be stopped or sunk. Either event could be enough to trigger World War III. The West Germans said shipping reports indicated about two dozen Soviet vessels were approaching the restriction zone. The crisis could reach a peak in the next 24 hours.

There was no time to find Sylvie after her return from the Altstadt to tell her about Pedro, or his escape from the Stasi agent – and her own questioning. She did not share anything about the afternoon adventure with her parents. They were subdued over their salad and sourdough supper. There was no mention of Cuba or that the meal could be the last as a family.

Their reluctance to talk about the missile threat was disappointing. It was understandable that they did not want to worry their daughter. But she was 13 and almost an adult. Even Herr Schumann had taken a risk to tell them. He treated them like mature students, capable of understanding the danger, brave enough to not panic. GDR kinder had a right to know about catastrophic events that threatened their existence. A part of Ingrid wished her parents had treated her the same way.

It did not diminish her love for Vati and Mutti. They were a close family. Ingrid often wished that she had a sibling – even a brother – to share their summer weekends at the allotment and the Steigerwald. Her own arrival had been a small miracle – the labour was extremely difficult – and her parents thought it wiser not to have another child.

That meant more attention for Ingrid. The influx of westpakete in the past year presented Mutti with more material to create beautiful dresses and shirts. Having to share Mutti's seamstress skills with a sister or brother would have halved her wardrobe of new clothes. It might have been reduced to a quarter if there had been a brother. She saw how boys at school were always ripping shirts and shorts in boisterous games of football, or tearing them on tree branches in the Stadtpark.

The television news service moved to other stories. Ingrid's knees were sore. She was about to ease away from the squeaky board to climb back under her feather bettdecke when her parents started talking.

Dieter Richter

'I THINK INGRID DESERVES TO KNOW WHAT IS HAPPENING IN CUBA,' SAID Dieter.

'But she is still young. She should be thinking of her studies, activities with the Thälmann Pioneers, the start of ice skating, having fun in the snow in the Steigerwald.' Angela waved an arm at the small television screen in the corner. 'Nice things – not the end of the world.'

Dieter clasped her hand again.

'Ingrid is a smart girl. Sensible. There will be talk at school tomorrow about the American threat. It is better that we prepare her.'

'And what will happen, Dieter? Kennedy might start a thermonuclear war that could destroy us. How do we explain that to a child?'

'We have to hope that it doesn't happen. Kennedy or Khrushchev must recognise the madness they have created. They are like teenage bullies waving big sticks at each other, daring the other to strike first.' Dieter shook his head. 'The world has seen enough of war and misery.'

'Will one of them back down? Who is prepared to suffer that humiliation?'

'Sadly, that is the heart of the matter, Angela.'

Dieter stood to add a briquette to the kachelofen. They were lucky to have received their winter quota early. It had taken many hands to shift and stack them in the cellar. Supplies always dwindled in a crisis; the powerful looked after themselves first.

'I understand Khrushchev's desire to have missiles close to the United States. The Turks are pointing nuclear weapons at the Russians' heads, just a few minutes from Moscow.' Dieter shrugged. 'I can't see Khrushchev wanting to take his finger of the trigger first.'

Angela pulled her cardigan tighter. 'We know how paranoid the Russians can be.' She shivered. 'I thought they would shoot us that night we were detained.'

Dieter walked over and wrapped an arm around his wife's shoulder. He had been just as terrified, caught by Russian soldiers while crossing the border with a pistol in his pocket.

It was before Ingrid was born, in the early days of the Socialist Unity Party regime. The border was porous, with barbed wire and minefields not yet completed. The enemy was defined – the West – but plans were still evolving to prevent GDR citizens from moving stealthily between the two zones for food and family reunions.

'I can still hear the Russians yelling "stoya! stoya!"' Angela said. 'The rifles pointed at our hearts.'

'That was scary. And unlucky. If they hadn't stopped to piss, we would never have been seen.'

They had had a small bag with cheese, sausage and coffee. The essentials were available in GDR shops, but the quality never compared to the West.

'Thank goodness the Russians were young, almost too scared to fire their guns without an officer.'

'I was more worried you might shoot first, Dieter. You might have got one soldier – but not two.'

Dieter remembered the temptation. He had been carrying a Mauser HSc, sneaked out of the armoury of the *Schlesien* before she was scuttled near Swinemünde in the Baltic. The ship had hit a British mine in the final days of the war, killing two crewmates. The future was uncertain; Dieter, like many veterans, had wanted a gun for protection.

'It was never a serious option, Angela. Besides, you had a better plan – stashing the pistol inside your fur muffler.'

The memory prompted a short laugh.

'I saw the soldiers were trying to hold their guns steady while buttoning their flies. I knew they would search you – but might be scared to touch a woman with her husband watching.'

'It was smart thinking.'

They had been marched at gun point to a shack a few hundred metres away. An officer huddled beside a small coal fire, not interested in Germans crossing *into* the East. It was the escapees who merited interrogation.

'And you were clever when the officer asked for our papers. You laid the muffler on the table, right in front of his eyes.'

That memory made them laugh, although they swiftly cut it short, not wanting to disturb Ingrid sleeping in the middle room.

'It was freezing outside, but I was worried a drop of sweat would fall from my brow as he checked our identities,' Dieter said.

'I was trying to stop my knees from shaking,' said Angela. 'Thankfully he was more interested in the coffee. It was a small price to pay for our freedom.'

That was one of their last covert shopping expeditions to the West. It was many months before they wanted to brave the border patrols again. The defences were becoming more robust as the East Germans took responsibility for security.

'Did you get rid of the pistol, Dieter, like I told you?'

'No. It is in a safe place where Ingrid will never find it.'

Angela nodded. 'You still have bullets?'

'Yes.'

Wednesday, October 24, 1962

Ingrid Richter

Ingrid arranged her blonde bob with a comb and hand mirror. It took seconds to control the locks, enough time to dream about when she could grow them longer, at least to her shoulders. She desperately wanted to use colourful ribbons to tie up her hair, like her school friend Petra Stelzer. Mutti said Ingrid had to wait until she was in the senior classes. Until then, the sharpest scissors would come out every fortnight to trim her fringe, sides and back.

Short, straight hair was convenient on days when she was late for school. Two days in a row was rare. Ingrid looked at puffy eyes rimmed with a tinge of darkness, evidence of a restless sleep: another nightmare.

This time it was Vati and Mutti in trouble, their daughter floating above the scene, witnessing the terror, unable to do anything about it.

They were running through the woods at night. Russian soldiers were chasing them, stopping every few metres to shoot at them. Ingrid felt the heat of the bullets before they gouged chunks from the trees. She saw Vati urge Mutti forward, then stop to aim a pistol at the Russians, but it would not fire. Her parents were defenceless and there was nothing Ingrid could do to save them.

Finally, they came to the wall – they were in Berlin, their backs to the bricks. The odd location did not register with Ingrid. Her focus was on her adored Vati and Mutti. The pistol was thrown away, their hands raised in surrender; they had nowhere to run. Ingrid felt the warm glow of relief; they would survive to give birth to her.

The terror returned when the Russians did not lower their weapons. More soldiers appeared. They marched into place beside their comrades, an officer with a sword taking charge. It was a firing squad. Ingrid had seen enough of them on the television. It was full of horrible movies about the brutal Nazis and Gestapo. Every child had those images permanently scarred on their brains. The officer ordered the soldiers to raise their rifles. Ingrid's screams were not heard. The officer told the soldiers to aim at her parents. The command to fire was accompanied by blinding light from 10 rifles …

The open curtain, morning chill and Mutti with the raised feather bettdecke had never been so welcome. The dream evaporated in seconds, overwhelmed by the joy of finding that she would share another day with her family. The Americans and Russians had not destroyed the world while she slept. The peace stick must have worked! Would it still be in the wall slot when she and Sylvie arrived at school? Would the glücksbringer continue to keep them safe?

'You're late again, Ingrid.'

Mutti's tone was gentler than the day before. Ingrid was not pressed about reasons for her tiredness, merely nudged along to get ready for school.

A boiled egg had been added to the breakfast. Ingrid happily peeled the shell and ate it between mouthfuls of buttered bread and marmalade. Mutti fussed around the kitchen as usual, tidying and cleaning. Vati had already gone to work. Ingrid's tardiness had ruined plans for a morning chat.

'Vati wanted to talk to you before school.'

Ingrid knew the topic but nodded vaguely. To acknowledge that would invite questions about two indiscretions: listening at the curtain last night and Herr Schumann's bombshell at school.

'Some kinder might tell you strange things at school.'

Ingrid added more salt to the egg. 'About what, Mutti?'

'About the Americans making threats against the Soviets because of Cuba. You know about Cuba from the students at the summer camp.'

'Yes, Mutti.' There was nothing to be gained by admitting to having met Pedro, Hector and Ermano in the Altstadt. That might change Mutti's mild tone.

'Well, the Americans don't like the Russians building military bases to defend the Cubans. They have threatened to attack the bases.' Mutti paused in the middle of the kitchen with the duster in hand. 'There is a chance it could lead to a new war.'

Ingrid knew what was expected. Was she a good enough actress?

'Oh Mutti! That's terrible. We've had too many wars. Can anything be done to prevent it?'

'Yes, my darling.' Mutti wrapped a protective arm around her daughter. 'The Soviet leader is a brave, strong man. He made President Kennedy look young and foolish last year when they built the Berlin Wall. Nikita Khrushchev will work out a clever solution.

'Don't be scared if one of your classmates says the world is about to end. They are panicking. Everything will work out. Vati will tell you more when he comes home for lunch.'

Ingrid was pleased her parents had decided to tell her about the crisis in the Caribbean. It was a watered-down version compared to Herr Schumann's scenario, but she knew Mutti was being protective, not wanting to worry her daughter. Everyone would have an opinion on Cuba after secretly watching or listening to the West German news services. Mutti knew it would be a stressful day if every child was worried about the skies filling with missiles and bombers.

'Thank you for telling me, Mutti. I'm sure you're right.'

That was Ingrid's best acting, showing no fear to her mother. Inside, her stomach was churning. Mutti's pep talk was welcome, but it could not drag fingers from the nuclear triggers.

'I'll let Vati explain it better.'

Sylvie was waiting in her usual spot on the driveway, dancing a few steps to warm her toes. Each day was chillier than the one before; polyester clothing was no match for Erfurt's autumn. The tinge on the grey clouds was a fraction darker.

'Hello, Ingrid. How are you?' She pointed at the sky. 'Nervous about the bombers – or whether the peace stick can give us another day?'

Ingrid wobbled her head: neither yes nor no. They started the trek to school with thumbs and fingers wrapped around the straps on their ranzens. Mittens would be required in the next few days. Ingrid usually shared one of her older pairs with Sylvie. They were much warmer than those Sylvie's grandmother knitted.

Her friend glanced several times at Ingrid's tired eyes. 'Did you have the nightmare again?'

A Trabant puffed past; noses wrinkled at the exhaust.

'I had another bad dream – a different one. It was about Vati and

Mutti. They were about to be shot by the Russians for crossing the border.'

'That's scary. What caused that dream?'

Ingrid looked around the street. There were three factory workers 60 metres in front, a schoolboy the same distance behind. There were no uniforms at the 31st Oberschule, but Ingrid presumed that was where he was heading. Habit made her whisper.

'I sneaked out of bed to watch the television news through the curtain.'

Sylvie drew closer. 'What is the West saying?'

'The American navy is going to stop Russian ships going to Cuba. Any ship caught carrying missiles will be sent back to Russia.'

A wind gust sprayed a fresh wave of golden leaves across the road. They would soon turn to mush; the trees were almost bare.

'The Soviets won't surrender. It's like the days of the pirates in the Caribbean. What do you think Khrushchev will do – order the Russians to shoot at the American warships or fire the missiles?'

'I—' a futile wave '—don't know.'

The ever-present brewery smells conceded ground to the fresh-bread aromas from Herr Wenkell's bakery. No customers loitered with the fat baker on the footpath. Worker and student on the streets were intent on their destinations. The quickest were the Frauen with their shopping baskets. Herr Wenkell waved through the window when he saw the girls, although the usual smile was missing.

'How did you get from the Russians and Americans going to war to dreaming about your parents being shot?'

'I listened to them after the news reports. They were talking about the Russians being trigger-happy. They used to sneak through the border on shopping trips before I was born. They wanted coffee, sausage and other stuff to trade, just like we now get in the westpakete. It was before the borders were closed.'

'How did they escape?'

'They bribed a Russian officer with coffee.'

There was no need to tell Sylvie about her father's pistol or that he still had it hidden at home. She was a friend, but Sylvie's gabby mouth could put Vati in a Stasi prison cell.

'I wondered why you looked so tired. Did anyone in 7A sleep

after being told World War III could start any day? My sister said I was mumbling all night, but I don't remember any dreams. Can you imagine having no time to say goodbye to our friends or family? You might never see your darling Pedro again.'

'I did.'

Sylvie stopped in the middle of the road. There was no immediate threat from a stray Trabbi, just a cyclist or two. 'When? Where? Is he still handsome?'

Ingrid looped an arm with Sylvie to resume the walk. First bell was looming. She noticed the boy from Friedrich-List Strasse was closer but had not overtaken them. That was surprising because their own pace was quite slow. She went back to a whisper. 'Mutti was sewing for the Colonel's wife, so I went into the Altstadt. I wanted to find a book in the library about nuclear radiation, see what we could do if we survived the missiles and bombs.'

'Pedro was there, at the library?'

'On the Domplatz. He and Hector and Ermano had been praying in the cathedral. They were worried about their families.'

'That's understandable.'

'They're going home – to fight the Americans.'

Sylvie stumbled, but Ingrid's grip kept them moving.

'What can they do against nuclear bombs?' Sylvie said. 'They'll be killed.'

Ingrid had been nursing the same fears since the meeting outside the cathedral.

'Pedro said it was their duty to their parents and to Cuba.'

Sylvie shook her head. 'Boys always want to be noble. What good is that if you are dead?'

There was no appropriate response, and they walked in silence the rest of the way to school. There was little time for Ingrid to share the rest of the dramatic afternoon around the Krämerbrücke. The priority was the peace stick. It had already given them one new dawn; they wanted thousands more.

They were surrounded by dozens of students as they made the final right turn. Ingrid slowed as they approached the retaining wall. Her heart beat increased. Talking about Pedro had momentarily distracted her from the most important mission of the morning: checking the peace stick. Was it still in place? Would the luck continue? It was a public examination that needed to be done discreetly.

'Don't say anything about the peace stick, Sylvie, even if it is gone. We can't draw attention to the wall. It worked for a day – there might still be more luck to help us. I'll stop to tie my shoe. You can be my shield to stop students tripping over me. We can both look, then move to the courtyard.'

Sylvie nodded.

As Ingrid knelt to fake the shoe tie, she saw the trailing boy stop at the end of the wall. There was no reason: first bell was close, no time to wait for slow-walking friends. She dismissed him as her eyes sought the peace stick. It was still there. Their glücksbringer had worked; they would be safe for another day.

She stood with flushed cheeks, Sylvie's eyes were wide and bright. Fortunately, she stayed silent. They hurried through the passage to the courtyard.

Angela Richter

Washing day in the communal laundry off the courtyard was always laborious. Water had to be heated in large copper bowls. That meant hauling briquettes from the cellar. Angela had learned to judge the correct amount required without being wasteful. She grimaced as the coal bucket clunked on the concrete floor. Did she need to be frugal if the world could end in the next few days?

'Don't be a silly washerwoman!'

She was alone. Her neighbour Gudrun Brendel was still in the cellar; there were six in her family to keep clean. More briquettes were required for her copper. The despair that had gripped Angela during the television news had been suppressed – for Ingrid's sake. There was a glimmer of hope the Soviets and the Americans might find a solution before they irradiated everyone. There was no need for the whole family to worry. It was time to be practical, to focus on the domestic duties.

Clothing and linen were washed with the help of a stampfer to agitate the water and move the heavier pieces around. Each item then had to be forced through the wringer, removing as much moisture as possible before being hung in the courtyard. There were communal lines in the attic for winter.

Angela's mind wandered as she watched the coals heat the bowl. Thoughts in the laundry usually drifted to West German television: commercials where smiling wives in colourful dresses breezed through the most irksome duty with sparkling machines. She looked at her practical, but drab, housecoat and dreamed of the day the GDR could copy the technology. A Miele washing machine mocked Angela from the back wall. It dated from the 1930s, the metal parts cannibalised during the war and never replaced.

A mid-week wash was the most convenient. Four of the six wives in the apartment block worked full-time jobs. That left Angela and Gudrun sharing the brick laundry a few steps down from the courtyard. They each had a stampfer. Gudrun's arms worked harder – she had three boys who played football.

The thud of a heavy coal bucket announced Gudrun's arrival from the cellar.

'Did you hear that the Stasi made a visit to Number 11 last night? Just after eight.'

Angela checked they were alone. She had known Gudrun since the Richters moved into Friedrich-List Strasse 13 years ago. She could be trusted. No previous political discussion had prompted a visit from the Stasi.

'No. Who were they after?'

'Lukas Bauer.'

The slap of wet clothing covered their voices.

'Did they take him away?'

'No.'

Angela nodded; did that mean Bauer was Number 11's informant?

'I wonder what was so important that the Stasi turned up instead of the VoPos. They usually choose more sociable hours.'

'It was probably a pep talk – keep an eye out for families who might think it is safer from nuclear bombs in the West.'

Gudrun snorted, turned a jersey, went to work on removing grass stains.

'Do you believe they will launch nuclear missiles at each other? I think not. Cuba is a spit of land in the Caribbean. Why would Khrushchev risk the world for an island full of blacks?'

The blatant racism did not shock Angela; the slur was voiced often enough before and after the war. Some people would never lose their prejudices. The Richters had learned a great deal about cultural diversity from the occasional boarders in the spare room.

The Polish mother and daughter had been lovely. A Bulgarian stayer became such a good friend he returned to visit with his family. There was a fascinating doctor from Beirut. He had kept them spellbound with stories about Lebanon and the changing politics of the Middle East. The new nation of Israel had defied Arab attempts to drive it into the sea. Doctor Ramia feared tensions would linger for many generations; Angela and Dieter were secretly pleased the Jews had a country they could call home.

Exposure to new cultures did not mean Angela loved all nationalities equally. The Russians were allies, but vocal support for the Soviet

Union was mostly lip-service for the sake of Dieter and Ingrid. She had fled East Prussia with her parents and siblings as the Nazis and Red Army carved up Poland. They could run no further than Hemme in Schleswig-Holstein. It was beyond the Russians' reach at the start of the war, inside the British zone of occupation by the end. That was where she met and fell in love with Dieter in 1946.

They could have stayed safely on the western side of the Iron Curtain. It was family that drew Dieter back to Erfurt. The eldest Richter son had to support his parents; Angela went with him as a dutiful wife. They never expected the growing paranoia of the Socialist Unity Party to permanently separate Angela from her family. Perhaps in a couple of days it would not matter; neither East nor West would be safe anymore.

Angela moved several items to the wringers, then they would be hauled out to the courtyard to dry. She had learned the frosts could help the drying process. It froze the water droplets in bed sheets. These could be shaken off before they were taken to the warmth of the attic. She watched Gudrun load another copper; it would take her at least another hour to finish.

The question about the merits of defending Cubans had been treated as rhetorical. Angela tried to navigate to safer waters.

'What are you preparing for lunch, Gudrun?'

'Lentil soup. You?'

'Semolina. No time for anything fancy on washing day.'

They laughed.

'Hendrik turns 13 on Friday. I wonder if the post will have something special for him from Hamburg.'

Young noses were pressed to the window for a week before birthdays and Christmas, hoping to see the yellow postal van arrive with a westpaket.

'Let me know if you get any cotton from your sister. I can trade you some coffee – or make a blouse for your daughter.'

'You are such a wheeler-dealer, Angela.' Gudrun smiled. 'Elsa grows so quickly. I never have enough clothes to fit her. I'll let you know if there are hand-me-downs. Elsa loves your designs; she always complains East German fashion is ugly. Teenage girls!'

Gudrun went back to the drudgery of wringing; a process Angela had never expected she might wish to do again. She admired her neighbour's faith in Khrushchev and Kennedy's ability to resolve the crisis. Could they settle their differences to ensure her daughter would grow up to raise her own family? She looked around the old laundry; maybe even the mundane could be appealing.

Ingrid Richter

THE MOOD WAS SOMBRE AS STUDENTS LOOPED THE COURTYARD DURING the long break. Snacks had been consumed, feet were mobile, chatter was muted. There was no new bombshell from Herr Schumann to set the tone. He had been silent on the nuclear threat: not a word about Cuba or the American navy waiting to attack Soviet vessels on the high seas. Piracy, as one boy whispered amongst the pack as they trudged into class after first bell.

There was no need for Herr Schumann to risk a visit from the Stasi. All the students had learned about the Cuban Missile Crisis from either legal or illegal broadcasts, many from both. Sylvie was puzzled there was no fresh information from their teacher. Ingrid had to grip her friend's arm tightly in class to signal there should be no questions.

Their courtyard pack had expanded to four with Renate and Katja, which prevented discussion of the peace stick success.

'Cuba has become the elephant in the room,' Ingrid said.

'What does that mean?' Renate asked. 'We could never fit an elephant in our classroom.'

They all giggled, a welcome feeling after strained morning sessions of German and maths.

'It's something my Opa often says,' Ingrid said. 'He reads a lot of books in German and English. He spends hours telling me wonderful stories when I visit. He says people avoid talking about an obvious problem, often because they are scared.'

'We heard what Herr Schumann said yesterday.' Katja's voice dropped to a whisper. 'Do you think the Stasi heard and told him not to talk about Cuban missiles again?'

Three heads nodded.

Ingrid glanced around the courtyard; most students idled at a snail's pace. Petra Stelzer was with two girls in front of them. Gerard, Kurt and Thorsten were diagonally opposite, heads bent in a private conversation.

'Kurt can be strange,' said Sylvie.

Ingrid thought for a moment, then nodded. 'He looks at life differently.'

'Yes,' said Renate. 'I was with Sylvie between classes this morning. Kurt was laughing about the next jugendweihe ceremony. His brother is 14 – ready to make the pledge to defend socialism and *peace-loving people*. Kurt said his brother was panicking the Party wouldn't present his adult papers because he didn't know how to stop a nuclear attack.'

'That *is* weird,' said Ingrid.

The chatter moved to the best coming-of-age ceremonies the schoolgirls had attended. The occasions were celebrated with much fanfare and presents. None wanted to point out the elephant – would there be any more jugendweihe?

'Have you noticed that eighth grader following us?' said Katja.

The pack turned as one. The boy stopped like a startled doe. Katja and Renate giggled. He was 10 metres behind and looked no different than dozens of other boys on the courtyard: slender, wearing a plain jersey, trousers, shoes. Boring.

Ingrid glanced at Sylvie; she raised an eyebrow. It was the boy who had followed them to school.

'Which one of you does he like?' Katja pointed a finger at Ingrid, then Sylvie. 'He lives close to us, and he knows we don't like him.'

'He's creepy,' Renate whispered. They all turned again. The eighth grader had dropped back, although he remained in the walking loop. Ingrid wondered how much of their conversation had been overheard.

'He followed us this morning.' Sylvie cast him an evil glance. 'He was standing in our street while I waited for Ingrid. I thought he might have a friend at Number 9.'

Ingrid was surprised. 'I didn't realise he was waiting.'

Sylvie shrugged. 'Who is he?'

'Matthias Kist.' Renate dismissed him, picking up the pace. 'He's just a boy, not a man like *my* Pedro.'

Ingrid and Sylvie shared a smirk behind her back. Katja missed it also. A raised eyebrow from Sylvie indicated she wanted some fun.

The competition for Pedro Barios had been fierce during the Baltic holiday. Sylvie's mother was not invited to share the cooking duties for the teacher trainees, thankfully. Otherwise, it would have been a four-way contest.

Sylvie dangled the bait. 'Have you spoken to Pedro since your return to Erfurt, Renate?'

'No. We have both been too busy with school.'

'The holidays finished in August; we are almost at the end of October. That is a long silence for *friends*.'

'We formed a special bond at Glowe.'

Ingrid noticed the change in Renate's tone. She was getting annoyed, probably wondering why Sylvie was interested in her friendship with the Cuban. Sylvie had never met him.

'But I thought Pedro treated you as equals?'

Katja stole a glance at Sylvie, then Ingrid, her brows knitted.

Ingrid was enjoying the cat-and-mouse game. It was a distraction from the nuclear threat, a reminder of their final night at the beach.

They had swooned over Pedro for eight weeks, each trying to find ways to spend more time with him. They had felt so grown up with the trainees. They were the only kinder at the camp, apart from Gerard. He tagged along when it suited, then disappeared to kick a football when they chased Pedro with puppy dog eyes.

They were sitting in a strandkorb on that last night, the beach basket sheltering them from the wind. The debate about who Pedro liked best had grown so heated they stewed in silence, with Gerard on the sand. He dared them to go to Pedro's tent and settle the question: who did Pedro believe was the most beautiful?

They did, to Gerard's surprise. And Pedro's. And his two Cuban tent mates. Honour was at stake for the young teens.

Ingrid's heart was beating like a piston when they entered Pedro's tent. They had agreed on the walk over that they would ask the question together; none would seem braver than the others.

The palpitations continued during the eternity they waited for Pedro to reply. His response made him more endearing.

'Each one of you has something beautiful.'

Sylvie the cat was still playing in the courtyard. 'Treating you the same at the beach does not mean you get the same treatment in Erfurt.'

Renate stopped, the furrow in her brow deeper than Katja's. 'What do you mean?'

'Perhaps he likes Ingrid better – but didn't want to hurt your feelings.'

'No!'

Katja was just as adamant. 'You don't know him. You can't say that!'

They turned on Ingrid.

'Have you been writing to Pedro?' said Renate. 'He never answered my letters.'

Renate's face was flushed. 'Have you met him? At the institute? You should not go there. That is unfair.'

'She didn't have to chase Pedro,' said Sylvie. 'He went to find her – in the Domplatz.'

Ingrid nodded as two jaws sagged. The chuckles finally overwhelmed her and Sylvie. They held onto each other as several groups passed, bemused by the only laughter at the school.

'Oh, you two!' Renate's hands were on her hips. 'You are always teasing us.'

Ingrid wiped her eyes. 'But it's true. I met Pedro in the Domplatz – yesterday.'

'He went there to find you?'

'No.' Ingrid put away a handkerchief she had been dabbing at her eyes. 'Pedro was in the square – with Hector and Ermano. We met by chance – they went to the cathedral to pray for their families in Cuba.'

She watched Sylvie's smile dim; every conversation went back to the crisis in Cuba.

'Pedro surprised me, but then I surprised them.' Ingrid smiled. 'I greeted them in Spanish. They said it was very good.'

Learning that the meeting in the square had been accidental was small consolation for Renate and Katja. They had lost ground in the battle for Pedro's attention. Ingrid knew the contest was over; should she tell them Pedro was going home to fight the Americans?

Sylvie beat her to it.

'You are all too late. Now I will never meet the most beautiful man in the world. They are going back to Cuba.'

'No!' Renate looked like she was about to cry. 'He will be killed!'

'They are going to bomb Cuba any day,' said Katja. 'Why go back to certain death?'

'Is here any safer?' The fun of the teasing had evaporated for Ingrid. 'You heard Herr Schumann – once they start firing the missiles, it's never going to stop.'

The silence was more pronounced. Few students were in the courtyard; the supervising teachers were waving them back to class. Ingrid heard a shoe scuff behind them. She turned to find Matthias

Kist still lurked nearby. How close had he been when they had talked about Pedro? Ingrid still had to tell Sylvie about her encounter with the Stasi agent. The walk home would be her next opportunity, as long as the stalker kept his distance.

Gunther Kist

A SCREWED-UP SHEET OF PAPER RICOCHETED OFF THE RUBBISH BIN AND rolled under a nearby desk at the Stasi office on Andreasstrasse. It mocked Gunther Kist for a minute until old habits forced him out of a rickety office chair with a heavy sigh. It was secrecy rather than tidiness that motived the second attempt to be rid of the document. It contained doodling about the runaway Cuban. Further investigation was not going to happen.

Word had come through from headquarters that the regional agents were to leave the Cubans alone. Their *unusual* behaviour – praying in the cathedral, running from the Stasi – was not deemed overly suspicious considering the political dramas in their homeland. Paperwork had been received – and approved – for the trainee teachers to return to Cuba.

The generals were impressed by the young Cubans' noble gesture to fight the Americans. Everyone in Berlin knew it was futile. Brave hearts and rifles were no match for nuclear weapons. Loyalty to Fidel Castro, the Revolution and their families should be rewarded. The indiscretion of running from the Stasi would be overlooked. Unless Pedro Barios survived the American bombers. A copy of Gunther Kist's report would be sent to Cuba's secret police. Anyone left alive in Havana next month could investigate Pedro.

The suspect had returned to the teacher dormitory after midnight. He spent the hours until dawn smoking and talking with his comrades on a balcony. There was no device close enough to record their conversations. It was more fuel to the pyre of Gunther Kist's suspicions, but he could not disobey an order. The most he could do was slap a palm against the desk.

'Still fuming about the Cubans?' Carsten Hartwig returned a telephone to its cradle, then wrote on a pad.

Kist waved a hand in apology. 'Sorry for being angry. I know Pedro is being devious. But Berlin refusing to let me investigate because they are *heroes* – going home to be martyrs – is nonsense.'

Hartwig was a large man, almost two metres, with thick dark hair and eyebrows with barely a gap in the middle. It limited his surveillance work but had not stifled his Stasi career. The 34-year-old joined a year after Kist and had already outshone him as a sharper investigator and leader. His personal list of spies in Erfurt was legendary in the office. He had bumped Kist's report up the line to protect his own back.

'I can approve a final *observation*. That won't contradict Berlin's order as you'll be watching them leave from the Hauptbahnhof.'

Kist's excitement peaked and troughed in eight seconds. Watching the Cubans depart was not going to solve the enigma of Pedro Barios.

Hartwig laughed. 'You don't think that it will provide the answers we seek?'

Kist shrugged. 'I would rather the Cuban spent a few days as a *guest* in our cells.' Kist smacked a fist into his palm. 'I could find out why he ran yesterday. If it was nothing criminal or treasonous – we can put him on the train to wherever.'

'No. Pedro is untouchable – but his local contacts are not.'

Kist tilted his head and waited for Hartwig to elaborate.

'I have been told the Cubans are catching the train to Berlin this afternoon.'

'But there is a more direct route to the West through Bebra. After that, I have no idea how many trains they will need to reach a port. But Berlin seems a backward step if they are in a hurry.'

'They are, and that is why they are flying from Schönefeld Airport to Amsterdam with Deutsche Lufthansa. They are booked on a freighter from Rotterdam tomorrow night.'

'Flying? Where do communist schoolteachers get the money to fly?'

'Exactly!' Hartwig smiled and folded his arms. 'I have learned that Pedro Barios arranged to sell something last night. The payment and handover will happen at the Hauptbahnhof. You might not get the Cuban, Gunther, but you might catch a black marketeer.'

Kist smiled. A disloyal ally was departing permanently while a local criminal would be inside the cells by evening. That was a better result than he could have contemplated five minutes ago. Life in the Stasi had a habit of changing rapidly. There could even be a turnaround in the other source of his frustration: the Richter family.

His visit to Friedrich-List Strasse last night had been worrying. Lukas Bauer said the Richters had an important connection – one of the top commanders in the Stasi. It had required all of Kist's skills to remain calm after hearing that information. He could not afford to have Bauer immediately running to his regular agent. Kist handled it professionally: a knee to the groin, two kicks to the kidneys, a warning to never talk about the visit. Problem solved.

Further discreet inquiries this morning had revealed the Richter family connection to Colonel Brecht was via the wives. Angela Richter was a talented seamstress whose fashion creations made Helga, the Colonel's wife, very happy. The daughter's name was Ingrid. Her involvement with the Cuban was suspicious. The Richter family was not totally off Kist's radar, but they could sit below the horizon for a while. Even a Stasi colonel could not protect a black marketeer.

Ingrid Richter

Music from Radio Luxembourg played quietly as Ingrid adjusted her blue neckerchief with the hand mirror. She was dressed for the Thälmann Pioneers' Wednesday meeting, but she would not be attending. Neither would Sylvie. Their curiosity about the nuclear threat – bombs and long-term radiation – was overpowering. Answers might be found in the regional library on the Domplatz; another visit into the Altstadt had to be risked. They hoped adults would assume they were on their way to a meeting rather than avoiding Pioneer duties.

Escape from the apartment was no problem for Ingrid; Vati was at the tailor's shop and Mutti was at Helga Brecht's home finishing her latest dresses. That should have been an encouraging sign. The wife of one of the Stasi's top officials in Erfurt was going about life as normal; did that indicate they held no fears about the city being flattened by American bombers? Ingrid tried to wring a smidgen of confidence from that thought.

Vati had used a reassuring tone to explain the Cuban Missile Crisis during their lunchtime meal. The Soviets and Americans were in a nuclear-armed standoff, but he was confident the Russian leader would prevent an attack. Nikita Khrushchev had proved he was a wily operator by climbing to the top job in the Kremlin. The US President had been elected on his good looks; a failed invasion of Cuba the previous year proved he lacked the diplomatic skills to beat the Soviet leader.

Ingrid had nodded through her father's analysis, hoping his trust in their allies would be proven correct. She did not question him about the range of the bombers or the nuclear fallout dangers. He had to get back to work and she knew their library visit could provide those answers.

The butterflies that had swirled in her stomach over the past two days had mostly settled. Not from the semolina. Possibly from Vati's calm manner. Perhaps it was the peace stick working its magic. She and Sylvie had checked it discreetly as they left school at 1.30pm: it was in place, no sign of curious fingers trying to extract it. They had another day to live; the politicians had more time to find a solution.

They were grateful there was no sign of the eighth grader who stalked them before and during school. Did Matthias Kist fancy Ingrid or Sylvie, or was he acting out a silly dare from one of his friends? They were inclined to think it was the latter when they were able to leave the school grounds by themselves. Boys could be so immature.

Sylvie's exit from home for the afternoon adventure was more contrived. They were early for the Pioneers; her mother was told they had to study a monument in the Stadtpark for a discussion. The girls were waved away without questioning.

The park was their first destination regardless of the fib. The walk to the Domplatz would take 30 to 45 minutes, depending on how much they chatted, which might cost them valuable time in the library. They decided to catch a tram from the southern corner of the park. It would take them under the Hauptbahnhof, through Anger, past the Rathaus and deliver them to the Domplatz. Ingrid could have taken that option the previous day but had worried that a solo journey might have prompted questions from adult passengers. Her own jugendweihe ceremony was almost 12 months away. Maybe.

'This feels exciting.'

Sylvie held her arm as they walked the 300 metres to Windthorstrasse. They would wait until the park to board a tram in case a neighbour saw them.

'We have our secret peace stick in the school wall, we are truants from the Pioneers, now we are sneaking into the Altstadt. Maybe the Stasi will want to recruit us?'

Ingrid shivered. 'Don't joke about that, Sylvie. And please don't mention it on the tram.'

There was a twinge of guilt as Sylvie rolled her eyes. Her friend's quirky sense of humour had not been dimmed by the tension of the past two days. They did not have to wait long at the park; a tram was soon trundling towards them on the narrow-gauge track. There were two carriages; hopefully the passengers were spread out between both. They did not want to sit close to an adult who might want to know what Pioneer activity required a tram ride.

The fares were cheap because most citizens relied on trams for transport. They had only seen a dozen Trabants and five Wartburgs since leaving home. They boarded the second carriage; there was an elderly couple and a worker with his cap tucked low over his eyes, possibly sleeping before a shift at the brewery near the park. They walked to the middle, at least four rows from the other occupants. The tall, grim conductor took their fares without saying a word. The girls had been warned not to engage them in conversation as they were often Stasi informers.

Sylvie had the window seat. 'I like the autumn colours, but I hate the bare trees. Winter makes me dream of Fiji.'

'Why?'

'The palm trees are green all year round.' Sylvie pointed to skeletal branches. 'They need them for shelter because it's so hot. And they are always full of coconuts. Have you ever drunk coconut milk? It's supposed to be delicious and healthy. You can rub it on your skin and lie in the sun all day. I wish we could go there.'

Ingrid did not want to puncture her friend's dream. The Party was unlikely to change its travel restrictions. 'Maybe one day.'

'Do you think anyone would bomb Fiji? It's thousands of kilometres from anywhere out in the middle of the Pacific Ocean. Why would you want to destroy a paradise?'

'Why would *anyone* want to bomb another city or country?' Ingrid shook her head. 'I can't imagine hating anyone that much. I might not like everybody – but I don't want to destroy them. Or the world. It seems silly to me.'

'Unless you're a Nazi.'

Ingrid glanced around the tram to see if the other passengers had overheard. All eyes were facing the front. They paused at the top of the park for the worker to exit. Another grime-coated tram trundled south. The dour transport reflected much of the city in the colder months; overcast skies sucked all the colour from Erfurt. Grand medieval houses highlighted their need for a clean. Paint was either in short supply or too expensive because most buildings were years overdue for a fresh coat.

The tram turned right over the Gera-Flutgraben, the safety valve for the city when the river was in flood. Then they passed under the train station. It was still an important hub, although the network was not as extensive as before the war.

'Do you remember coming to say farewell to Herr Meister last year? That was a fun day. We had ice-cream after his train left for the West.'

'There must have been a hundred students and parents. I was surprised when he cried.'

Herr Meister was their teacher from first to fourth class. He did not have to cut barbed wire, sneak through minefields or avoid trigger-happy border guards to leave the GDR. He simply boarded a train at the Erfurt Hauptbahnhof and went West after he retired. The East was happy to be spared a pension for a citizen who was no longer productive; the West was content to pay the price for a refugee from a dictatorship.

Their former teacher had no living relatives in the East; most had died during the war. There was nothing tying him to the GDR. His students were secretly told in the final teaching days that he longed to visit famous shrines at Lourdes in France, Santiago de Compostela in Spain and Fatima in Portugal. Postcards to the 31st Oberschule briefly confirmed his dream had been completed. They were removed from the notice board within an hour.

'It seems strange that the Volksarmee guard the border all day and night to stop us from going to the West.' Sylvie gestured out the window. 'Yet we are allowed to celebrate and wave goodbye to a valued citizen when they turn 65.'

Their tram had emerged onto the plaza in front of the Hauptbahnhof. There were no large farewell gatherings for pensioners, just a few groups scattered around the triple-arch entrance. Ingrid's attention focused on a group of four – three exotic men and a local woman – standing between the tram track and the front of the building. She knew them all: she had seen the Cubans at the Domplatz yesterday; the woman had served her semolina for lunch. She gasped as Mutti exchanged something with Pedro Barios.

'What's wrong, Ingrid?' Sylvie swivelled towards the plaza. 'You've gone white. What did you see?'

The tram was moving north towards Anger. Ingrid was confused. Why had her mother been meeting Pedro and his friends, and what had they swapped? Her mother was the best westpaket wheeler-dealer she knew. What could she trade with Pedro who was about to leave the country? The most immediate question was: should she tell Sylvie? Her dilemma was solved by a passenger in the first carriage pulling the cord to stop the tram.

'Come on, Sylvie. We have to get off.' Ingrid was grateful Sylvie responded without further questions. She hoped her friend would treat it as a fresh lark.

They were on Bahnhof Strasse, 200 metres from the station. They were alone, which made it safer to talk.

'Pedro and his friends were outside the station. We have to go back.'

Sylvie squealed. 'I'm finally going to meet the most handsome man in the world!'

'I don't know.' Ingrid was almost running.

'Why not? Why can't I say hello?'

'Because ... something was strange.'

They separated to race around an elderly man. He cursed at their rudeness.

'Sorry!' Sylvie apologised for them both.

The pace finally eased when they approached the station forecourt. It was flanked by a hotel and the station façade and large enough to play a game of football. Ingrid pulled Sylvie close; they hugged the stonework until they could shelter behind a taxi and guests at the hotel entrance.

'Look. There they are, holding their bags near the entrance.'

'Let's go then. They won't be boarding immediately. We can ... oh!'

Sylvie had seen what had shocked Ingrid.

'What is your mother doing here? Is she saying goodbye?'

They watched as Angela shook hands with each of the Cubans. It was a formal, if not fond, gesture. That did not quell the resurgent butterflies in Ingrid's stomach.

'Did your mother meet them at the camp in Glowe?'

'Yes. She even joined one of our Spanish lessons, to help me practice at home.'

Sylvie smiled. 'That explains it. Maybe she wanted to wish them farewell in Spanish – like you did in the Domplatz.'

'Maybe.'

Ingrid wondered whether to let Sylvie believe that was her mother's only connection to the visitors. Everyone in the neighbourhood knew that Angela was a canny trader; most had made secret westpaket exchanges. Should she tell Sylvie her mother was making a last-minute deal with a foreigner? The entrenched secrecy of life in the GDR made her cautious, even with a friend.

Angela turned right to exit the forecourt while the Cubans moved to the entrance. Ingrid wanted to rush over. Her excuse could be to introduce Sylvie. Pedro, Hector and Ermano would be naturally polite. Most of all, she wanted to know what her mother was doing. It was the man who emerged from under the arches that ended notions of a proper goodbye with Pedro. It was the Stasi agent.

Ingrid feared he was going to arrest Pedro. The Stasi man was dressed differently: a shorter jacket, darker hat, spectacles and a thin moustache. It did not fool Ingrid. He glared at the Cubans as they walked inside the station. Then he hastened towards the tram line on Bahnhof Strasse – the same direction Ingrid's mother had taken.

'Oh no!'

'That's alright. We can go inside. They probably need to buy tickets. Come on.'

'We have no time for Pedro. Look.' Ingrid pointed to the agent who was exiting the square. 'That's the Stasi who chased Pedro yesterday.'

'Why doesn't he arrest your Pedro?'

'Because I think he's following Mutti. We must warn her.'

Sylvie didn't hesitate. She grabbed Ingrid's arm and they ran along the hotel wall in pursuit.

At the corner, they saw the Stasi agent walking with his hands in his jacket about 40 metres behind Angela Richter. Ingrid's mother was unaware of the danger. Ingrid had two options: call out to attract Mutti's attention or run to her? Either choice could cause problems: how to explain their wanderings in the Altstadt instead of being at the Thälmann Pioneers.

A tram rumbled towards Anger; Mutti would not hear a shouted greeting. They followed the pursuer and the pursued. The tram slowed as it passed the agent; his eyes were on Angela. She opened her purse and retrieved some coins. Mutti was going to catch the tram; she could escape the Stasi. To Ingrid's horror, the agent sprinted as the doors opened and Mutti entered. He squeezed on-board a few seconds later.

'Come on, Sylvie. We have to catch the tram at another stop.'

The trams were never fast because of the proximity to pedestrians. The schoolgirls dodged shoppers and street signs while trying not to trip on cobbles and rails. But young Pioneer legs were no match for electrically powered wheels. They almost caught up in the square outside the Hauptpost in Anger as an elderly woman exited slowly. The doors closed and the tram pulled away when they were 20 metres short.

'I can't run any further.' Sylvie was bent over, hands on her knees.

Ingrid puffed just as hard. Should she leave her friend, hope to catch the tram in the Fischmarkt? There was always a queue waiting for transport outside the Rathaus.

No. Ingrid's legs felt like jelly; Mutti's fate rested with the Stasi.

They took a minute to recover their breath, then set off at a steady pace along Schlösserstrasse. They frequently checked over their shoulders for a new tram on the same route. The only traffic was on foot or bicycles.

'Why is the Stasi following your mother?'

'She gave something to Pedro.'

They crossed the river.

'Was it a going-away present? Something to remind him of Erfurt and the GDR?'

'I don't think so. It looked more like a trade. Pedro gave her something too.'

They were approaching the Fischmarkt; the only trams were trundling towards them.

'What would your mother be selling to Pedro? They don't need coffee or soap. Maybe it was chocolate? That would be tastier than train food.'

'No.' Ingrid knew it was not chocolate bars from the family's westpaket supplies. They always went straight into the buffet in the lounge, which was kept locked. Vati and Ingrid had a sweet tooth – treats would be gobbled on the first evening if Mutti did not act as guardian. She dished out the chocolate two pieces at a time to make it last. Ingrid knew their supply was getting low; Mutti would never risk a rebellion in the Richter home by selling the last Western chocolate.

They heard the rattle of an approaching tram as they were about to enter Marktstrasse. There was no need to return to the stop in the square; the Domplatz was barely 200 metres away. Aromas from a bakery near Allerheiligenkirche stalled Sylvie. She stared through the window at the last éclairs. Treats had been ignored on the way to and from school the past two days.

'Can we stop for a moment?' asked Sylvie. 'Running always makes me hungry.'

'You get something – I can't eat.'

Ingrid stayed outside. The ancient buildings were a perfect setting for a grim fairy tale. They were three to four storeys high; several had crumbling rendered walls. Many leaned menacingly towards the network of cables that powered the trams. She would not be surprised if a witch or goblin poked their heads out a window.

Sylvie emerged from the shop eating an éclair and holding another.

'The baker gave me two for the price of one because he wants to close.' She held the spare out to Ingrid. 'Are you sure you don't want it?'

The choux pastry filled with cream always looked enticing. Éclairs were Ingrid's favourite; this one had an extra-thick layer of chocolate.

'Oh, alright. You'll get fat if you eat both.' She licked a creamy end.

Normally they gulped éclairs, the treats too tasty to be eaten daintily. Still puffed from their run, they nibbled slowly as they walked the final metres to the Domplatz. Ingrid did not want to acknowledge the possibility an American bomber could make it their last. She looked at the dark clouds as they arrived at the plaza. There could be a hundred planes overhead with nuclear bombs, but they would never see them.

There was no sign of her mother or the Stasi agent. It would be impossible to miss them as only a handful of pedestrians were crossing the square in various directions. The tram lines swung to the right onto Andreasstrasse where they ran past the Stasi headquarters. Did the agent sit back with a smile and let the tram do his work, delivering a suspect to the prison door? That thought almost soured the éclair.

Ingrid faced a conundrum: should she go to Vati's tailor shop to tell him about Mutti? She might be in the Stasi headquarters up the road, or she might still be on the tram. If that was the case, Ingrid would be accused of crying wolf, which would embarrass her parents. She was worried about her mother, but there was no proof she was in the hands of the Stasi. That agent might like to follow citizens all day. Mutti might not have anything incriminating on her; there would be no reason for the Stasi to hold her.

Ingrid turned from the Stasi end of the city to where Sylvie had crossed the cobbles to the Domplatz. She followed her to the obelisk.

'Why are we here? The library is over there.' Ingrid pointed to the northern corner.

Sylvie sighed. 'Looking at the churches made me think of Martini. It's only a couple of weeks away, but will we get to celebrate this year?'

Thoughts of a sea of paper lanterns sprang to mind for Ingrid: people from all over Erfurt filling the square for a Christian event in a secular state. November 10 marked the birthday for the former resident and Father of the Reformation, Martin Luther. St Martin of Tours, the city patron, was honoured the following day. Erfurt had created a unique tradition, more popularly known as Martini. Children led the way to the square with their lanterns to remember the Martins.

'I love going to the shops to select our lanterns.' Sylvie swung her arms wide and twirled. 'My brothers always have a bratwurst with mustard on a bun.' Sylvie giggled. 'I usually bite the ends. They try to steal my Martinshörnchen with the jam filling. Then we go home to count the hours until we can parade to the Domplatz. We're always fighting over the lanterns until they're lit.' Another sigh. 'It's such a fun festival – I hope we get to celebrate again.'

Ingrid's Martini days were just as enjoyable, although as an only child not as adventurous. She remembered being allowed to carry the lantern for the first time in class 1. It had made her feel proud and grown up. The religious connections had no relevance; it was the excitement of the community festival, of the city coming together, that made it so memorable.

Leaves fluttered across the stone as a breeze reminded the schoolgirls the first snowfalls were only a few weeks away. Ingrid looked at the massive churches that dominated the city. The Dom was the most formidable, like a stone battleship with its rounded façade and tall, narrow, stained-glass windows. It rested on a dry dock supported by a series of arches. Three green-tinged spires formed the bridge at the rear. In the centre was the clock tower that housed the famous Gloriosa bell. Every child in Erfurt knew it dated back to the days before Martin Luther; it launched Martini at 6pm with the first ring.

Severikirche, across the stairway, was imposing but never made

Ingrid think about battleships. It had three green spires facing the Domplatz and a squat bulk running away from it. Neither structure looked inviting; Ingrid had never seen if the coloured windows looked prettier on the inside.

Sylvie interrupted her observations.

'Do you want to say a prayer that your mother will be okay? And Pedro?'

'I wouldn't know what to say. Do you?'

'No. My parents have never taken me to church. My father said his faith died in the Ardennes, along with many of his comrades. Martini is the closest my family gets to religion.'

'I think it's the same with many soldiers and sailors, although Vati never talks about his war years. All I know is the ship he served on: the *Schlesien*.'

'I wonder if praying offered them hope when they were fighting the Americans and British – like our peace stick.'

'Maybe. Pedro, Hector and Ermano said they felt better after going to the cathedral yesterday. If you really believe in something, perhaps those good feelings spread.'

'I wonder who will protect us better – Pedro's god or the peace stick?'

An answer to that escaped Ingrid as another wind gust encouraged her to return to the original mission: investigating nuclear bombs and their radioactive fallout. What would happen to the survivors after the Americans and Russians ran out of missiles?

Sylvie pointed to the Petersberg Citadel beyond the churches. It had been protecting Erfurt since the late 17th Century, although the landlords had changed several times. Prussia, Napoleon, the German Empire, the Nazis and the Soviets had occupied one of the largest town fortresses in Europe before the Volksarmee was given the keys to the doors. Would the people's army welcome citizens in a nuclear crisis?

Sylvie clapped her hands. 'We should have thought of it earlier. We can shelter in the citadel when the bombs and missiles start flying!'

Ingrid looked at the massive stone walls. The highest were 26 metres, the thickest six. It was funny how those facts from a lesson last year stuck in her mind. Probably because it was just after the Berlin

Wall had been built.

'Remember Herr Schumann telling us about the tunnels inside the walls?' Sylvie pointed. 'How could any bombs reach us there?'

Ingrid thought of her namesake, Katharina. The Augustinerkloster basement was supposed to have been protection against the British planes. Nuclear bombs were more powerful than everything that was dropped on Erfurt during the war. But Ingrid did not want to burst her friend's bubble.

'The army controls the citadel. I guess they might let us in if the bombers come.'

'I'm sure they would. The whole town will probably have the same idea. We need to get here first.'

'What if we're in school, or in our beds? How long would it take to get here?'

Sylvie's eyes were alight. 'I think we should do a trial. Tomorrow. Time ourselves from school and home.'

'We don't have watches.'

'I'll get one from my brother. He leaves it at home when he plays football.'

'Would we have to run all the way?'

'No. That might look suspicious. I think we run when nobody is watching, then walk. That will give us a good indication. I'm sure I can run like the wind if I know there is a nuclear bomber on the way.'

Ingrid did not want to point out the flaw in that argument: would they hear the bomber? At least it was another reason not to despair if the peace stick let them down.

'That's a good idea. Petersberg Citadel offers some protection, which makes our homework even more important. We must find out what to do after the bombs have fallen.'

Ingrid hooked an arm through Sylvie's and turned towards the library. They hurried across the square with a cold wind at their backs. The research might be chilling, but at least it would be warmer inside.

The library stood taller than the surrounding buildings. It had four floors of collections and a high, peaked roof that could probably store a similar number of books. The grand façade made it worthy of a hotel entrance, although it required some maintenance.

They waited for a tram to pass south before crossing. Ingrid gasped.

'There's Mutti – on the tram!'

'Should we catch it?'

The tram had made the decision; it rolled around the bend into Marktstrasse leaving no time to catch up. Mutti was free, there was no sign of the Stasi agent. Perhaps a session in the library could help her decide how to explain everything to her mother. The girls should have been at the Thälmann Pioneers, not running around the Altstadt. She worried that her mother would be more upset about that deception than being a target for the Stasi.

The library catalogue had led them to a large book without the help of a librarian. They carried it to a quiet corner near the arched windows. The statistics were as awful as the photos. Sylvie whispered them as they sat shoulder to shoulder.

'The first atomic bomb on Hiroshima contained about 15,000 tons of TNT. It destroyed eight square kilometres of the city.'

Sylvie paused, wet her lips.

'An estimated 70,000 Japanese citizens were killed instantly, and 100,000 were dead from injuries and radiation sickness by the end of 1945.

'The final casualty figures remain unknown as more people died in the following years from cancer and long-term radiation effects.'

The schoolgirls sat in silence for many minutes as they looked at photos of the devastation in Hiroshima and Nagasaki. The second bomb was plutonium; it killed almost 80,000 people and destroyed 30 per cent of the city.

Ingrid looked out the window. 'If they dropped a bomb here on the Domplatz, it would destroy our homes and school.'

'Unless we're inside the citadel.' Sylvie pointed at a photo of Nagasaki. 'That church is still standing after the blast. The roof is gone, but the walls and spire are mostly intact. Anyone below ground could have survived.'

Sylvie gestured towards Petersberg Hill. 'We know there are tunnels under the fortress. They're much thicker than church walls – we would have a better chance.'

Ingrid nodded. 'There is still the radiation to worry about. What can we do about that?'

A book on radiation sickness was found. Most of the research was based on the Japan bombs and testing by the Americans and British during the past decade.

'See.' Sylvie indicated a page with tips on how to avoid the worst effects of a nuclear bomb. 'The scientists say we must get inside a building to avoid radiation fallout. We need clean clothes and water to wash our bodies if we don't get to the citadel in time.'

Ingrid read along with her friend.

'We'll need four litres of water a day for at least three days, non-perishable food, a battery-powered radio, and torches. That is a lot to find and take to the citadel.'

'We should carry tins and torches on our trial tomorrow. It will give us an idea of the weight.'

'What about water? That is more important.'

'We have a few empty Vita Cola bottle at home. You must have some too.'

Ingrid shrugged. 'Maybe one. Mutti says too much cola rots my teeth. It's a birthday and Christmas treat.'

'Look for other bottles. We can fill them with water and hide them in the laundry. We'll squeeze them into our ranzens before running to the citadel.'

Ingrid's chin rested in her hands until her eyes drooped; Sylvie had been turning the pages. There was a lot of advice: some of it good, much of it gloomy. It would be much easier if the peace stick worked. *Please be in the wall in the morning.*

Tomas Schumann

Ancient timber stairs creaked as Tomas Schumann climbed to his second-floor apartment in Anger. It was within a stone's throw of the Hauptpost and the tram line. Climbing two flights at the end of school was the most exercise he wanted in a day. He was keen to reach 65, possibly even follow his friend Meister to the West. Exploring great cities like Paris, Rome, Madrid and London appealed. But Schumann did not see a need to maintain the fitness or weight of his army days to enjoy retirement.

He placed a shopping bag of potatoes, cabbage, cheese and sausages on the floor as he retrieved the door key from the leather satchel he had inherited from his father. The apartment consisted of four rooms and a short corridor. To the left was the bedroom and a lounge, to the right the bathroom and kitchen. The left-side windows opened to a cobbled courtyard, home to a few cars: Trabbis and the Wartburg owned by a VoPo captain. Crime was never an issue in the area.

Guilt sat heavily on his shoulders. He had avoided talking about the Cuban Missile Crisis with his class. That was unfair; he had thrown the world crisis in their laps, then failed in his most basic duty – to educate young minds. It was a familiar survival instinct that kept him silent, initiated by a warning from Grau before the first class.

'The spitzels were gossiping before you arrived. Most people know that you told 7A about Cuba. Hold your tongue, my friend.'

There had not been much new information that Schumann could have shared with the class. The United States was six hours behind the GDR; the blockade was still several hours away when his students assembled for first bell. It had been easy to heed Grau's advice, until the inquiring and worried eyes of his students pierced his heart. They wanted to know if American bombers would be using their courtyard as a target. If they could dream of surviving to study and play another day.

Schumann had protected his back by turning around and launching into the lesson. He justified his decision, as he wrote on the blackboard, that he had alerted his students to the danger. It was up to their parents to keep them safe. Fathers and mothers needed to share updates on the crisis – or not.

It was a pathetic excuse that had niggled at Schumann through every class. He was not a coward; British bayonet wounds and American shrapnel were evidence of his willingness to defend the Fatherland. But morally, he had let down 7A to protect himself. He could not tolerate that person: tomorrow he would atone.

Most of the shopping went into the small refrigerator, the potatoes were left on the table. Several letters had been collected from the box: party literature, a bill, an envelope from a former teaching colleague in Berlin. They shared a passion for chess.

Schumann walked across the corridor to the lounge. It was a good size for a bachelor. A large faded red rug covered most of the timber floor. Pastoral prints of Germany during the 19th Century hung on two walls. A television that was usually tuned to West German broadcasts was in the corner near the window. He turned it on, the volume low.

Beside it was a bookcase that almost reached the ceiling. There were 10 shelves, all full: mostly German classics, educational tomes, a few Western thrillers that the Party would deem a corrupting influence.

A well-used armchair rested within easy reach. A matching chair bracketed a small timber table with an ivory chess set. Grau, who lived around the corner, would be over soon to play the pre-dinner game that had never started the previous evening.

The letter from Berlin was still in hand as Schumann approached the sideboard beneath the window. Another three matching chess boards were laid out, the games well advanced. The mail exchanges occurred every two or three days, one move per game. Schumann had paper, envelope and stamp ready for his reply. He moved the timber pieces as directed by the letter. In the first game it cost Schumann a pawn. In the second a bishop was taken off the board. In the third, Schumann saw an opening created where he could checkmate his distant opponent with a few return letters. He walked back and forth between the boards. Games one and two required more thought; the third contest was an assured victory. But would he get to claim it?

A much larger and more critical strategic game was being played between Nikita Khrushchev and John Kennedy with the fate of the world at stake. Schumann believed the Russian was proving to be a better player. The fresh president had been outwitted when the Berlin Wall went up overnight. The porous borders were plugged; the GDR and Soviets had trapped the Western Allies in a ghetto deep inside communist territory.

Admittedly it was a posh ghetto, with all the luxuries of a Western lifestyle: better cars, fancier clothes, modern home appliances, fresh fruit and vegetables. And best of all – freedom of movement beyond national borders.

Schumann understood that the Russian leader was playing a long game. Khrushchev could wait until the Americans, French and British tired of subsidising the democratic pocket deep within GDR territory. The old fox had probably already selected a date when the Americans would close Checkpoint Charlie in West Berlin.

Schumann fiddled with the dead bishop from the second board as he considered the troublesome game where his opponent held an advantage, but he could not stick with the task in hand.

His logical mind believed Khrushchev's attempt to set up a nuclear base in Cuba was both brilliant and foolish. The savvy communist leader had taken advantage of a green president who had suffered two diplomatic humiliations in mere months: the failed Bay of Pigs invasion by Cuban expatriates occurred in April; Berlin was permanently divided in August. A handsome smile and a pretty wife might have charmed the rest of the world, but Kennedy was losing on the global chessboard. Checkmate could be hours away.

Schumann made a note on a pad for two of his games. He could probably rescue one, the second might be a struggle. He laughed. Threats of giant mushroom clouds stretching around the globe could not dim his competitive spirit.

West German television had lauded Kennedy since his election. He was a Pacific War hero for having saved his PT boat crew. The GDR considered Kennedy inept for getting sunk by the Japanese destroyer he had been hunting. It was a valid point. But what Schumann recognised in the young president was a fellow survivor. He fought back from the potentially career-ending episode to sail into the White House. That was impressive in Schumann's opinion.

A knight was shifted on the third chess board; another note was made on the pad. That checkmate was inevitable.

Kennedy's pride would be wounded by the events of 1961; he could not afford a third public humiliation. Yelling at the Russians for a few days, then still allowing them to build a nuclear arsenal in the Caribbean was not going to appease his generals. Hubris and the safety of 186 million Americans demanded that Kennedy act. That action could end every chess game forever.

Schumann went to the refrigerator for a Braugold pilsner. He wouldn't usually drink two nights in a row, but these were strange times. He sat heavily in the armchair by the bookshelf, the foaming glass on a mat nearby. He doodled on the pad, not quite ready to add the usual chatty notes to accompany the chess moves. There was a new niggle: had Khrushchev underestimated the American?

The chilled beer was sipped as Schumann turned to the television for a news update. The American blockade of Cuba was underway; at least 25 Soviet ships were known to be approaching the island. The crisis could come to a head in the next few hours.

A bell from the street entrance made Schumann move to the kitchen without changing the channel; Grau was his only visitor. Another pilsner would be ready by the time his friend climbed the stairs. A sudden thought made him listen to the tread on the floorboards: one person, not a Stasi arrest squad.

'Hello, old friend. Here's a thank you for saving me from the Stasi.'

Grau grunted, swallowed some beer, then saw the foreign broadcast.

'You live dangerously, old man. What if that had been the Stasi coming through the door?'

'I probably would have given them the beer.'

'They would have kicked your old bones down the stairs, then drunk *all* your beer.'

The comrades laughed and settled into the armchairs beside the chess table. Schumann had a feeling the white pawn would not move any time soon.

Grau gestured at the television with his glass. 'What are the imperialist aggressors saying about our brave Cuban and Soviet allies?'

'A bit louder please, Jürgen. The VoPo captain across the courtyard can't hear you.'

They sniggered. There was no telephone in the apartment to tap and old schoolteachers should not warrant wall bugs.

'What's happening with the blockade?' Grau asked.

'Apparently the first Soviet vessels are a couple of hours away. That is when everything could unravel.'

'Do you think the Americans will commit piracy?'

'They were cunning. They got unanimous support from the Organization of American States. That gives them a legal basis to call it a *quarantine* instead of a blockade.'

Grau shrugged. 'Call it what you like: what will Khrushchev do if the US Navy tries to board his ships?'

'Moscow radio says the Soviet Union won't use nuclear weapons against the United States unless "aggression is committed".'

Grau placed his beer on a mat beside the chess set. 'I would call armed US sailors boarding a Soviet boat aggressive. But does it warrant launching a nuclear missile?'

'A sane man wouldn't, but we are not threatening a Russian bear.'

Beers were sipped in silence. Both stared at the chess pieces, although Schumann didn't think his friend was contemplating the opening moves.

'I was interested by the tone of the Soviet response,' Schumann said. 'Moscow's statement was relatively mild. Sure, there was the usual belligerent warning that the whole Soviet bloc is ready to fight. But the Kremlin called for the United Nations Security Council to convene immediately. Perhaps that indicates Khrushchev is prepared to look at a diplomatic solution.'

'I think he's buying time to complete the missile sites. Kennedy said the US has evidence of the construction, but we don't know how close they are to firing.' Grau snorted. 'I bet Khrushchev is working his Cuban crews around the clock to get them ready to launch. A few wasted days with diplomats talking at the UN will suit him nicely.'

Schumann leaned over to pick up his king. 'The old fox is playing a game on two fronts. Did you see the Moscow report makes no mention of the Soviets building ballistic missile bases in Cuba? They say the assistance is purely for the *defence* of communist allies.' The ebony piece was replaced after a speck of dust was removed. 'They are keeping the peasants in the dark about the true reason for the American anger: nuclear missiles 150 kilometres from US beaches. That is dangerous.'

'Lying by omission – not an unusual tactic for any government, communist or capitalist. I can see the United Nations getting bogged down in silly debates about what is a defensive weapon and what is offensive. The result will be the same if a frustrated general wants to punch the launch button before his opponent.'

Schumann rose with an empty glass. He held out a hand for Grau's.

'Perhaps another beer and a game, my friend. At least we can control this chessboard.'

Ingrid Richter

INGRID STOOD WITH HER BACK CLOSE TO THE HOT TILES OF THE KACHELOFEN in the lounge. It was twice her size, almost reaching the ceiling. She would nuzzle against the side of the masonry heater whenever she was sure that Vati had his eyes on the television. It was tuned to an action drama as it was too early for the West German news broadcast. Mutti was tidying the kitchen after their supper. It was a familiar routine most nights.

'Put two briquettes into the oven and move away to let some heat into the other rooms.'

Mutti could see through walls.

'I'll be through shortly and we can have some chocolate.'

Ingrid carefully used tongs to open the waist-high door and stoke the fire. The heat made her cheeks redden, although it could not remove the fearful chill that had infiltrated her bones at the library. The research on radiation was more horrifying than either of the schoolgirls had expected.

Pans rattling and cupboards closing indicated Ingrid could risk another minute or two against the tiles. The heater was her favourite furnishing in the room. The two armchairs, sofa and table were stylish and well maintained, and the chintz curtains were always clean. Her parents were very house-proud; Mutti was always on the lookout for ornaments to decorate the timber buffet and walls.

Her latest deal had netted a rack of three small plant baskets. It hung at the other end of the sofa, fronds lazily reaching out towards the television. Ingrid wished they could magically change the channel. The GDR schedule rarely appealed in the evenings.

Family photos of aunts, uncles and cousins dotted the walls. She might lack siblings to play with in the courtyard every day, but there were two cousins to make special Erfurt occasions exciting. She hugged one of Mutti's colourful hand-sewn cushions as she wondered whether they would meet again during Martini in three weeks.

It had been another strange day. It started with the weird eighth grader following them to school and ended with their return from an eye-opening hour at the library. In between was the shock of seeing Mutti being followed by the Stasi.

The kitchen rumblings had gone quiet. Mutti would soon be unlocking the buffet for a treat. Would that be the time to raise the matter of the Stasi agent, or would it create more problems? Vati might not be impressed with his daughter or his wife.

There had been no opportunity to speak to Mutti alone before supper. Her parents had talked quietly in the kitchen while Ingrid completed her homework in the lounge. Herr Schumann had made up for the previous evening with extra mathematics and German literature.

The conversation during the meal mostly focused on Opa. His back was causing him great pain. The GDR system was efficient – if you had the right connections and good westpaket contents. Vati and Mutti had discussed what to trade for stronger pain relief. It was not the right time for Ingrid to reveal the Stasi problem or her own truancy. And not just today. Ingrid would have to find a way to explain Tuesday's visit to the Domplatz where she had seen the Stasi agent pursuing Pedro.

Two restless nights made Ingrid sleepy. Not even the chocolate could perk her up. Mutti ushered her through the curtains before eight, when the West German news aired. There was a brief moment for Ingrid to voice her fears as they hugged goodnight. The warmth and closeness with Mutti made her decide that conversation could wait until the morning. Sleep might provide her with the right words.

Gunther Kist

'My advice is to keep your mouth closed, Gunther.' Carsten Hartwig raised his pilsner and sipped. 'You are no match for Colonel Brecht, regardless of what he might have done. You have no evidence, and the Colonel won't be invited to the cells to have a confession beaten out of him.'

The colleagues sat at the best table in Das Paridis on the corner of Semmelweisstrasse and Tchaikowskistrasse. The pub was half full, although no drinkers ventured close or even looked at the pair. They could sniff out the Stasi better than their favourite beers. Two agents locked in an intense discussion had spooked several of the regular clientele into making an early departure.

The pub was midway between the agents' homes, although neither was a regular visitor. Kist would drop in occasionally for fruehschoppen on Sundays during summer. The drink before lunch was a chance to think about cases away from the distractions of work and the family. Matthias would collect him when his meal was ready.

'But the Richter woman delivered something to the Colonel. A deal was done with the Cuban at the Hauptbahnhof and she went straight from the square to headquarters.'

Pedro Barios being allowed to walk free without an interrogation irked Kist. Knowing that something probably illegal had taken place, and Kist could do nothing about it, compounded the frustration. He slapped the table.

Several drinkers flinched. No one said a word. One patron returned his glass to the bar without finishing and exited.

'It's not fair, Carsten. We are the shield and sword of the Party. We're supposed to weed out trouble wherever we find it.'

'You might have identified a corrupt senior officer, but without the goods you will only ruin your career. He has a plausible defence – the Richter woman works for him.'

'She works for his wife. Why would the Colonel give a bundle of Deutsche Marks to Ingrid's dressmaker?'

'How can you be certain they weren't Ostmarks?'

'I was close enough to see the colour – I'm sure they were five Deutsche Mark notes.'

'Did he spot you?'

'No, I was behind a pillar. They left headquarters and walked across to a bakery. He bought some rolls, came out and gave her the money.'

'That doesn't make sense. The baker wouldn't have given him Deutsche Marks.'

'I'm sure it was a ruse to get him out of headquarters.'

'You only saw him pay her, not the exchange.'

'That would have happened when she went into his office. I couldn't follow.'

Hartwig picked up a handful of nuts provided free by the manager.

'The only case you *might* have against him is dealing in Western currency.' He threw in several nuts as he talked. 'But that can be explained.'

Kist threw his arms wide. 'I know she bought something from the Cuban. She hopped on a tram, rode straight to Ministry headquarters. I followed her all the way. A few minutes later Colonel Brecht goes to a shop, buys bread, then gives money to the intermediary. To me, that is enough to interrogate both. If we start with Angela Richter, we will soon get evidence on the Colonel.'

'Or you could expose the Colonel's secret informant.'

Kist paused with the beer midway to his mouth. He swallowed air and replaced the glass.

'No. She is a known westpaket trader. That's how Helga Brecht gets all the glamorous material – Angela Richter deals with her connections.'

'Exactly.' Hartwig smiled smugly. 'You are providing the Colonel with his own defence. We turn a blind eye to westpaket trading because everyone benefits. Angela Richter is popular in the community. She must hear a lot of gossip. The Colonel will say that he was paying a spitzel.'

'In Deutsche Marks?'

'They can help her reach targets that our currency might not tempt.'

Kist's head sagged. The beer held little appeal. Three probable criminals were going to escape justice. It was unfair after all his hard work.

Hartwig finished his beer. He looked around the room, but no drinker would meet his eye.

'You are a good investigator, Gunther, but you must learn to think like a politician. They have an instinct for protecting their backs. They gather information on their opponents, file it away, then use it like a dagger when it can cause maximum damage. You don't have anything that can hurt Colonel Brecht.'

Hartwig stood, buttoned his thick jacket.

'I understand you, Gunther. You are black and white when it comes to your duty to the Party. I know you won't stop making discreet inquiries. You will try to build a case against the Colonel or the dressmaker. My advice is: don't get caught. And remember – we never had this conversation.'

The big man tapped the brim of his dark hat and left.

Kist felt a collective exhalation as his superior walked out the door. Carsten Hartwig looked like a poster boy for the Ministry for State Security, although he rarely went into the field. The younger man was destined to command a desk in Berlin. It would be wise to hold onto Hartwig's coattails. Accusing a senior officer of corruption could bring great rewards if there was a conviction, or it could be career ending. Hartwig was canny enough to ride the crest of any office success while ensuring failures buried the ambitious field agent.

Kist scooped up a handful of nuts as he left the pub. No acknowledgment was made to the manager. Respect for the Stasi was important; it never had to be returned. He headed north on Semmelweisstrasse, intent on a wide loop home via Friedrich-List Strasse.

There would be no second visit to Lukas Bauer. It was likely the informant had curried favour with his handler by declaring Kist's interest in the Richters despite the kicking. Another stop might start a chain reaction through the hierarchy on Andreasstrasse; the result could be a difficult interview with an officer senior to Carsten Hartwig.

A low-key solo effort was the only way Kist was going to expose two corrupt enemies of the GDR. He whistled as he slowly walked past Number 10. Matthias should be awake when he reached home. It would be interesting to hear about his spying mission on the Richter daughter at school.

Thursday, October 25, 1962

Ingrid Richter

Sleep came swiftly for Ingrid although it was interrupted by another harrowing dream. She knew it was not reality, right from the start, yet it was impossible to break free. All she had to do was open her eyes; that would break the cinematic sequence running through her head. No, Ingrid remained fixed to the staircase between the cathedral and Severikirche; below, her mother was doing endless laps of the Domplatz under the gaze of the Stasi. It was nonsense; the agent would dash back and forth between the obelisk and fountain. Each time he was wearing a different disguise: a beard, no beard, a hat, no hat. His surveillance was obvious; Mutti was oblivious. Ingrid tried to warn her at every circuit, but Mutti never looked at her daughter. She was preoccupied, waiting for someone.

The climax came when a Stasi officer marched into the square with a dozen soldiers carrying rifles. Mutti stopped her pacing; the agent halted his prowling. Who was going to be arrested or shot? Ingrid shouted at her mother to run. Mutti never heard the words. They were drowned by a tearing noise. They all looked to the sky – the roar of an approaching bomber grew louder. Ingrid leapt off the staircase to reach her Mutti – and was shocked awake as she fell onto the bedroom carpet.

The impact sounded like a bombshell to Ingrid, but her father's snoring continued in the master bedroom. Ingrid scampered back beneath the warmth of the feather cover, her breath already frosting. Condensation would spread from the thin glass window to her bed within a few weeks. She hated leaving that warmth to get dressed for school on those mornings.

Ingrid pulled the cover tight around her face. She was wide awake, her brain seeking explanations for the nightmares: the concentration camp, Russian border guards chasing her parents, the Stasi targeting Mutti, the American bomber.

What did that symbolise? How close were the American planes now? And their missiles? There was no clock in the middle room; she had no idea what Khrushchev and Kennedy had achieved while she slept. Had they ordered the generals to act, or was the threat of nuclear annihilation keeping them in check? An ear was turned to the window; nothing was stirring – or flying – outside. The peace stick had done its job so far; would it continue?

Ingrid snuggled deeper under the covers as she waited for the first glimmer of dawn. She was 13, in the top class at school, destined for a university education. That indicated a high level of intelligence. Yet, her best hope for holding back the world from a nuclear abyss was a stick in a wall. It was almost as fanciful as the fairy tales she loved to watch on television: children in danger were rescued; wolves, monsters and evil men were vanquished. Good triumphed over evil, that was the message. With nothing better to cling to than hope, what harm was there in believing in the magic of a peace stick?

Thoughts turned to Pedro and his Cuban friends. They were on a train rolling through the darkness of Western Europe. Possibly the second or third train since leaving Erfurt. Her knowledge of international shipping routes was limited. A study of the dykes in the Netherlands had revealed that Rotterdam was a major port, as was Marseille in France. The Cubans could be headed to either, looking for transport back to their homes.

Ingrid could understand the desire to be with family in a crisis, but she worried how noble she might be if her home was directly threatened by the nuclear might of the United States. The GDR was in danger as an ally of the Soviets but not to the same extent as Cuba. The Russians were building nuclear launch sites close to America. There was a chance – a tiny hope – that any war might be limited to the Caribbean.

Gerard, Kurt and Thorsten had been arguing about that possibility between the fifth and sixth classes. Thorsten was positive the US Air Force could pinpoint all the launch sites with non-nuclear bombs. If the Americans did not use nukes, there was no need for the Russians to fire their missiles. Thorsten argued that many of the American planes would be shot down with surface-to-air missiles. Military losses on both sides might satisfy honour for the Soviets.

Ingrid remembered Kurt growing red in the face. He yelled at Thorsten that Soviet prestige could not suffer that humiliation. If the American planes attacked, there would be no way to stop the generals from using *every* weapon in their arsenal.

The outburst had silenced the usual between-class mayhem. It inflamed Ingrid's fears for survival. How many other nightmares was the crisis causing? Would the trauma of these few days linger in impressionable minds? She closed her eyes with another wish: that Khrushchev and Kennedy would see the folly of destroying the world. They must, because in World War III there would be no winners.

'Come on sleepy head, you're late again.'

Ingrid shrivelled into a foetal position as the feather cover was thrown onto the floor.

'I've pulled the bettdecke off five times. It's almost seven; you'll have to eat your breakfast as you walk.'

Ingrid rubbed bleary eyes. A moment ago, she had been wishing for world peace; now she might have to run to avoid detention. She had been buzzing after the dream; that energy had been sapped by the final snooze. The morning routine was compressed into 10 minutes; Ingrid stumbled out the door with the ranzen half on her back and buttered bread with honey in hand. Her stress was compounded by a failure to complete the most important morning task: talking to Mutti about the Stasi agent.

Sylvie was jiggling on her driveway. 'Finally! I'm puffed from trying to keep warm. What kept you?'

'Another dream.'

'Oh. Bad?'

'Not as scary as Monday and Tuesday night. I dreamed that Mutti was being chased by the Stasi agent in the Domplatz. An officer and soldiers with guns arrived. Then we all heard the roar of an American bomber overhead.'

They barely looked as they crossed the road; the Trabbis in their neighbourhood could be smelt from half a block away. Ingrid finished her breakfast.

'What happened then?'

'I fell out of bed.'

Sylvie's giggles set off Ingrid. They bumped shoulders as they held their ranzen straps.

'Did you wake your Mutti?'

'No – the roaring I heard was Vati snoring. Nothing can drown him out.'

The laughter brightened Ingrid's mood. They were almost back on routine for school. Their pace would get them to the wall to check the peace stick before first bell. There was no time to panic if it was gone.

It was the third day of the world crisis and life in Erfurt was progressing as normal: the brewery smell was typically strong; workers trudged to their factories, offices and shops; students hurried to school. Low clouds obscured the sun; missiles and bombs could sneak through without warning.

Neither slackened the pace as they reached Tchaikowskistrasse. The bakery was ignored. Herr Wenkell would be by-passed again after school if they were going to do their survival run to Petersberg Citadel.

'Did you bring your brother's watch?'

Sylvie pulled a battered watch without straps from her jacket. 'The leather frayed; he has to wait for a replacement. He won't know it's gone.'

'I never got to speak to Mutti about the Stasi following her.'

'Oh. I meant to ask about that. Will you tell her after school?'

'Maybe. I'm not sure Vati will be happy with either of us. I haven't worked out a way to warn her and not get into trouble.'

The streets were filling with students as they neared school. A group hovered at the intersection with Am Schwemmbach.

'Be honest. Both times you saw the Stasi man you were on your way to the library. It's natural we want to learn more about the nuclear threats.'

Ingrid could see that possibly working, although her mother would see a flaw in her decision. 'Maybe. Mutti would ask why I went to the Altstadt instead of the school library.'

The students at the corner ambled towards the entrance, leaving one straggler. Or was he? It was the eighth grader who had followed them yesterday.

'Look, Sylvie. It's that boy again. He's waiting at the corner.'

Sylvie glared at Matthias Kist as they approached. 'Who are you staring at?'

Ingrid was surprised by her friend's bravado towards a senior student. So, it appeared, was Matthias.

'Nobody.' Matthias shuffled his feet, fiddled with a strap on his ranzen. 'I'm waiting for someone.'

Sylvie was not easily deflected. 'It's almost first bell. I don't think you would risk detention for a friend.'

A sneer replaced the confusion. 'Who are you to question a senior student? I should report your rudeness.'

Sylvie scornfully dismissed him and marched towards the entrance. Ingrid hurried behind. Matthias did not follow.

'He looks nasty,' Ingrid said. There was no reply as another surprise awaited them at the entrance. A boy was leaning against the wall, obscuring the peace stick. 'Do you know who that is?'

'No. I think he must be a fifth grader. Look – he's reading the latest *Mosaik*.'

It was the most popular comic in the GDR. The adventures of the time-travelling Digedags were eagerly consumed every month. The stories had strong technical and educational themes to keep Party bosses happy. There was enough humour and irreverence to make students laugh. Much of the appeal was in Dig and Dag exploring places young readers could only dream about. Less fortunate students would have to beg friends to read their copies.

Sylvie took the lead again. They had to move the boy to see if the peace stick remained in place.

'Hello.' Sylvie leaned in to look at the pictures. He was short of a growth spurt; an older girl showing interest made him cringe. 'What issue is that?'

'Seventy-one.'

'I haven't bought that copy.'

The fifth grader tilted further to the right. Ingrid still couldn't see the peace stick. Sylvie leaned in for a closer look at the cartoons.

'What are Dig and Dag doing this month?' Sylvie's shoulder was almost touching him. The lad tilted further but did not budge.

'They are helping Master Noodlebaker make a magnificent cake for Lord Groggy.'

'Oh yes, I can see that.' Sylvie put a finger on the comic. 'Do they end up making a big mess?'

She reached to turn the page. The lad could lean no further, he had to shuffle. It was just enough. Ingrid could see the end of the peace stick – they would have another day without nuclear bombs and missiles.

'You can read my copy, Sylvie. Come on, first bell must be seconds away.'

They looped arms and scooted through the entrance.

'The peace stick is still there?' Sylvie asked.

'Yes. Well done – another minute and that poor boy would have given you the comic to get you off his arm.'

They were the only students in 7A giggling as they assembled. Ingrid looked at Petra, Gerard, Kurt and Thorsten standing nearby. They were subdued, reflecting the mood of most in the courtyard. She looked at the long class lines: hundreds attended the 31st Oberschule, and most would be petrified by the growing animosity between the Soviets and Americans. They did not have a peace stick like Ingrid and Sylvie to boost their spirits. Thirty seconds later they marched steadily into class. Herr Schumann was their first teacher.

Matthias Kist

MATTHIAS KIST WATCHED LINE AFTER LINE ENTER THE SQUAT, GREY building. His father told him repeatedly that children were the future of the German Democratic Republic; their path to perpetual loyalty to the Party needed to be guided and observed. Some – like Ingrid Richter and Sylvie Witzenhause of 7A – required greater scrutiny.

It was interesting to see they were the only students smiling as they prepared for class. Many of their classmates were constantly looking to the sky, terrified the clouds shielded American bombers. Not Matthias. His father was an integral part of the security apparatus; Gunther Kist was positive there would be no World War III. Hence, there was no need for his son to worry about nuclear bombs falling on Erfurt. The Soviet Premier was too clever for the Americans. His father was convinced the Soviets would end the crisis in a stronger position, President Kennedy would suffer more humiliation. Control of all Berlin – the ultimate communist goal – would soon be theirs.

Matthias relished the surveillance task assigned by his father. Initially he was required to check on Ingrid. His father said the daughter and mother had aroused suspicion of anti-social and corrupt behaviour. Exactly what they had done was not explained. That was secret information for sworn Stasi officers only. Matthias understood. One day he hoped to stand alongside his father as they protected the GDR from all foes, foreign and internal.

This was perfect training, although Matthias would not share all the details of the morning confrontation. That was twice in less than a day that he had been caught out by his target. Make that *targets*. The Witzenhause girl should be added to the suspect list. She travelled to and from school with Ingrid; they also spent much of their time together outside of the classroom. Sylvie had to be involved. The feisty challenge at the street corner was unprovoked. Luckily no other students were close enough to hear. Sylvie would never treat Matthias that way again. In a few years he would be able to do more than report her for discipline. Matthias had heard plenty of stories about the work done in the Stasi cells on Andreasstrasse.

Matthias shuffled along the corridor. He was a lone wolf; no other student whispered to him. Keeping your distance from any Stasi connection was instinctive. Classmates knew Matthias was the son of a Stasi agent, destined for the Ministry of State Security after completing military service. There would be no need for university. Protection of the Party was paramount for the Kist family.

He passed an arched class entrance; inside Ingrid and Sylvie awaited second bell. Would their first lesson be with Herr Schumann? The teacher's defeatist message about World War III had spread through the school. It was a mystery that the old fool had not been hauled away for interrogation on Tuesday evening. Apparently, Herr Schumann had been wiser yesterday – there was no more terrifying talk about nuclear missiles destroying the world several times over. His father had praised him for reporting the alarmist teacher.

Thursday breakfast at the Kist apartment had turned into an eager briefing session. Matthias was to report any more indiscretions by the teacher. He was to step up his scrutiny of Ingrid Richter wherever possible: to and from school, between classes, the long break.

After lunch, he would need to hide near her home on Friedrich-List Strasse. She had been caught wandering the Altstadt and contacting targets in another case. Ingrid's explanation was being treated as doubtful following suspicious activities by her mother. No carrot was needed to inspire the son, but his heart burst with pride to know that senior Stasi officers would be aware of his skills.

Matthias took his seat for a Russian lesson. He was one of the few to embrace the language of their ally. It would be invaluable in his future career. He would focus for the next 45 minutes. The following lesson – art education – would allow him time to plot how to get close to the 7A girls without being spotted.

Second bell quashed a niggling thought about the retaining wall at the school entrance. There was something about it that made the girls stop each time. Maybe a closer inspection was required.

Tomas Schumann

Herr Schumann stood with shoulders squared, hands behind his back, Class 7A at attention in front of him. Pioneer leader Hans Rathmann addressed his classmates.

'Be ready!'

'Always ready!'

Hans turned to their teacher.

'I report that 7A is ready for the class.'

He saluted and resumed his seat.

'Thank you, Hans. And good morning. Before we start our lesson, I want to issue an apology and an update on the terrible crisis facing the world.'

Confused faces stared at Tomas Schumann; he was walking on eggshells. A teacher offering an apology had probably never happened to these students. His authority was supreme in the classroom. It was personal integrity that compelled him to treat his class as intelligent students, not mindless robots swallowing Party dogma.

'First, the apology. On Tuesday I shared information about the crisis in Cuba and the threat it posed to the world. I know it shocked and upset you to hear that World War III could be just minutes away. That was a fact that I believed you had a right to know about immediately. At that stage, there was no guarantee we would have a Wednesday class.'

There were several gasps. Perhaps some of the students had never fully grasped the implications of his warning, or they had chosen to block the ramifications.

'Fortunately, common sense prevailed in Washington and Moscow. Threats were still being uttered, but no general pressed the trigger. We had our Wednesday class.'

Schumann swallowed.

'I regret that I did not provide an update on the negotiations yesterday, which might have left many of you confused and terrified. It was like I threw a big rock into the pool where you were swimming and left you to struggle in the waves. For that, I am sorry.'

He could have talked about moral cowardice, but it might be a wasted exercise. They were mature students with inquiring minds; they would reach their own conclusions.

'I'm not privy to what Comrade Khrushchev and the American president are discussing. However, I should have shared the small amount of public information available with you. Our future is at stake; we have the right to discuss it openly.'

There were several murmurs.

'I shall tell you what I hear until the crisis is resolved.'

Many heads nodded, Ingrid and Sylvia among them. Their eyes seemed brighter than their classmates'.

'You are aware that the Americans have set up a naval cordon around Cuba. They want to check every vessel. Naturally, the Soviets are angry. The Americans believe their blockade is legal; the Soviets say it's piracy. The biggest worry for the world is what will happen when the United States tries to board a Soviet boat. If a battle starts, will it quickly escalate to something larger and catastrophic?'

Schumann watched most heads nod along with his summation. There would not have been an information vacuum yesterday. Parents and friends would have provided enough details to keep them abreast.

'I'm pleased to say that the Soviets are doing their best to ensure there is no loss of control. Some of the ships sailing to Cuba have veered away. They have every right to go about their business on the seas without interference from the Americans. However, given the aggression shown by Washington, they have chosen a wise course while talks continue.'

Hans Rathmann clapped in the front row. Schumann held up a hand to stop others joining him.

'This is welcome news, Hans, but we are not out of danger yet. Not all of the Soviet ships have changed course.'

Hans instantly raised his hand.

Schumann nodded.

'Have they been stopped by the Americans?'

'There have been no news reports about any boardings. We don't know how close the ships are to the US Navy.'

'They could be hijacking the Soviets at any minute.'

'Possibly.'

'Which means our Soviet allies will have to retaliate.'

The spark of hope that had glittered in most student eyes waned swiftly. Schumann tried a new track of reassurance.

'As a former soldier, I was trained to keep your opponent guessing. To never reveal your strengths or direct line of attack.' Schumann smiled grimly. 'It kept me alive in two world wars.'

Brows furrowed again. He could see the class were wondering where this tack was taking them.

'Comrade Khrushchev has been a fighter since the start of the Bolshevik Revolution. He is a great leader, older and wiser than the young US president. He would not let important Soviet ships cruise into an American trap. There is unlikely to be any military equipment on the boats approaching the blockade.'

Thorsten Koehler joined the conversation with a raised hand.

'Yes, Thorsten.'

'The American navy won't find any weapons, but any boarding is still a slap in the face for Soviet honour. They must retaliate.'

'They might not have to. It could turn out to be the American military and President Kennedy who are humiliated.'

'How?' Gerard Mueller did not bother to raise his arm. Schumann was comfortable; he wanted to encourage them to be analytical. Apparently Western schools encouraged free-ranging debates.

'If the sailors don't find missiles or building materials for weapons sites, then it will be the Americans who will be seen as the aggressors. The ships might be carrying much-needed grain or oil for Cuban citizens.

'It would be a diplomatic disaster for the Americans. We only have their word that the Soviets are building offensive missile sites. There has been no evidence. Kennedy talked for almost 20 minutes on television on Monday, yet produced no photos. The Cubans survived a US-sponsored invasion last year. The world understands that the Cubans have every right to defend themselves against further attacks.'

Schumann watched Thorsten and Gerard nod. Their friend Kurt Neubert had been listening carefully.

'Are you suggesting, Herr Schumann, that Comrade Khrushchev might be prepared to suffer a small indignity for a greater prize?'

'Quite possibly, Kurt. I'm not the Soviet premier, just a humble schoolteacher who would like to reach retirement.'

That prompted laughter from most students.

'I don't think Premier Khrushchev or President Kennedy want to blow up our planet. Both will need to be clever to extract themselves from this mess. Other world leaders will be important in doing that.'

Kurt tilted his head. 'Why should they be involved?'

'Because the British, French and other heads of state will be offering their opinions to President Kennedy. They don't want World War III. Cuba has little relevance to Europe and the NATO allies. They will be doing everything they can to stop an outbreak of hostilities.

'Soviet diplomats will be whispering in their ears about the American Jupiter missiles in Turkey and Italy. If the US commanders launch, they will be crashing into the heart of Moscow within a few minutes. The Soviets have been under threat for many years. Why should the Americans be upset about a defensive base in Cuba to stop another invasion?'

Schumann looked around the faces. This was disturbing content for young minds. Yet, they all sat straight, absorbing every word.

'As I talk to you, there are undoubtedly negotiations going on across the world. The United Nations could play an important role in defusing the standoff. The Acting Secretary General, U Thant, has called for a moratorium for two to three weeks.'

'What does that mean?' asked Kurt.

'A suspension or postponement. Let tempers calm down. U Thant wants the Soviets to stop their military supplies and for the United States to lift the blockade. It would remove the trigger point of boats being searched illegally.'

'That sounds sensible.' The voice was female: Sylvie. 'Could he get Comrade Khrushchev and President Kennedy to meet at the United Nations until they find a solution?'

Schumann turned to Sylvie. 'Yes. That is a practical idea – to us. Getting the two most powerful men in the world to agree to that suggestion is another matter.'

Sylvie propped her chin with a hand. 'Why is it that all the wars are started by men?'

There were sniggers from several boys, although Kurt, Thorsten and Gerard were not among them.

Hans did not wait for their teacher to answer. He pivoted towards Sylvie.

'Because girls know nothing about war.'

'That's my point, Hans. Why does every disagreement have to end up in a war? Men always want to pick up a gun to settle their differences. What is wrong with talking, like we do when we have a problem?'

Schumann stood at the front of the classroom and let the discussion flow. Sylvie raised a valid point – most heads of state were men. Women and children had little hope of preventing 'patriots' from plunging their nations into bloody and futile conflicts. World War II showed there were few sanctuaries for the innocent. There would be no hiding from the next catastrophe currently being orchestrated by two angry, stressed men and their minions, most of whom were men.

'Girls are too weak to fire rifles or throw grenades,' Hans insisted. 'You're better behind the front lines in hospitals, doing the nursing.'

'Hans!' Ingrid Richter's exasperation silenced the room; several discussions had broken out between boys and girls. 'Sylvie is not talking about the physical acts of war. She is asking why we ever need to have wars. There are no winners – just lots of death, tears and destruction. Sylvie is saying men don't think clearly when their pride is wounded. Women can be more rational, prepared to compromise and find solutions that don't involve bullets.'

Schumann was impressed with Sylvie and Ingrid's logic and arguments. They were intelligent girls who would be a credit to the GDR – if they stayed. Or survived the next few days. The Soviets had deferred the start of the conflict, but tensions were still high.

It was an appropriate point to bring the class back to the lesson of the day: the founding of the GDR in 1949. He picked up a text from the table behind.

'Okay class, open your books.' Schumann watched as his students complied. 'I will continue to update you about the crisis when I have more information. Now, turn to page 33.'

Ingrid Richter

THE COURTYARD SHUFFLE DURING THE LONG BREAK LACKED ENERGY. It was normally above snail's pace but never likely to raise a sweat. The momentum was enough to keep the supervising teachers happy; the rules were being obeyed, although no future Olympians were being groomed. The inertia was caused by frequent stops to check the skies: no bombers, time for another circuit.

Ingrid pulled her jacket tighter; the temperature had dropped another degree. She and Sylvie had no need to check for danger from the sky. Herr Schumann's update had fuelled survival hopes that had been reignited by the peace stick before first bell. The thought of the boy with the *Mosaik* comic made her laugh.

'That was funny watching you make that fifth grader slide along the wall this morning.'

'I didn't think he was going to shift. I thought I might have to kiss him – that would have made him run.'

Their laughter attracted Renate and Katja as they cut across the yard from their 7B classmates.

'Why are you two the only happy students at the 31st Oberschule?' asked Renate.

Sylvie shrugged. 'There is nothing we can do about men playing war. Enjoy life while we can.'

The newcomers dropped into step with their friends.

'We heard you were being provocative in class, suggesting men were silly to make war instead of finding solutions to problems.'

Ingrid looked across the yard; Hans Rathmann was talking to a group of boys and girls. He pointed in their direction. Her stomach lurched when she saw their eighth-grade stalker listening.

'Was it Hans who told you?'

'Yes,' said Katja. 'He says girls don't fight, so we shouldn't decide who the men go to war against.'

'Silly boys.' Ingrid shook her head. 'They grow into stupid men who never learn. If they used a bit of common sense and less pride, there might not be any need for wars.'

'Enough about depressing topics.' Sylvie turned to Renate and lowered her voice. 'Have you heard any more about that new British band from your cousin in Hamburg?'

'Yes!' Renate's eyes crinkled. 'Heidi saw them again – they get better with every performance.'

Ingrid was mystified. 'What band are you talking about?'

'The Beatles. They're from Liverpool and Heidi says they are gorgeous. They wear their hair long, like beatniks, and their songs make everyone want to do the twist.'

Beatles, beatniks, the twist: Ingrid was a Western music novice. Vati never strayed far from classic German composers on his record player. Radio Luxembourg had modern music, but she never listened between the songs to learn the important information.

'Heidi sent pictures of her friends doing the twist,' said Renate. 'It's hard to tell if I'm doing it right.'

'How is it supposed to go?' asked Ingrid.

Renate looked around the courtyard. 'I can't show you here. But think of what you do with your hula hoop. You wriggle and twist and then raise one leg.'

They all laughed, which attracted stares from parading students. The bamboo GDR copies were heavier than the plastic American hula hoops. It took strong hips and tummy muscles to keep them rotating.

'Heidi says it's great fun. The Beatles have been playing at the Star Club, which is like a theatre. They mostly dance in front of their seats because the music has a vibe that makes you want to move.'

More giggles. Ingrid would love to see a mass audience twisting together. Would they look like a bunch of drunken snakes?

'The Beatles have just released a single – "Love Me Do" on one side, "PS: I Love You" on the other.' Renate fluttered her eyelids, prompting more chuckles. 'Heidi is going to send me a record in our next westpaket.'

'Won't the Stasi intercept that? They'll call it Western sedition or propaganda.'

Renate shook her head. 'She's going to replace the label with a polka one.'

A rain shower sent students scattering towards the corridors. Katja and Renate went to the far end for their next class. Sylvie bent to tie a shoe, and Ingrid saw Matthias Kist lurking in a doorway a few metres away.

'Are we still going to—'

Ingrid dragged her friend back towards the entrance. The rain was heavier, blowing through the open doors.

'Why are we going back out – it's wet.'

'That Matthias was standing nearby. I didn't want him to know our afternoon plans.'

Sylvie looked down the corridor; the numbers had thinned. Matthias stepped away from the door. No pretence: he was watching them.

'He was listening to Hans talk about Herr Schumann's class.'

'Why is he so suspicious? We've done nothing wrong. I want to tell him to get lost.'

Ingrid grabbed Sylvie's arm.

'No. We have to be smarter than him.'

'How?'

'By not doing anything out of the ordinary. Maybe he'll get bored and bother someone else.'

Sylvie did not look convinced. 'What if he follows us home? And hangs around until we go to the citadel.'

'We won't carry anything – we'll just time the walks. We might never have to run to the Altstadt if Comrade Khrushchev continues to be clever.'

Angela Richter

Angela laid out the ingredients for lunch on the kitchen table. It was going to be a variation on her jägerschnitzel. Traditionally, it was made with slices of jagdwurst: ground pork drenched in flour, egg and breadcrumbs, fried in oil until golden brown. Normally Angela accompanied it with letcho – a tomato-based sauce with peppers – and spirelli. Ingrid loved the noodles.

The meat component of the dish would not change; the difference would be the sauce. She was making a rich mushroom gravy. It was extravagant as lots of butter, extra onions and fresh pilz were required. The crisis in Cuba encouraged Angela to ignore her frugal nature; the Deutsche Marks from Colonel Brecht had not gone into the usual hiding place.

She brushed aside a lock of hair with the back of her hand; her fingers were already coated with flour. The mission for the Stasi boss had been easy. Angela was the intermediary with the Cubans: the payer and collector. It was a one-time deal as Pedro and his friends were already gone from the GDR, never likely to return. Thinking about what awaited them in Cuba made Angela sad. They were nice boys; loyalty to their family and country could see them sailing home to a warzone.

The meat was methodically floured, egged and breaded as Angela thought about the past two days. They had been turbulent, inflaming fears that had simmered since the start of the atomic age in 1945. They were personal terrors, never discussed with Dieter or Ingrid. GDR citizens were never told about the nuclear arsenals that were building around them. It was the illegal broadcasts from the West that kept them apace with every bomb or missile test, each new member of the nuclear club.

Angela knew the British and French had their own nuclear weapons. The capitalists would line up with the Americans against the communists in the Soviet Union. A nuclear war could never be contained. Cuba might be obliterated in a flash; Europe would follow soon after. Her German family in Erfurt and across the border in the West could do nothing to avoid that destruction. Just as in the last war, they would be the innocent victims at the mercy of madmen.

Angela remembered being swamped by feelings of helplessness in the final year of Hitler's Third Reich. They had been squeezed between two attacking forces: the Americans and British in the west, the Russians from the east. There was nowhere to run; it was a matter of who would capture them first. Stories about the brutalities inflicted by the avenging Red Army spread through the contracting Fatherland. It was a trauma that escalated every day as the cannons drew closer. It was a relief when the town's final surrender was to the Western forces. If the missiles were launched in the next few days, there would be no solace for anyone when the shooting stopped.

The breaded meat was laid on a plate to settle before frying. She peeled the outer layer off the onions and chopped. Tears formed but were quickly brushed away. Next, the mushrooms were halved and quartered. She checked the clock, calculated cooking times to ensure perfect jägerschnitzel would be ready for when her husband and daughter arrived for mittagessen.

Ingrid would have to do the dishes as Angela had another fitting at Helga's home near the Augustinerkloster. Coincidentally, that was where she had been on Tuesday when Pedro knocked on the door. He had something to sell to the Colonel. That much Angela learned at the time. It was only when she returned yesterday afternoon that Helga begged her to act as the go-between.

Angela was happy to help. It was a straightforward transaction, like the many deals East Germans conducted every day to improve their lives. There was no need to be concerned, especially when you were helping a colonel in the Stasi, although Angela had to admit to a slight unsettling feeling after leaving Pedro at the Hauptbahnhof.

The feeling that she was being followed had grown gradually. She had carefully scanned the tram, but nobody was paying her undue attention. The sensation had returned today while shopping for the meal she was about to cook. She had not recognised any faces from the tram or Altstadt; a man in his 30s had seemed a little familiar, but she had not noticed anyone with such a beard yesterday.

Angela ignited the gas, poured oil into the fry pan and focused on more important duties. Dieter would be home in 10 minutes.

Gunther Kist

A TUFT OF HAIR POKED FROM A JACKET POCKET AS THE STASI AGENT CHEWED on a hot bratwurst smeared with mustard. It was delicious, but he was not happy. Kist had deferred a surveillance task from Carsten Hartwig to spend the morning following Angela Richter. It had been fruitless.

She shopped, gossiped, returned home. It looked like a typical day. Money had changed hands at several shops, but bodies had obscured the transactions. Angela Richter could have palmed away the Deutsche Marks given to her by the Colonel, or payment could have been in Ostmarks. A morning away from an assigned duty had produced no evidence she was a black marketeer.

Kist stood at the edge of the Fischmarkt. The Gildehaus looked inviting, but he was gobbling lunch from a street vendor. He licked sauce from a thumb as he pondered what to put in his report at the end of the shift. There was nothing worthwhile to share with his supervisor. That might worry many workers in the GDR where diligence was expected to keep the socialist state running smoothly.

Stasi agents had learned to be flexible with the truth. Kist's assigned target was known to be indiscreet with customers about his views on the Socialist Unity Party. It would be easy to cobble a charge of Crime Against the State. It would be the felon's word against a sworn protector of the Party. No contest. Falsifying the charge was no problem; doing all the paperwork was another matter. He might need a citizen or two to be appalled by the sedition they had heard. Kist did not want the distraction. He would stop by the bakery where the target worked and *encourage* him to keep his mouth shut. A kicking behind the building might ensure the message was clear.

That thought cheered Kist as he disposed of the wastepaper in a bin. A bit of bullying would make up for the frustration of the morning. The bakery was about 20 minutes away from the Altstadt. That would give his stomach time to settle.

Ingrid Richter

SYLVIE WANDERED AROUND THE RICHTER LOUNGE AS INGRID WASHED plates, cutlery and pans from the family lunch. It was her duty if Mutti went out for an afternoon dress fitting. That was usually several times a week as her seamstress skills kept her in high demand. Vati returned to the tailor shop as soon as he finished eating. The threat to humanity did not reduce the demand for clothing.

The mushroom treat with the jägerschnitzel had been a delicious surprise. It was a messy clean-up for Ingrid, but worth it. The last of the knives and forks were left to drain on the cloth while Ingrid emptied the two bowls that sat in the pull-out drawers beneath the kitchen table. One was for washing, the other for rinsing.

Sylvie returned to the kitchen.

'Your mother has a lovely eye for colours. She is very creative – a dressmaker, a decorator, great cook. I wish I could live here.'

'I always wanted a sibling.' Ingrid picked up another cloth to dry the dishes. 'But if you were my sister, you might boss me around. If you were younger, I would boss you around. We couldn't be friends.'

They laughed.

'A good point. You see how my family works.' Sylvie returned to the lounge. 'He's still outside the bakery.'

'Can he see you through the curtain?'

'I don't think so.'

Matthias Kist had dogged them all the way home from school. He had been sitting on the retaining wall as they departed, almost in the same spot as the boy with the Digedags comic that morning. His hands had rested on the top brick, one row above the peace stick. It was reassuring their symbol of hope was in place, less so the presence of Matthias.

Any thoughts that he was a love-struck teenager had been blown away by Renate before the final class. She whispered to Ingrid in the corridor: school gossip claimed Matthias was the son of a Stasi agent. He was believed to have reported several teachers for crimes against the State. Renate feared he was going to report Herr Schumann. Sylvie's comments and questions in class might make her a target also.

Sylvie adjusted the curtain for a better view as Ingrid entered the room. 'I think he needs surveillance lessons from his father. Your targets shouldn't know they're being followed.'

Part of the Matthias mystery had been solved, but not all. 'First it was Mutti being followed by the Stasi. Now it's us.'

'Or maybe it is you,' Sylvie said. 'Your mother aroused their suspicion, and now they're checking on the whole Richter family. Is there an agent watching your father sew suits?'

'Apart from receiving something from Pedro, I don't see why the Stasi would bother with Mutti, Vati or me.' Ingrid slumped onto the sofa and wrapped her arms around a patterned cushion. 'Mutti is friends with the Colonel's wife.'

'Did you warn her about being followed from the Hauptbahnhof?'

'No.' Ingrid rested a chin on the cushion. 'We had such a lovely meal. Everyone was chatting and laughing about silly things. There was no talk about nuclear bombs or missiles. They were talking about life as normal. Vati wants me to go with him to the Schrebergarten after school on Saturday.' A shrug. 'I didn't want to spoil the mood.'

Sylvie looked back to the street. 'If Matthias keeps following us, you will have to say something to your parents. Your mother might have to alert the Colonel.' She pointed across the road. 'We've heard the Stasi use children as informants, but I'm sure they don't use them to follow schoolgirls.' She turned back to Ingrid. 'Perhaps it's his father following your mother. They might be running an illegal operation.'

'I never thought of that.'

Sylvie flicked the curtain. 'This is getting boring, watching a watcher watch us.'

They laughed.

'Shall we lead Matthias to the citadel? That won't enlighten him, but it will help us prepare in case the bombs start falling.'

They agreed to dispense with the ranzens. It would be a walk without any side trips to scare themselves at the library again. They had seen what nuclear bombs could do to people and buildings. Their best hope if the Americans sent their B-52s was to reach the tunnels at the citadel.

Sylvie pulled on her jacket as Ingrid loaded the kachelofen with more briquettes. She had to ensure it stayed alight until they returned. Mutti would be curious if it had to be relit; she always had to shift Ingrid from in front of it.

'Okay, the walk from school took 13 minutes,' Sylvie said. 'That was faster than our normal pace.'

'We won't be stopping for éclairs if the bombers arrive.'

'The most direct route is along Löberstrasse. I think it will be about two kilometres to the Domplatz, another few hundred metres from there to the citadel entrance.'

'Come on. That will mean a round trip of more than an hour. We need to get back before Mutti – she will want to check my homework.' Ingrid looked across the road. Matthias was gone. 'The junior spy has given up. Let's go before he comes back.'

Matthias Kist

Hunger had finally driven Matthias into the bakery for a roll. He had not eaten since breakfast; no warm meal would be kept at home. His father had not warned him about the challenges that agents faced on surveillance. Matthias had to sneak around the back of the shop to pee against a brick wall.

The cold was kept at bay with a warm jacket. Boredom was a bigger issue to contend with. Matthias had watched the ground-floor apartments on Friedrich-List Strasse for more than an hour; the only reward was an occasional twitch of a curtain from a window on the left. He could never tell his father that the girls were aware of his surveillance. He would do his duty and follow them if they left home. Perhaps his presence might curtail whatever mischief they were involved in.

Stomach juices gurgled as Matthias surveyed the offerings on the shelves. He had only a few pfennigs: not enough to buy tasty fillings. The baker said nothing as Matthias pondered the option of rye or sourdough. He could not have missed the schoolboy behind the tree in front of his shop. Fortunately, he was smart enough not to question the son of Erfurt's best Stasi agent. Matthias pointed to a roll, received it without any courtesy, dropped the coins on the counter and walked out.

Matthias leaned against the tree, pulled a chunk from the roll, put it in his mouth – and almost choked. The girls were close to the intersection with Semmelweisstrasse. They were walking quickly, hands in their jackets. He had been inside the shop for less than a minute. Had they been watching him watch them? That was sneaky; had they used his need for food to escape the apartment? Matthias smiled. They were not smart enough to get away from the son of a Stasi man.

The first lump of bread was forced down. A second bite was taken, the roll then stuffed into a pocket. He was on the job; a couple of bites would sustain him for a while. He stayed about 100 metres behind. They did not bother to look back when they reached Arnstädter

Strasse. The stadium and other sport facilities were to the left; the girls went right.

Their pace did not slacken as they joined Löberstrasse just before the flood canal. It was obvious to Matthias they were heading for the Altstadt. They passed under the rail bridge and were soon among the old buildings. They showed no interest in shops or other pedestrians. Matthias had to slow when they reached the major intersection at Reigerungstrasse. They did not appear to be looking for him, but Matthias stayed close to the wall when possible.

Ingrid and Sylvie finally diverged off Lange Brücke, ducking through side streets for a different crossing over the Gera River. Matthias did not believe they were trying to avoid him; their pace remained the same and they appeared fixated on a destination. Neither had paid any attention to the ancient architecture above them. Next was An den Graden; ahead was the Domplatz.

Were they going to the churches? His father said the Richter file showed no indications of religious beliefs. The school system never encouraged holy curiosity. Several dozen adults stood at the base of the stairway. That was more than Matthias would have expected for a weekday. Were they going to a service, or had they attended one? He had overheard his mother say that the crisis in Cuba had resurrected their elderly neighbour's faith in God. He could not see Frau Weege amongst the crowd.

The subject was discarded as his quarry scurried past the mostly elderly churchgoers. They turned left at the end of the square beneath the high walls of Petersberg Citadel. Again, they never bothered to check if they were being followed. Lauentor was an unusual choice. There was nothing along there to interest schoolgirls, only the citadel entrance. They continued for another 100 metres. Then they stopped at the slope to the citadel. They looked at something in Sylvie's hand, nodded and smiled. Matthias was confused. Why would they rush all the way from their home to the fortress?

No answer arrived before the girls turned back towards the Domplatz. Matthias slipped into the trees that bordered Maximilian-Welsch Strasse. Ingrid and Sylvie paid him no attention as they returned across the square towards Marktstrasse. They paused for barely 30 seconds before a tram arrived and whisked them away. It would have been a wasted effort to chase them to the tram; Matthias did not have the fare.

It was going to be a weird report for his father that evening. The girls went on a half-hour walk to the citadel, then caught a tram home. That was the most likely destination on that track. Matthias could never reveal he had been unable to follow them all the way.

A stomach rumble reminded him lunch had only been partially eaten. He retrieved the roll and chewed hungrily. There was nothing threatening to the Party about the schoolgirls. They did not talk to anyone or do anything illegal. The wall at the school entrance, which attracted Ingrid and Sylvie's attention before and after classes, produced no evidence of treason against the State. It was just bricks. Would it help his father if Matthias created something sinister about the friends? He mulled that possibility as he retraced his steps to the river.

Tomas Schuman

THE PILE OF ESSAYS STACKED IN FRONT OF TOMAS SCHUMANN IN THE staffroom was slowly moving from his right to his left. Some merited longer examination, fewer corrections and encouraging remarks. A couple prompted weary sighs and head shakes: wasted assessments. It was a ritual repeated many times through the school week.

'Imagine if you were given a Mark for every essay you have corrected in your career, Tomas. You could afford to retire to the casino at Monte Carlo.'

Jürgen Grau dropped a similar pile of student work on the table. The veterans usually commandeered the corner several times a week. The burden of assessment was more palatable with a friendly discussion.

'If you're giving me Deutsche Marks instead of Ostmarks, I'll be content to sit at the roulette table for a decade. Maybe with a pretty waitress to bring me wine.'

The laughter was hearty, as usual. The casino fantasy had sustained them through dark nights in the trenches during World War I. It started before a patrol through no man's land; Grau had inquired what his friend would do when they captured Paris. Schumann said he would ride his luck to the tables at Monte Carlo. Neither made it to the south of France before the Iron Curtain fell.

Grau pulled an essay from the pile. 'I heard you've been educating 7A in the finer points of international diplomacy again.'

'Yes.' Schumann jotted a note in a margin. 'I felt I had an obligation to be honest to my students.'

'Regardless of what the Party and Stasi think about honesty?'

'I'm too old to worry about them anymore, Jürgen.' The essay moved to the completed pile. 'Those kinder have a right to know what the demagogues are doing. It's not fair if a thermonuclear war erupts while they sleep.'

Grau snorted. 'That might be a blessing. A quick end rather than watching the bombers approach. Or dealing with the aftermath.'

'I'm a little more positive. Did you hear the Soviets stopped most of their boats before the blockade?'

'You mean the ones carrying the nuclear missiles. They couldn't afford to sail up to the American navy with the warheads on their decks. But Khrushchev hasn't backed down. Soviet boats are still heading to Cuba. What will Kennedy do – search or let them pass?'

Schumann lifted his eyes from a page. 'Do we know what shipments they carry?'

Grau lowered his voice. 'Western radio suggests they might have grain or oil.'

'Nothing to help build a missile site, yet enough to edge us over the cliff if the President enforces his blockade.'

A nod, a notation; Grau's essay was shuffled. 'Khrushchev is playing another cunning hand. Kennedy was made to look weak and indecisive following the failed invasion in Cuba and the wall going up in Berlin. He needs a major diplomatic victory to appear strong, both for his voters and the Western alliance.'

'If he fails to stop and search, he will look feeble at home and on the world stage.'

'Yes. If he does board a Soviet vessel, that's a green light for the Kremlin to retaliate.'

The teachers worked in silence for a few minutes. Diplomacy was like their favourite game, with more at stake than a black or white king.

'I see the crisis has occupied your thoughts as much as mine,' Schumann said. 'You try to sound blasé, but I know you are deeply worried.'

Grau dropped his pen on the table and slumped in the chair. 'I fear the wily fox might have miscalculated this time. I can see the justification for wanting nuclear missiles close to the United States. The Americans have them in Turkey and Italy. Their submarines could be even closer in the Baltic and the Black Sea. But why did Khrushchev do it secretly? He can shout all he likes about defending Cuba from invasion, but this method makes him look sneaky. It hands some of the moral high ground to the Americans.'

The essay assessments resumed.

'The other thing that worries me, Tomas, is the American generals. They have a young commander in chief. He was merely skipper of a patrol boat during the war, and he lost that. Now he has the power of the entire army, navy and air force at his fingertips. I bet the hawks in his government are screaming at him to unleash their biggest weapons. They don't want Khrushchev to draw first blood.'

'Surely America's own morality will stop them from launching the first missiles? Japan caught them asleep at Pearl Harbor; they were able to harness that moral indignation for a crushing victory. It justified what they did to Hiroshima and Nagasaki. Wouldn't the Americans be seen as hypocrites if they launched a strike against Cuba and the Soviets?'

'Probably. There might not be many left alive to debate that issue.' Grau went to the sink and poured a glass of water. He held a glass up for Schumann; he shook his head. There were only three other teachers in the room. The rest were working in empty classrooms or doing after-school activities with Young Pioneers.

Another essay was shuffled from right to left, the grade no better or worse than the previous paper.

'What if the American air force tried precision bombing? They could knock out most of the Soviet sites with conventional weapons. Khrushchev might see that any retaliation would condemn the Russians to massive losses compared to the Americans.'

Grau shook his head. 'We saw how ineffective bombers were during the last war. The British and Americans had to use overwhelming numbers to ensure a few bombs fell in the right place. If Kennedy doesn't get the nuclear sites on the first strike, then it's all over.'

Schumann lifted a new essay, then replaced it.

'I can't imagine the pressure Khrushchev and Kennedy are under. It's move, counter-move. They must make decisions that could lead to the destruction or preservation of the human race. That kind of pressure must do strange things to the mind, Jürgen.'

He tapped the pen against the essay.

'We saw the best and worst of mankind during the wars. There were brilliant commanders whose levels of humanity were corroded by the depravity we experienced. In some it produced strength and depths we never knew they had. For many, it was overwhelming. Who can predict what impact this duress is having?'

Grau looked up from his current assessment.

'There is another factor to consider, Tomas. We talk about two men, but how much control do they both have away from public scrutiny? The hawks in Washington and Moscow will be pushing for military solutions. That is their instinct, regardless of the mess it might leave for the world. Will it come down to an air force or army general thinking they are patriots, that they must act for the welfare of their citizens? I think there is an apt proverb for this situation.'

'Pride goeth before the fall.'

'Exactly.'

Silence returned; the paperwork piles altered in height.

'One thing that has intrigued me, Jürgen, is the evidence of these Soviet missiles.'

'As in, we haven't seen it?'

'Yes. It might strengthen the American case if they produced photos.'

Grau wiggled a hand. 'Khrushchev has already acknowledged they are building the sites. It's a case of semantics over whether their purpose is defensive or offensive.'

'The American spy planes must be constantly flying over Cuba to check on the launch site progress. That is breaching the Cubans' sovereign territory. What would happen if they shot one of the American planes down? Would that be the trigger?'

Ingrid Richter

INGRID LAY ON THE CARPET IN FRONT OF THE KACHELOFEN, HER MATHEMATICS homework laid out in front. Three fresh briquettes on their return from the citadel mission had made the room warm, her eyes drowsy. It had been a successful reconnaissance: they could reach the outer walls within 45 minutes from school, 30 from home. They might be safe in the tunnels – if the Volksarmee allowed them inside. Sylvie was certain it would not be a problem; the soldiers would run underground as soon as the nuclear war started. The gates should be wide open.

Ingrid struggled with an equation in her book, her eyelids drooped, the figures on the page blurred. Maths was not her favourite topic. She wished someone could invent a simple gadget that did the calculations for her.

The schoolgirls had laughed on the tram when Matthias was left behind in the Domplatz. He would be annoyed and confused, no idea why they walked to Petersberg Citadel then returned home immediately. The junior spy probably thought he had been clever, that his clumsy pursuit was not seen.

They were too clever for Matthias, but Ingrid knew the homework would defeat her. She pushed it away and rested a tired head on her forearms. Inspiration might come after a brief snooze. It had been a traumatic week: the horror of the concentration camp compounded by the threat to their existence. Then the Stasi was showing unwanted interest in her family. No wonder sleep at night was so restless.

Her eyes had been closed for only a few seconds when the front door closed. No time for nightmares.

'I'm home, Ingrid.'

Ingrid stretched like a cat, arching her back. It was dark outside. The clock on the buffet showed 5.07 – she had slept for almost an hour.

Mutti entered the room, pulling off gloves and an overcoat. Mutti always looked elegant, even after several hours fussing around clients with their dress designs.

'It's snug in here.' She swept through the curtains to the middle room. 'Did you finish your homework?'

'No, Mutti. I fell asleep. I'll do it now.' Ingrid scampered across the carpet to rest her back against the sofa. Distance from the warmth of the ceramic heater might sharpen her thoughts.

Mutti returned in a cardigan. 'Are you feeling alright, dear? You've been doing a lot of sleeping this week – I can barely wake you in the mornings.'

'I'm fine, Mutti, just a lot on my mind.'

Mutti stopped at the door to the hall. 'Do you want to talk about anything?'

Was this the moment to share her concerns about the Stasi agent? And his son. Ingrid's head still felt foggy from the unexpected nap. Could she articulate her fears and explain her actions over the past few days without upsetting her mother?

Mutti settled the issue by sitting on the sofa.

'Come here, sit beside me. We haven't had a chance to chat for a while.'

Ingrid let the book slide off her lap and settled in beside her mother.

Mutti draped an arm around her shoulder. It was comforting, like when they read books together after kindergarten.

'I know it was a shock to hear that the Russians and Americans might start another war. Is that what has been upsetting you?'

Ingrid nodded. 'We feel so vulnerable, Mutti. Everyone at school. We've done nothing to hurt the Americans or Russians, yet their problems might destroy us. We'll never grow up to have jobs, our own families. If we survive a nuclear attack, we'll be stranded in a poisoned wasteland. Why do men we've never met – who will never know us – want to destroy us? Why should they have that power?'

No further words were necessary as mother and daughter hugged tightly. They stayed like that until Vati came through the door 15 minutes later. He struggled out of his overcoat, damp from an autumnal shower. He moved a stand closer to the kachelofen, hung the coat to dry.

Ingrid wiped tear tracks from her cheeks.

'What's wrong?'

'Ingrid's upset about the crisis in Cuba. She's worried it might lead to a nuclear war.'

Vati joined them on the sofa and spread an arm around his family.

'I don't think it will come to that. The Russians don't want to destroy the world. Neither do the Americans. There is too much pride at stake but at least they are still talking after three days – we must trust they will find a solution. Something that will satisfy Khrushchev and Kennedy.'

It felt good in her parents' embrace. Ingrid wanted to be reassured. Would the politicians prove as wise as her father and mother? She hoped they would. As they huddled, Ingrid knew the missiles were not the only threat to her family. There was the Stasi. Was it the right time to share that danger?

The comfortable feeling made Ingrid hesitate. They were sharing a special moment, perhaps even brought about by magic from her peace stick. The Richter family had no control over matters outside their apartment. Why not let the happiness at home linger?

It did for another 10 minutes until Mutti broke the spell.

'I need to make the supper. Dieter can attend to the heater and you, young lady, need to finish that homework. There will be school tomorrow.'

Gunther Kist

SUPPER AT THE KIST APARTMENT WAS THE FIRST SHARED BY THE FAMILY since Sunday. That was the routine most weeks: his wife, Magda, at the table with Matthias and the twin eight-year-old daughters anxiously watching the door to see if the husband and father would have time to join them. Kist knew they understood the duty of protecting the Party was uppermost. A good Stasi man never worked standard office hours.

The salad, egg and bread were consumed without much chatter. The girls were left to clean the dishes, with Magda supervising, while Kist discussed his son's surveillance work.

'They walked to the citadel and then went home again?'

'Yes.'

'They spoke to nobody on the way?'

'No.'

'That is strange behaviour for schoolgirls but not illegal.'

Kist paced the small room.

Matthias sat on the edge of the armchair his mother normally used.

'What about school – did you see them do anything suspicious?'

'No.' Matthias sat up straighter. 'But I heard from an informant that Sylvie Witzenhause said strange things during class.'

Kist stopped in front of his son.

'Apparently, Herr Schumann started a debate about Cuba. He even *apologised* for not telling them anything on Wednesday. That must have made Sylvie bolder because she was rude to their Pioneer leader. Hans Rathmann was explaining the requirement for men to fight wars. She questioned why there had to be wars.'

Father and son snorted.

'Sylvie blames men for starting wars. She said it would be better to sit down and talk – like women.'

An incredulous shake of his head was all that Kist could offer to that notion. He started to pace again. 'They are radical ideas but not against Party policy. That nonsense will be slapped out of her one day.

'That teacher is a worry. He is the type to encourage anti-social ideas among impressionable students. I have passed along your earlier report about his revelations on Tuesday. I think my supervisor will assign an agent to examine his loyalties in the next few days.'

Kist stopped to lay a hand on his son's shoulder.

'I know, of course, that you will not say anything about that to your classmates. Even if they haul him out of school for interrogation. You must stay below the radar, Matthias. Never let them know you are destined for the Ministry for State Security.'

Matthias nodded, a smile barely suppressed.

'We don't have any new evidence against the Richter family, but instincts tell me they are guilty of crimes against the Party. Perhaps they are getting more cunning at hiding their corruption. I followed the father this afternoon.'

Young eyes lit up with anticipation. 'Did you catch him making black market deals or doing something wrong?'

'Not yet. He was too confident. Nobody in the GDR should be that self-assured. Unless they are trying to hide something. I'm certain we'll find it.'

Matthias clutched his knees and rocked on the edge of the armchair. 'Will you take him into Andreasstrasse for interrogation? A good beating?'

Kist smiled. His son was a good match for a career in the Stasi. He was not squeamish about the need for rough treatment.

'Not yet. One day, hopefully. I must build my file on them. I'm sure the wife – Angela – will flip when she knows we have her Dieter in a cell. Working for a Stasi colonel won't protect her when he starts talking.'

Kist winced when he saw his son's eyes light up even more. He should not have revealed that valuable tidbit. Carsten Hartwig was aware that Kist was hunting big game. The supervisor could be guaranteed to keep his mouth shut unless his star field agent bagged the prize. A corrupt colonel could be career-enhancing for more than the sergeant.

Ingrid Richter

THE HEAT FROM THE LOUNGE BARELY REACHED THE CURTAIN TO THE middle room where Ingrid huddled. Mutti had been firm. She declared her daughter was too stressed by the standoff between the Soviets and Americans; bed was the best place. The desire to know what was happening in Cuba, Moscow and Washington was too overwhelming for Ingrid. It required another sneaky viewing of the West German television news from the curtained doorway.

Her parents' armchairs were closer, obscuring the television screen. Ingrid was reliant on the audio, which only just reached her hiding place. It seemed Herr Schumann might have been too optimistic about the confrontation looming at sea near Cuba. Some Soviet vessels had changed course; others were still cruising towards the US Navy.

The news service believed an oil tanker had been cleared to proceed to Havana without boarding. The next vessel that might cause a confrontation was also a tanker. The *Grozny* was carrying deck cargo, which intelligence sources suggested could be missile fuel tanks. It was expected to reach the blockade zone on Friday evening. Would the Americans want to board to verify the cargo? Any boarding would be viewed as piracy by the Soviets.

The television reports moved to diplomatic efforts to find an agreement. The moratorium request by the United Nations Acting Secretary General had not found favour with either the Americans or Russians. The West German reporter said that Moscow had not responded, while Washington said U Thant's request did not go far enough: they wanted an immediate freeze on construction at the sites in Cuba and verified withdrawal of any missiles.

Ingrid stifled a yawn, pulled the bettdecke closer; they were still in danger. Politicians were refusing to bend. They would rather blow up the world than show weakness. It was madness. How many millions lived in the Soviet Union and the United States? They would be the first to die in a thermonuclear war. Didn't their leaders care about them? If Ingrid could see the futility of everyone dying, why couldn't the old men understand? She hoped the peace stick would work its magic for another 24 hours.

The West German news service moved to domestic stories. Ingrid prepared to return to bed without alerting her parents. The squeaky floorboard had to be negotiated. Then her father spoke quietly.

'I was followed home from work this evening.'

Ingrid parted the curtain slightly.

'Oh.' Her mother had taken her father's hand. 'Are you sure?'

'Yes. He wasn't subtle about it.' Her father looked towards the curtain. The gap was barely a crack; there was no backlighting to betray her. 'He was a stocky man, in his late 30s. Dark hair, hat, factory worker clothes. Not the sort of person who would bother hanging around our tailor shop.'

'Did he have a beard?'

'No.' Her father pivoted in his seat. 'What makes you say that? Have you been followed?'

'I … think so.' Her mother also looked towards the doorway. The gap had been reduced. Ingrid was safe.

'When?'

'Yesterday at the Hauptbahnhof and today while shopping.'

'What did you see?'

'It was more of a feeling.' Her mother shrugged. 'There was nobody obviously staring at me. But I felt eyes watching me on the tram, then around the shops today.'

'Did anyone stand out?'

'Not really. The only possibility was a man in his 30s that looked familiar, although he had a beard today. That's why I dismissed him – you can't grow all that fuzz overnight.'

'You can always put on a fake.' Her father leaned forward and rested his arms on his knees. 'The Stasi are getting more creative with their disguises. I've heard they have a room full of beards, moustaches, wigs and hats at their headquarters. They change their clothes frequently if they want to stay hidden.'

Ingrid watched her father stand and pace the lounge. She prepared to run for her bed.

'It sounds like the man who followed me. Yet he didn't seem to mind being seen. That's when they want to intimidate their targets.

Make them do something silly.' The pacing stopped. He spread his arms wide. 'But we haven't done anything to make the Stasi suspicious.'

Her mother raised a hand to her mouth. 'The Stasi don't view the world the same way as us, Dieter.'

'I know that, but they make the rules. How do we find out what put us on their radar?'

'I have an idea.'

Her mother walked to the buffet where the chocolates and other westpaket goodies were kept locked away from the sweet tooths. She produced a key for the cabinet from her cardigan.

'What have you been doing, Angela?'

Ingrid heard the change in her father's tone. It was not anger, more like fear.

'Nothing dangerous, Dieter. Or illegal.'

The cabinet was unlocked. Ingrid could not see what was retrieved. Her mother shuffled items that sounded like books. The next sound was a gasp from her father.

'Where did you get that?'

It was another change in tone; fear was replaced by awe.

'The Cubans. Remember the trainee teachers we met during the holiday on the Baltic? They wanted to go home urgently to defend their country from the Americans. They needed cash to fly to Holland. They wanted to sell this.'

Ingrid desperately wanted to see what her mother had traded. There were so many possibilities, but nothing she could imagine that would pay for an international plane ticket. And where would her mother get the money? She risked nudging the curtain a fraction wider. Her parents were staring at something laid on a flat surface of the buffet. It was impossible to tell what.

'Is it authentic?'

'We believe so.'

'We?'

'The Colonel and me. The Cubans heard he was a collector. Their leader went to his home on Tuesday afternoon because he didn't want to be seen at Stasi headquarters. Pedro wouldn't say how it was obtained. He claimed there were loyalists in powerful positions everywhere in the GDR. They were committed to never letting the Reich die.'

'But this is the opposite of what the revolutionaries achieved in Cuba. Why would he want it?'

'He's a smart collector, like the Colonel and me. Pedro knew the value would increase over time. Revolutions always need money.'

Ingrid watched her father pick up a book from the buffet and move under the light. It was one of Mutti's stamp collections. She was an avid collector, like many in the GDR. That solved part of the puzzle, but not why the new addition was so valuable. It also explained Pedro's flight from the Stasi agent. He couldn't get caught with contraband, not when he was wanting to fly home to fight the Americans.

'It's incredible. Do you know how many were printed?'

'No. Pedro never revealed anything. Not who sold it or how he made contact. This would be a very deep and private market. I don't know how he would have found the money to buy it in the first place.'

'If he paid for it.'

'Oh. I never considered that. I wonder if the Colonel did.'

The stamp book was replaced on the shelf.

'If the Colonel bought the stamp, why do you have it here?'

Ingrid could see the side of her mother's face; she was smiling.

'He doesn't know about this one.'

Her father was stunned.

'You mean Pedro sold two stamps, and you passed only one to the Colonel?'

Her mother laughed. 'The Colonel thought only one was being offered. When I went to their home on Wednesday, Helga asked me to act as the go-between. I had a better eye for authentication, and she knew my skills as a trader. A price was asked on Tuesday – if I could negotiate a better deal, I could keep half the difference.'

A smile spread across her father's face. 'The poor Cuban was no match for you, Angela.'

'We had a good haggle.' Another laugh. 'But he had to buy his train tickets. Plus, we were on the square in front of the Hauptbahnhof. He was getting nervous. I trimmed 15 per cent from the price and Pedro handed over *two* identical stamps.'

'The Colonel saves money, gets his *unique* stamp and has no clue about your cleverness.'

'Exactly.'

Ingrid closed the curtain as her mother packed away her prize. The television was switched off; they would be going to bed soon. She rose carefully, still reluctant to leave without learning about the special stamp.

'I wonder if the Cubans were under surveillance – if that's how the Stasi spotted you, Angela. And finally turned to me.'

'That might explain it. But if they followed me from the train, they would know I have a connection with the Colonel. That should make any field agent nervous.'

'Unless it's a rogue agent. I wonder if Pedro offered the stamp to other collectors first. They might want to know who bought it. This stamp is valuable but also extremely dangerous.'

A chill gripped Ingrid. Just when her Stasi fears had been subsiding. Her parents knew about being secret police targets; there was no need to reveal her adventures in the Altstadt. If the Stasi man and his son were on the trail of that stamp, what would they do next? Should she warn Mutti and Vati about the agent's son? A lamp by the television was switched off, Ingrid's cue to scamper to the bed. She only just caught her father's final comment.

'I never thought I would see anything like that – Yuri Gagarin as a Nazi.'

Tomas Schumann

Most of the tomes on Tomas Schumann's shelf had been read at least once. Many had been enjoyed twice; a treasured few had been worthy of three readings. He surveyed them from his favourite armchair, trying to decide whether the next book should be an old read or new; whether it should be thick or thin.

The West German television had been replaced by a radio broadcast of Beethoven interspersed by news updates. New York was six hours behind the GDR; it had become the new epicentre for the Cuban Missile Crisis. Moscow and Washington's responses to U Thant's diplomacy were being filtered through the United Nations headquarters and the waiting media.

Schumann reached for a recent addition to his collection: *Catch-22* by Joseph Heller. A satirical American novel about a war that Schumann had been on the losing side was an unusual choice. The book was highly recommended by a liberal colleague. It was less than a year old, sneaked through the border in a westpaket; now dog-eared from frequent use. The blurb appealed, but would there be time to finish?

The morning's optimism had been tempered. The flashpoint at the Cuba blockade had not been averted, merely delayed. Khrushchev had been cunning enough not to expose ships loaded with weapons to American scrutiny. That would have been a public relations disaster for the Kremlin. The world was largely in the dark about the extent of the Soviet operation in Cuba. President Kennedy could still be portrayed as the aggressor.

It was known that a second tanker was maintaining its course for Cuba. Khrushchev's pawn was ignored; a knight was on the board to test Kennedy's resolve at the blockade. Would he risk the Russian wrath with a boarding or let the ship sail through untouched? That decision would be made on Friday. It seemed the world had not emerged from the darkest hours of the crisis.

Catch-22 was opened, the pages carefully adjusted so there would be no further damage. It might be passed to other free thinkers, such as war veterans like himself and Heller, the author, who saw first-hand the futility in using armed conflict to settle differences. Perhaps young Sylvie Witzenhause had a valid point: only men started wars – should they be stripped of the power?

Schumann considered the two males gambling with the world's future. Was it a game to the Soviet leader? If so, he was playing on multiple fronts, which was always a risk. Hitler might even concede that after 17 years reflection in hell.

Publicly Khrushchev appeared to offer hope of a peaceful resolution. It was announced that Khrushchev welcomed U Thant's initiative to discuss 'all the problems which have arisen'. However, with the Russians, there were always hooks to every deal. Khrushchev was telling the world he was ready to talk, but only if the blockade was lifted. Your move, President Kennedy.

Schumann settled into the chair. It was late, but he would probably read for an hour or more. Former soldiers preferred to keep sleep at bay in stressful times. Old memories were harder to quell in the dark.

Friday, October 26, 1962

Ingrid Richter

It had been Ingrid's ambition to meet the first man into outer space. Yuri Gagarin became her hero when his *Vostok 1* orbited the Earth in April 1961. She did not care that the Soviet Union had won the race with America to be the first. It was the thrill of escaping Earth that captivated her. Rocket missions to the Moon and Mars were no longer science fiction stories; they would happen in her lifetime. Could she dare to believe she might enjoy that weightless experience?

Yuri was an international star from the moment he landed. His charisma beamed from open-top car parades in every city. And now he was in Erfurt. Ingrid cheered with her friends as the limousine parted the adoring crowd on the Domplatz. The black Mercedes slowed near the obelisk where Ingrid perched on the lower steps. Yuri stood to wave. He smiled, then thrust his right arm out in a salute that was banned on both sides of the Iron Curtain.

Ingrid was horrified when the cosmonaut's car stopped at the obelisk. Yuri remained at attention, the right arm thrust skywards. The palm was gigantic, obscuring her champion's warm smile. All she could see was the awful hakenkreuz: the most despised Nazi symbol. Ingrid tried to retreat through the throng. Everyone was saluting Yuri in the same manner; everywhere she turned swastikas were thrust into her face. She tripped, sprawling beneath a sea of flailing Nazis.

It was Mutti who saved her, again.

'Ingrid, Ingrid.'

The legs evaporated; the tangle on the cobbles was her bettdecke and pillow. Another dream. Horrible, but not as terrifying as the start of the week when she had to escape a gas oven.

'I was hoping an early sleep might refresh you.' Mutti lifted the cover back onto the bed. The morning chill made Ingrid scramble into her school clothes.

'What were you dreaming about this time?'

Should that remain secret? Telling Mutti about Yuri being a Nazi would reveal her own spying. She wanted to know how a stamp could portray the holder of the Order of Lenin as a Nazi. But it was too risky; Ingrid hated to think her parents would consider her a snoop.

'I don't remember, Mutti.' She pulled on a blue jersey. 'It's gone now. I'm okay.'

'Hurry up then. You're not as late as yesterday. You'll have time for a boiled egg.'

Amazingly, the egg did not make her stomach rebel. Was she getting used to the nightmares, or was dreaming of Yuri Gagarin as a Nazi not as extreme as missiles and concentration camps? Another surprise waited at the kitchen table. Vati was still drinking his coffee, the smaller radio tuned to a West German station.

'Morning, Vati. What's happening in Cuba?'

Vati tousled her blonde bob. A couple of swipes straightened it again without grumbles. It was part of the morning routine when they shared the first meal.

'A lot of watching for the US Navy at the blockade. The Soviets are not risking any vessels that might have weapons.'

'What about in Cuba? What do we know about the missiles?'

Vati placed his cup on the table.

'The Americans released photos at the United Nations last night to prove the Russians are building missile sites.'

Ingrid stopped her egg peeling. 'Are their missiles ready to fire?'

'We don't know. There might be something more on the television news tonight.'

A bite of sourdough with honey was taken; the methodical peeling resumed.

'There is some good news. Both Khrushchev and Kennedy are willing to talk to the United Nations about finding a solution.'

Ingrid salted the egg. 'Are Khrushchev and Kennedy going to New York? To sit down together and talk?'

Vati stood and brushed a crumb from his suit jacket. 'No. That's not the way heads of state do things. They work through diplomats, like U Thant at the UN.'

The honey, bread and egg combination were washed down with a mouthful of milk.

'Wouldn't it be easier if the two men who have the problem meet face-to-face? Make them sit in a room until they find a solution that doesn't involve blowing up the world.'

Vati smiled. 'Yes. That sounds much more sensible. But that's not how the world works.'

A kiss was planted on Ingrid's forehead as her father exited the kitchen. Mutti was already at work in the master bedroom with the sweeper.

Ingrid shook her head. Why was it so hard to make men see common sense? Nobody won in a thermonuclear war. Khrushchev and Kennedy should be eager to find a way out of the mess they had created. The breakfast dishes were washed, rinsed and left to drain. Mutti would tidy them away. Her mind considered simpler ways to resolve the crisis in Cuba as she completed her morning preparations.

Politicians wanted to win, probably more than most people. If Cuba was not going to provide a winner, why not choose a resolution method that did not destroy every living thing on the planet? Could they play chess? Backgammon? Cards? There was a multitude of possibilities that could provide a winner and loser without shedding a life.

Or was blood the key to a satisfactory result for men? The loser had to be bloodied in some way. Ingrid had no brothers and Vati was a gentle man, but she knew that some men liked to fight. She had heard their neighbour complain about her husband getting involved in brawls at his local inn. There was something in the physical nature of men that women would never understand.

Rather than line up armies of millions to be slaughtered, why not let national pride be decided by two knights? Just like in medieval times. They could get on horses with armour and joust. That used to settle honour without excessive bloodshed.

Ingrid pondered other non-violent solutions as she packed the mathematics homework into her ranzen. Maybe a few more women politicians would prevent these catastrophes. Why not Mutti? She was smart, caring, organised, a good negotiator: the perfect female candidate for the Socialist Unity Party.

'Bye, Mutti.'

The farewell was overwhelmed by the sweeper and a hesitation. Who would do the cleaning if Mutti went to be a politician in Berlin?

Sylvie was in her usual place on the driveway, jogging to keep warm under leaden skies. Rain was forecast.

'You're on time, but do your eyes indicate another nightmare?'

'Just a restless night. Too much thinking about Cuba.'

The Yuri dream would not be shared; she could never explain her mother having a controversial Nazi stamp involving the first man into outer space. She checked the street for the junior snooper: no signs of Matthias Kist. Ingrid dropped into step with her friend. The first aromatic wave from the brewery caught up with them as they crossed the road. The autumn leaves were soggy from an overnight shower.

'What are we going to do this afternoon?' Sylvie held out a hand as a few drops fell. 'We've done our reconnaissance of the citadel. We know what to expect during and after a nuclear missile attack. Should we start gathering food and candles for our survival kit?'

'We'll have to see later. Mutti has been out every day this week. I'm not sure what she will be doing today. It might look strange if we're caught taking cans from the pantry. And where would we hide them?'

Sylvie giggled. 'My brother and sisters would tell my mother if I hid them under the bed.'

They waited for a Trabant and cyclist to puff past, the factory worker only slightly less noisy.

'Mutti stores a lot of dressmaking patterns and material under my bed. She's always ferreting under there.'

'What about the shed at your Schrebergarten? It's not used much after summer.'

'No, although Vati wants me to go with him while he digs some weeds tomorrow. It's too far away to collect food when the missiles and bombs start falling.'

It was only as they reached Tchaikowskistrasse that they noticed their shadow. Matthias Kist had waited further along the route, knowing they usually passed that way.

Sylvie was the angriest. 'I'm sick of him. I'm going to tell him to leave us alone.' She was across the road before Ingrid could grab an arm. Matthias did not cower from the running Sylvie; he squared his shoulders and stood with hands on hips. Sylvie pointed a finger in his face.

'You have no right to follow us, Matthias Kist.' The junior agent flinched but held his ground. 'Your father might be a Stasi agent, but you're not.' A handful of students stopped to watch the confrontation. 'You stay away from Ingrid and me.' She turned the finger from Matthias to Ingrid. 'Her mother has powerful connections – a Stasi colonel. That's more important than your gutter trash father.'

Ingrid's face reddened. Having the connection was valuable – flaunting it was wrong. She grabbed Sylvie's arm.

'Come on – we'll miss first bell.' She looked at Matthias. He looked unshaken. Had his father already shared that information about the Stasi boss? She could not resist a parting jab. 'I'm sure Matthias got the message.'

They hurried towards Häslerstrasse. Ingrid sneaked a glance; Matthias trailled a long way behind the students who had witnessed the eighth grader being put in his place by a girl.

'Please don't mention Mutti's connection to the colonel again.'

'It worked.' Sylvie smiled. Matthias was more than 80 metres behind.

'The connection hasn't stopped his father following Mutti and Vati.'

Sylvie stopped. 'Your father? The Stasi are following the whole family?'

That was an awkward slip. Ingrid hadn't worked out a way to share that information with Sylvie without explaining the Yuri Gagarin stamp. Ingrid walked towards Am Schwemmbach; Sylvie followed.

'Vati mentioned it last night during the television news.'

'What did your mother say? Have you told her she was being followed?'

That was a dilemma. Ingrid could not lie; her whole education at school and home was about being honest. Revealing her mother's secret stamp deal with the colonel and Pedro could ruin that special connection. The stamp could also be illegal. Prison might seem like a lesser problem as the world grappled with a nuclear crisis, but Ingrid did not want her parents being thrown into a Stasi cell.

'Mutti … thought she had been followed from the Hauptbahnhof.'

'We know for certain. Did you tell her we saw the agent chase her onto the tram?'

'I couldn't – I was listening from the curtain. Mutti sent me to bed early because I've been so hard to wake up in the mornings.'

They were 20 metres from the school entrance. Ingrid wanted to shift focus from family matters to the peace stick.

'Look, there's no one standing at the retaining wall.'

They checked behind for Matthias. He had not reached the main road. Their path was clear for a slow pass and check.

Sylvie was more concerned about the Stasi.

'Did your parents have any idea why the Stasi might be curious?'

'They were talking quietly.' Ingrid shrugged. 'The television was playing.'

It was true, if not totally honest. Ingrid could live with that if it protected her family.

A few steps later they were abreast of the peace stick.

Sylvie reacted first. 'Oh no. It's sticking out.'

About four centimetres of the stick protruded from the hole. Another student must have found it. Had they removed it to investigate or merely played with it while they sat on the wall and waited for friends?

Sylvie covered her mouth with a hand. 'Do you think the luck has been broken?'

Ingrid stood sideways against the wall as students rushed for the courtyard.

'No.' She nudged the stick deeper, away from curious fingers. 'I'm sure it's still providing protection. There will still be Saturday school. And we need to hurry if we don't want detention.'

Ingrid looped arms with Sylvie as they entered the school. She risked a final glance; had her stop at the wall been noticed? More importantly, did Matthias Kist see anything? If he saw the stick and their interest, would he remove it out of spite? They turned a corner for the courtyard without another sighting of the eighth grader.

Angela Richter

The floors were clean, the beds made, the dishes returned to the cupboard. Angela surveyed her lounge for anything out of place. The sofa cushions required straightening. There was no need for realigning. Dieter and Ingrid understood her quirky rainbow design; they had to go red, orange, yellow green, blue, indigo, violet. Angela loved the splash of colour that had taken a lot of trading to source.

Shopping was next on the agenda. There was some leftover jagdwurst. A few extra onions, paprika and a broth would flesh it out for a tasty wurstgulasch. It was unusual to have two rich dishes in a row. At most it would be three meat dishes for lunch in a week. Angela decided the fears generated by the crisis in Cuba warranted hearty meals to cheer her small family. She needed some noodles, bread and butter. There was always something required for the pantry most days. She enjoyed the outings; it was a chance to meet neighbours, gossip and organise trades. She was expecting a westpaket from her parents next week.

Angela looked at the locked cabinet that held the new and most important stamp in her collection. Yuri Gagarin could not be shared with her philatelist friends. It would be the same for Colonel Brecht. Word would sweep Erfurt within hours if either was to display their treasure. The lure of the forbidden drew her to the buffet.

She unlocked it and pulled out the blue album. All stamps needed to be kept in dry, dark places. Her Yuri Gagarin gem would require its own discreet location. That was a work in progress. Angela could not risk a fellow philatelist stumbling upon it when viewing her collection.

She used tongs to hold the stamp; it was pristine, no sign of damage or skin oil. Running down the white border on the left was the abbreviation for the German Democratic Republic: DDR. Below it the cost: 40 pfennigs. The main image was like the hundreds that flooded the market following Yuri's space mission: he was standing in an open-top car, the bonnet covered in flowers. Yuri was dressed in his military uniform and cap. A local dignitary always squeezed into the camera frame. In this case it was the East German head of state, Walter Ulbricht. Crowds lined the road; the Brandenburg Gates were in the background. The men waved. It was Yuri's right-hand salute that made the stamp unique.

Angela picked up a magnifying glass to investigate the most contentious element – the swastika on Yuri Gagarin's palm. It was rough but identifiable as a hakenkreuz. It had not been drawn on the stamp by a cunning fraudster; it was part of the print. Angela did not believe that the hero of the Soviet Union had drawn a swastika on his hand before parading before thousands of East Germans. Every step, wave and greeting that Yuri made in tours outside the Soviet Union was covered by television or photographers. It would be suicidal to display banned symbols, even if he secretly had Nazi sympathies. Which Angela doubted. The Russians would have thoroughly vetted the first man into space before launching him onto the world stage. Yuri Gagarin reflected the technological success of the Soviet Union; nothing would be allowed to tarnish that public relations image. The original stamp available throughout the GDR had been professionally changed.

Angela was certain neo-Nazis were responsible. They shed the uniforms of the SS in 1945 but not their loyalty. They were silently present in every level of German society on both sides of the wall.

The Nazi connection did not make the stamp any less valuable. The Neos were giving the Soviets a poke in the eye while fuelling the lingering ambitions of the faithful. The Third Reich had not been buried forever in the rubble of Berlin. The value of the stamp rested with the number printed. There must have been more than the two that Pedro offered for sale. The network of philatelists was wide in East Germany; there were tens of thousands collecting. Angela and her friends had never heard whispers involving Yuri Gagarin and swastikas, an indication the print run might be low. Illegal stamps like that would be impossible to keep secret. Especially if the neo-Nazis wanted to embarrass their Russian conquerors.

This was a special stamp that would need to stay confidential. She would find a small album to keep it private and safe. Angela would be able to enjoy the thrill of owning a rare and controversial stamp, but that knowledge could not extend beyond her family. One day she would tell Ingrid about the stamp and its significance. Angela suspected it might never change ownership in her lifetime.

The tongs eased the stamp into a clean envelope, which was slipped inside a flap at the back of an older album with a modest collection. It would be safe for the moment; crime in the apartment blocks on this side or Erfurt was rare. The cabinet door was closed and locked. The key went into her purse. It was time to shop for more mundane things.

Gunther Kist

THE STASI AGENT FINISHED A BREAD ROLL AS HE WATCHED ANGELA Richter leave her apartment. Kist stood beside the same tree that his son had used the previous day. It was a good surveillance location; the bakery kept the hunger at bay while he waited. There was no concern about concealment from the fat baker inside. A silly comment about Kist watching for American bombers had been dismissed with an icy stare. The baker was sweating after 30 seconds; payment for the roll and éclair was waved away.

Kist had changed his facial appearance again – no beard or moustache – as it was important that neither Frau Richter nor any neighbours remembered him. He was about to launch a new level of intimidation after spooking the husband, Dieter, the previous evening. He was overt about his interest in the tailor, wanting him to report the close attention to his wife over dinner.

It had worked; she was twitchy when leaving home, glancing back and forth along the street. Angela might even have looked across to the bakery. Not that she would have seen anyone; Kist was mostly concealed by the tree. There was no danger of losing sight of her. It was obvious from the bag that Angela was going to the shops. That would be a waste of Kist's time; onions and talk would be her focus. Kist had another plan, a subtle trick to work on their paranoia. He was going to enter the Richter apartment.

He watched as Angela disappeared around the corner. Kist paused another minute to eat the cream and chocolate treat. It was okay, not as good as the bakery near Stasi headquarters. He had to wait for a Trabbi to putter past before crossing the road.

Kist approached Number 10 with a purpose. He had a set of keys in his pocket; they could open almost every apartment door in Erfurt. Luck was on his side at the entrance; it was wedged partially open. No residents loitered in the hall or stairway. He found the Richter's name on the first door to the right. That was surprising; he knew they were on the ground floor, but Matthias gave him the impression their apartment faced the street. Perhaps he had watched the schoolgirls from the driveway.

Voices emerged from the upper floor: female. It could take a minute to find the right key; would the women hear the jingling and scraping? He considered walking back to the street to let the women depart. Would they double his workload by locking the entrance door? He had a few seconds to decide. The voices came no closer. It was probably top-floor neighbours gossiping in the hall. Time to act.

The third key worked. He faced a corridor with three doorways on either side. The first on the right was a bedroom: neat, compact, double bed and wardrobe. Kist started with the bettdecke; he ruffled it at a corner. Enough to make it obvious to Angela, not sufficient to indicate it was anybody other than her husband or daughter.

There was not much he could do with the bathroom: there was the boiler, bath, towels. Most likely tomorrow would be the family bath. The lower towel was dumped on the floor. Had it slipped?

The kitchen was as tidy as the rest of the house. No food was left on the benches, the table was clear of the breakfast dishes. Kist opened the refrigerator; there was sausage, milk, cheese, gherkins. He left the door ajar, just enough to make Angela wonder if she had been careless.

The lounge was next. It was typical of most in East Germany: a sofa, armchairs, television, sideboard, family photos on the wall. The cushions provided the best opportunity to mess with Angela's mind; they were laid out in an obvious pattern. He switched the end two on the sofa.

Collectively, the apartment interference should jolt Angela and Dieter Richter. It was better this way. Trashing their home would have been easy and fun, but it would have been treated as a burglary or vandalism; the intimidation factor would have been wasted. It was preferable they understood the Stasi had penetrated their inner sanctum and could do it again at any time. They could not call the VoPos; a few household displacements were not evidence of any crime.

Kist did not bother locking the door as he left. He was beginning to appreciate the psychological terror these tactics created. For a dozen years the Stasi had relied upon brute force with wayward citizens. Several colleagues had been testing this subtler approach. Kist could see the merits in both – they reinforced the Stasi's control of the citizens.

Tomas Schumann

Class 7A sat silently as Tomas Schumann strode to his desk. It was their first class of the day together; an update on Cuba and the state of the world was required. Schumann had struggled with what to share. There was no thought of reneging on his promise to keep them abreast of the Khrushchev-Kennedy standoff. He would honour that pledge until the bombs fell or the Stasi dragged him away. It was more a case of analysis, how to interpret the latest diplomatic moves. Did they offer hope of a resolution, or would the Soviet and American leaders' best efforts be thwarted by trigger-happy generals?

'Hello, class.'

The reply was uniform and respectful. They were attentive, hungry for information about a far-away conflict that threatened their lives. Schumann guessed that for many students he might be their only source for information on the threatened nuclear holocaust. On the streets, East Germans would only whisper about the danger. If adults were so reluctant to talk frankly, what would they share with their worried kinder?

'We shall start again with Cuba.'

Heads nodded from front to back row. Sylvie and Ingrid appeared the most enthusiastic.

'Overall, the American blockade around Cuba remains in place. The first potential flashpoint was averted when the most contentious Soviet vessels were held back. The Americans investigated an oil tanker – the *Bucharest* – but allowed it to continue to Havana without boarding. That avoided any need for military retaliation.'

Schumann could see a dozen students for whom this was fresh information: they smiled.

'Another ship is expected to reach the naval line today. We can only hope that common sense prevails again.'

Most heads nodded in support. Only the Pioneer leader, Hans Rathmann, seemed disappointed. Some people were born for confrontation.

'There is some encouraging news to share. The United Nations is taking a lead role in the negotiations between the Soviet Union and the United States. Acting Secretary General U Thant will talk separately with representatives of Khrushchev, Kennedy and Castro in the next few hours.'

That announcement was greeted with murmurs of approval; surprisingly Ingrid Richter was shaking her head.

'Talking is always a good sign, although I should point out the Americans are remaining belligerent,' Schumann said. 'They won't lift the blockade until the United Nations can independently verify the missiles have been removed.'

Rathmann raised his arm. Schumann nodded.

'Sir. We only have the Americans' word that the Russians are sneaking nuclear missiles into Cuba. It could all be a ruse by the United States to justify an attack on communist nations.'

Schumann rocked on the balls of his feet for a moment.

'Actually, the Americans have produced evidence. Last night their ambassador to the United Nations displayed spy plane photos of the bases under construction.'

Rathmann's jaw dropped. Obviously, his parents never deviated from East German news reports.

'Can we be sure they aren't fake, Sir?'

'I'm not an expert on nuclear missiles or launch sites.' Schumann smiled at a few titters. 'The pictures I saw looked authentic.'

That probably confirmed for most of the class that their teacher was getting his most important news via Western services. Schumann was not concerned; the Stasi could charge him with subversion whenever they liked. Unless they caught him listening or watching West German broadcasts, how could they prove it? Even if they fabricated a case, it might never get to court. It was the Stasi's obsession with trivialities that was one of Schumann's greatest disappointments.

'The diplomats have a lot of work to find common ground between Khrushchev and Kennedy. We can only wish them well. Now ...'

Schumann turned to pick up a mathematics textbook. When he faced the class again, Ingrid's arm indicated a question.

'Yes, Ingrid.'

'Sir, I think it is commendable the Russians and Americans are willing to talk.'

Schumann nodded, waited. He suspected Ingrid was about to outline the wrinkle in the negotiations.

'What I don't understand is why the two leaders don't sit down and talk through the issue. Sending messages back and forth takes time and often the original meaning gets garbled.'

Ingrid turned to her friends Sylvie and Gerard. 'Recently we played a game called Whispers at Gerard's birthday party. There were 10 of us in line. Sylvie whispered a message in my ear, I passed it along to Kurt and so on. Finally, Gerard had to announce what was said.'

Ingrid shrugged.

'It didn't make sense, Sir. The message became confused in the space of a minute. What hope do we have if Khrushchev and Kennedy play whispers across the ocean, through countless diplomats? There are already language differences from Russian to English and back again. Wouldn't it be simpler to put them and their interpreters in a room – maybe even in a neutral country – and make them stay there until they work out a deal to protect the world?

'If the matter is urgent – like Cuba – why not create a dedicated phone line between Moscow and Washington? That would save many hours or days of worry for us.'

It was childish innocence that attracted nods from most of the class. Schumann understood that it could never work in an adult world dominated by men, egos and expansionist ideology.

'That is a logical and sensible way to handle this crisis. Unfortunately, diplomatic solutions can be like chasing a runaway school bus downhill. They develop their own momentum. Everyone wants to stop it but coordinating the people who can is a difficult task. At this stage, getting talks started through the United Nations is like a driver catching up with the bus. Will there be enough time to apply the brakes before crashing?' He shrugged. 'Cuba is still an evolving situation. We can only hope that goodwill and clear thinking can stop the missiles.'

He held the maths book aloft.

'For now, we have to plan our own future – the next exams.'

Schumann smirked at the groans from front row to the back.

Ingrid Richter

The wurstgulasch was delicious; Ingrid soaked up the last of the spicy broth with her bread. Vati ate all his meal but not with the same relish. Mutti pushed most of her mushroom sauce around the plate. It would go into a container to be reheated later.

Ingrid was not sure about their glum mood. She had arrived home as the steaming plate was being laid on the table. Her tardiness had been caused by a late exit from school due to the pesky Matthias Kist. Sylvie spotted him lurking by the retaining wall containing the peace stick as classes ended. They wanted to make another check it was safely beyond the reach of prying fingers.

They waited in the inner courtyard, taking it in turns to sneak to the edge of the building to spy on their spyer. Finally, he left after 15 minutes. They checked the wall – the stick was secure. Another 24 hours for Khrushchev and Kennedy to make their own peace. They hustled home, using an alternative road to Tchaikowskistrasse.

Ingrid looked at the pile of dishes waiting to be washed, rinsed and dried. She wanted to delay that task a few more minutes.

'Is everything okay, Mutti? You've hardly touched your lunch.'

'Oh, yes. I'm alright. I was just thinking about the break-in. Frau Richter was very upset. Nothing was taken – it was the invasion of their privacy that is upsetting her so much.'

They were not the only Richter family at Friedrich-List Strasse 10. The other Richters were almost a mirror image: name, three family members, a ground-floor apartment. They were not related; their daughter was four years older, almost ready for university; their apartment faced the driveway.

The gist of the story had been shared at the start of the meal. The rest had to wait until the plates and dishes were stacked and the water was boiled. Mutti had met Brigitte Richter as they returned from shopping.

'She was sure she had locked her apartment. I've seen her do it myself often enough. We know the children upstairs often wedge the entrance door open. Brigitte's would be the first target for any burglars.'

Ingrid listened as she filled the washing and rinsing bowls.

'I stayed with her, just in case there was someone inside. There wasn't, but Brigitte knew instantly that someone had been messing around in the apartment.'

'What had they done?' Ingrid asked.

'The bed cover was disturbed, a towel was on the floor, the refrigerator door was open.'

'Is Brigitte forgetful?'

'No. She is house-proud like all of us in the block. The real giveaway was the cushions.'

'What happened to them?'

'Brigitte loved my rainbow design in the lounge. It wouldn't be polite to copy me, but she made her own pretty colour pattern. They are never out of place – until she came back from shopping.'

'Stasi.' Her father's voice was firm but flat. The only sign he ever displayed of being annoyed.

'Why do you say that Vati?'

Her parents looked at each other. There was a subtle nod from her mother.

'There have been rumours about the Stasi using a new intimidation tactic.' Her father stood, put his hands in his pockets and paced the small kitchen. 'If they don't have evidence to interrogate suspects, they break into their homes and move things around. Nothing is taken – it's a warning to keep people in line.'

'Why would they pick on the Richters?' Ingrid knew them to be a quiet family.

Her father stopped pacing. 'We think the agent might have gone to the wrong apartment.'

'Oh!' Ingrid should have made the connection herself. Both Vati and Mutti had been followed. She had also been targeted by the son of a Stasi agent, most likely the same one who had been investigating her parents. Ingrid had to think quickly – she had vital information but could not openly declare it. She had to subtly reveal the connection to Matthias Kist.

'That means the Stasi are interested in us?'

Vati nodded. 'Your mother believes she was followed while shopping on Wednesday. There was definitely an agent following me home from work last night.'

'Why?'

Her father returned to his pacing. 'You know your mother likes to trade with neighbours – coffee, chocolates, material. The Party normally doesn't worry about deals from westpakete.' Vati stopped, shrugged. 'This time we think the Stasi might be concerned about illegal items. Not that your mother would ever trade anything like that. Perhaps someone sent a secret report – the Stasi always investigates.'

Ingrid added a splash of cold water and swished detergent with a fork. The plates were slid in by fingertips. It would take a minute to cool enough for her hands to clean the crockery.

'Was it the same agent who followed you both?'

'We think so.' Her mother searched a cabinet for a container to store her leftover meal. 'I think the same man followed me shopping yesterday morning. He was clever, using a beard one day to make me think he was someone different. Your father and I compared what we saw – we're sure it was the same agent.' The final gulasch-coated plate beneath the suds. 'If we could identify him, we might be able to find out why he's so curious about us.'

There was Ingrid's opportunity. She gingerly tested the water. Still too hot.

'I might be able to help.'

'You?' Her father stopped pacing. 'How?'

'There's been a boy at school who has been following Sylvie and me this week.'

Her parents grinned. Did they think it was a teenage crush?

'At first, we thought he might be interested in one of us but was too scared to say anything.'

Her father chuckled. 'I can remember being nervous around girls at that age. Is he a nice boy?'

'No. Definitely not. He's been following us to and from school, popping up in different locations, and trying to listen to our conversations during the long break.'

'Some boys lack the right social skills.' Her mother sealed the leftovers container and put it in the refrigerator. 'How old is the boy? Is he in the same class? Year?'

'He's an eighth grader. Nobody likes him.'

'Maybe he needs some friends.'

'He's creepy, and his father is in the Stasi. He's told classmates he's being groomed to join the Ministry for State Security.' Ingrid tested the water; she could wash the dishes without scalding fingers. 'The way he followed us was like an agent, not a love-sick puppy.'

Ingrid saw her parents exchange an incredulous look. She put in the final nail.

'Do you think it's likely that his father has been following you? That he did the break-in at the Richters' apartment?'

Vati nodded. 'Highly probable. What's the name of the boy?'

'Matthias Kist.'

Do you know his father's name?'

'Gunther.'

'Okay. You need to finish the dishes before the water gets cold. I have to get back to work.'

Her father kissed her blonde bob and went to collect his coat. Mutti followed. Ingrid could not hear their hallway conversation over the rattling of the plates. A minute later the front door closed.

What would her parents do? What *could* they do? The Stasi were all powerful; no citizen could accuse them of bullying or intimidation. Everyone knew the Stasi made the rules and interpreted them any way they liked. If Vati confronted Gunther Kist, it could lead to his arrest. Her family had done nothing wrong, merely innocent trading of luxuries that were not available in East Germany. Even the Stasi bosses took advantage of westpaket deals. Colonel Brecht and his wife, Helga, had been a valuable connection for her mother. Could that business relationship be their salvation from an inquisitive underling?

Her mother returned to the kitchen with her coat and gloves.

'I have to go out for a while. Do you have homework to finish?'

'A bit of Russian, but we don't have another class until Monday. Sylvie was going to come over for the 2.30 movie. Is that okay?'

'Yes.' Her mother turned for the door and stopped. 'Don't tell Sylvie about the Stasi following your father and me. I'm sure it will turn out to be a misunderstanding.'

'Okay, Mutti.'

Ingrid finished rinsing the last of the dishes as the front door closed. There would be no concerns about lying to her mother. Sylvie already knew everything about the Stasi interest in the Richter family.

Gunther Kist

THE STASI AGENT WAS PROUD OF HIS MORNING'S WORK. HE HAD SQUEEZED the Richter apartment realignment into the surveillance schedule assigned by Carsten Hartwig. Subtle intimidation was an unexpected thrill. Kist was more used to physically menacing the disloyal; messing with their heads was a new weapon to be savoured and refined.

Ironically, he could not share the experience or feelings with his colleagues at Andreasstrasse. Not even Hartwig. He had been warned to stay away from Colonel Brecht's connection. Or was Angela Richter more likely to be an informant? Regardless, Kist was using his experience and initiative to rattle a suspicious family.

Dieter, to be fair, had not displayed any treasonous behaviour towards the Party. He was a well-respected tailor with no secret reports of anti-social comments or criticisms of the Party. His file at headquarters was slim. His wife's file was no thicker. However, Angela warranted further investigation, from Kist's perspective, after the exchange with the departing Cubans at the Hauptbahnhof.

The daughter, Ingrid, was no innocent. There was no law stopping a 13-year-old girl being in the Altstadt unsupervised. She had the first contact with the Cubans, meeting them in the Domplatz just before Pedro disappeared near the Augustinerkloster. That was enough to put her on Kist's list of suspects. His son's own observations during the school day indicated unacceptable behaviour ran through the female line in that family.

Kist glanced up from the reports of his other duties. They were mundane: two smart-mouthed shopkeepers had been reminded the Party set policy on international matters like Cuba. Their files were fatter than the Richter family combined. No doubt Kist or other agents would need to remind the men again about being too liberal with their chat. Would that involve a visit to the cells, or should Kist employ his new tactic of tweaking their biggest fear: who has been poking around in their drawers at home?

The shopkeeper report was ready for Hartwig's inspection and comments before filing. Kist remained in his seat; the supervisor's desk was surrounded by four agents. There was nothing to fear; he had participated in many field operations with all of them. Their reports were on Hartwig's desk; they should be preparing to leave the office for afternoon duties. Kist could hear the conversation; the subject made him reluctant to join them.

The topic was the Cuban Missile Crisis. Everyone was fixated on the next moves by the Soviets or Americans. The consensus was that the world might be safe if they could keep the rabid American generals away from the nuclear missiles.

Kist wanted to shout at his colleagues that it was never going to happen. Sure, the Americans were greedy, arrogant and stupid. Their generals were dangerous warmongers. They loved blowing up cities and nations. But they were not going to destroy a world full of capitalist luxuries because of a peasant country like Cuba.

Their president would huff and puff, but he was not going to risk everything to blow the Russians off Cuba. They would learn to live with a metaphorical knife at their throat, just like the Soviets had since the Americans sent Jupiter rockets to Turkey and Italy. Mutually assured destruction was the best defence for any nuclear nation. It had kept the status quo since the Russians' first test in 1949. The Stasi agent seriously doubted either combatant wanted to risk everything now.

Kist doodled on a pad as he waited for the gathering around the supervisor to break up. Hartwig liked to bond with his field operatives, since field work was beyond his skills because of his unforgettable size and features. The four agents would eventually be ushered back to work; there were always dissidents trying to subvert the Party. Until then, Kist pondered new ways to crank up the pressure on the Richters.

Ingrid Richter

The fairy tale movie on East German television lasted barely five minutes. Ingrid and Sylvie had seen it at least three times in the past two years. They used to love the escapist plots: they were wildly fanciful, exciting, often bleak, but usually offered a happy ending. Maybe the schoolgirls were growing too old for them, or the state of the world was too distracting. They had opened several Richter family photo albums for better entertainment.

'Your parents are such prolific photographers. Who is better with the camera?'

'Mutti.'

'There are so many of you as a baby. You were so cute.'

'I still am.'

They rolled on the sofa in fits of laughter before settling back with the album.

'Dieter and Angela always look so elegant together. When was that photo taken? You could cut cheese with the creases in your father's trousers.'

Ingrid liked the photo: it was before she was born. Mutti in a tan overcoat and small bonnet, Vati with a stylish jacket and buttoned shirt. They were all black and white prints; colour film was too expensive.

The next pages held at least four photos, charting Ingrid's progress from a babe in arms.

'I love that white kinderwagen. It's so beautiful; look at the curves and swirls. Does your mother still have it?'

'No. I don't remember it – only these pictures. Mutti probably traded it for something else once I could walk.'

That prompted more laughter.

'Look, there you are, holding onto an iron fence. They might have been your first steps. Is that out the front of the apartment?'

'Yes. But look at how rickety the bars are. I remember workers replacing it a few years later.'

'You were always up to mischief. Look at you, twiddling the dials on the radio.'

'It's funny how we don't remember everything from those early years. Vati told me I used to annoy him by changing the channels during the news bulletins or concerts. He had to get out of his chair to retune the programs. Vati says he's going to invent a device one day that will change the channels for him.'

Sylvie turned another page. It was a collection of six photos of Dieter holding Ingrid's hand as they herded geese on a farm.

'I know that village. It's Grossvagula. We visit a couple of times a year. They give us lots of pork sausage and farm produce to bring home. I love playing with the animals.'

Another page was turned, the protective paper pushed aside.

'Oh! I remember that Christmas. It was my first doll – Heidi. Her kinderwagen was almost as good as mine. Maybe Mutti traded my original for that?'

'The Christmas tree looks magical.'

'It was the first time I remember having to wait outside the lounge with Oma and Opa while Mutti and Vati decorated it. It was as bright as the sun when they opened the door.'

There were many Christmas photos from that season, most with Ingrid and her new doll. Several with her mother reading a new bedtime story.

'Oh, there's you and a friend pushing your kinderwagens on the street, just like little mothers with your scarves, jackets and babies. Who was she?'

'That was Kersten.'

'What happened to her? She doesn't go to our school.'

Ingrid recalled the pang of first loss.

'She disappeared. They lived a few doors along from us. I asked to go visit one day, but Mutti said they had gone. The whole family left in the night.'

'Oh.' There was no adult to hear, but Sylvie still whispered. 'They escaped to the West?'

'Yes. Not that I understood that at the time. I was upset she didn't like me anymore because she never said goodbye.'

Sylvie nodded. It was accepted that families who managed to flee

East Germany could never communicate with those who remained. Mail would draw attention and suspicion from the Stasi.

'Mutti told me a few years ago that the Stasi had emptied the family apartment within a day but never told the neighbours what happened to Kersten or her family. We hope they made it to the West without getting shot or blown up in a minefield.'

They turned the page to happier memories: the family and friends dressed to perfection in Steigerwald, Vati and Ingrid eating blueberries. Another page, another year: Ingrid eating zuckerwatte and riding a miniature horse at a circus.

'I remember my hands being sticky from the candy floss when I held the reins.'

'You were fortunate as an only child.' Sylvie pointed at the pages filled with Ingrid roller skating, ice skating and twisting with a hula hoop. 'I had to share all those toys with my family– we were always fighting to get our turn.'

They laughed.

'I always wanted a sister or brother. Maybe it wasn't so bad getting special treatment from my parents and grandparents.'

The albums continued to chart the growth and progress through school: first day, Young Pioneers, sports adventures. There were lovely photos of her first teacher, Herr Leuschner, entertaining the class with games on a school outing to the forest in summer. They were happy, carefree days. Memories that made Ingrid sigh when they found a class photo in front of a monument.

'Look at us – so young.'

Sylvie misinterpreted the sigh. 'Short hair for everyone – even me in those days. Shorts for the boys. It can't have been too warm – most of us are wearing cardigans.'

'Hmm.'

Ingrid's change in tone made Sylvie lift her eyes from the album.

'You don't want to look at any more photos?'

'Yes, yes. Sorry. I do.' Ingrid hugged the indigo cushion. 'Looking at these pictures makes me wish we weren't under threat from the Americans.' She pointed at a photo of herself doing gymnastics with cousins in their lush garden and playing with a watering can and hose. 'That's what our lives should be about. Being children, having fun. Not worrying about whether some stupid men on the other side of the world will decide if we get to wake up in the morning.'

That sat in silence, slowly turning pages, enjoying the precious memories that could be snuffed out at any moment.

'Do you think other children are doing the same as us? Are they terrified in Russia, America, Cuba? Even further away – in Fiji. None of us should be involved, yet our fates are linked by two angry men.'

Ingrid had no answer; her eyes stayed on the pages until they reached the most recent additions: the trip to the Baltic Sea a few months ago.

'I wish I had been able to join you at Glowe. It would have been so much fun, and I would have met Pedro. I'm sure he would have said he loved me best.'

They squealed as they fought over the album to find photos of the Cubans. Ingrid knew there weren't any, but it eased the tension created by thoughts of the world crisis beyond their doors.

'Look at all that sand. I've never been to the sea or played in waves. Was the water cold?'

'Some days, especially if the wind was blowing. It got warmer with every week we spent up there.'

The page turned to a photo of Ingrid, Renate and Katja posing on a cliff in front of a misty sea. They looked like triplets with their short blonde hair. They were dressed for a hike rather than frolicking on the beach.

'I remember that day. Vati took the camera on our three-hour walk to Kap Arkona. Vati loves walking, but he's not a great organiser. We didn't have any food or drinks. We felt like collapsing, but Vati would jolly us along, saying we would be able to see the West from the cliffs.'

'Did you make it?'

'Yes. The mist had lifted. We could see the Danish island of Møn. Vati said it had chalky white cliffs, not that we could tell. All we could see was the low outline of the coast. But—oh, Sylvie. It was such an amazing feeling. I remember looking across the water and thinking, there is freedom. If only we could be there.'

'Really?'

'Yes. It was so strange. We all know about the Berlin Wall, the border minefields, that travel outside of East Germany is almost impossible. But I never felt that restriction until I saw the island.'

Sylvie laughed. 'Maybe you were hallucinating because of the lack of water?'

Ingrid shrugged, then flicked through the remaining photos from the Baltic. It was her first family holiday and it had generated feelings and memories that she wanted to keep for a long life.

'How did your father know about the white cliffs at Møn?'

'I think he must have sailed there during the war.'

They had reached the end of the Ingrid album. 'Do you know anything about his war years?'

'Not much. He never talks about that time. I think there are some photos here.'

Ingrid went to the shelf where the family albums were stored. The thinnest had her father's name and the dates: 1935-1945. She opened it. The first photo was her father as a young man, most likely in his 20s. He was bean-pole thin, wearing a dark uniform with double-breasted buttons. The trousers were flared. Vati was beaming, jauntily leaning against a wire and timber-framed fence. He wore a cap with his ship's name on the banding: *Linienschiff Schlesien*.

'He looks so handsome.' Sylvie turned the page. 'I wonder if the first photo was before the war.'

The next image was of a teenage Vati with his familiar thick, wavy brown hair. It looked like it was taken soon after his recruitment as there were no indications of ranks on the uniform. There was only one insignia, which chilled Ingrid. She quickly turned the page before Sylvie noticed it. The next photos appeared to advance Vati through his early career and ranks. He never gained a kilo or lost the smile. The hateful insignia remained in place on his right breast: an eagle above the hakenkreuz.

The swastika was missing in a group of photos where the crew were dressed in white uniforms. They did not appear to have been taken in the old Germany. The locations looked more tropical. The crew stood beside the ruins of a damaged building in one, among twisted rusting cylinders in the next, on the deck of their ship smoking pipes in the third. The sailors were young, happy, goofing around.

'I guess these were taken before the war.' Sylvie turned to a page with a group at a table in a garden. They all had beer bottles; the man sitting opposite her father had a swastika band on his left bicep. Sylvie did not comment.

The *Schlesien* and its crew featured in the next photos: sailors rowing a skiff, two massive guns pointing over the warship's bow. That was another surprise for Ingrid. A Christmas postcard of the whole vessel confirmed the *Schlesien* was a battleship. She thought Vati had served on a minesweeper. Or had she misinterpreted a conversation Vati had with her uncle? It was something to do with minesweeping duties. Perhaps the big ship was the protector.

Sylvie turned another page. It revealed officers holding wreaths in front of a military honour guard; it was obvious from the crosses in the cemetery. The *Schlesien* had suffered casualties.

'I wonder how they died. I guess your father never talked about the battles they fought at sea.'

'No.' Ingrid closed the album and returned it to the cabinet. That was enough family history for her emotions to deal with. A week filled with shocks had delivered another twist. It started with the horrors of the concentration camp. That escalated to the threat of nuclear Armageddon. Fear had been swamped by a new wave of guilt: Vati had been part of Hitler's war machine for a decade.

Angela Richter

THE TRAM TRUNDLED PAST THE GILDEHAUS, THEN THE RATHAUS IN Fischmarkt. Erfurt citizens went about their business; occasionally a man or woman would glance at the sky, either searching for rain or bombers. Angela Richter saw the people and ancient landmarks but paid them no heed. She was lost in thought: had they done the right thing?

The post-lunch conversation in the hall had been brief, the decision rapid. It had been Dieter's idea: they had to discourage Gunther Kist. The only way to do that was to use her connection to the Colonel. They agreed Helga should be approached first.

The trouble stemmed from Angela's trade for the Stasi boss. Collecting stamps was not illegal; paying for a stamp that portrayed a hero of the Soviet Union as a Nazi sympathiser could land Angela and the Colonel in prison. This was a matter best dealt with – from Angela's perspective – away from Stasi headquarters.

Normally Angela's visit to the Brecht home near the Augustinerkloster were by appointment. Helga was surprised to find her dressmaker at the door.

'Hello, Angela. I didn't think we had a booking for today. Please, come inside; it's cold out there.'

The Brechts lived in a three-storey townhouse, as befitted a senior official in the Stasi. It had been built a century or two after Martin Luther lived in the nearby monastery; modern Western features had been discreetly added since the war. Angela had never seen beyond the downstairs room that had been converted for dressmaking and fittings. It was warm and comfortable; Angela followed her host.

'I see you don't have your kit. Is there something else I can help you with?'

Helga waved her to one of the two dining chairs in the room. They were probably discards after a new setting had been installed upstairs.

'We have a problem with that stamp from the Cubans.'

'Oh? Helmut seemed happy it was authentic. It's certainly

controversial, but nobody else is likely to see it, apart from Helmut's trusted friends. Your name won't ever be discussed, although the Colonel was very impressed with your negotiating skills.'

Angela shook her head. 'No, it's nothing to do with the stamp itself.' She had to be careful here; in theory, Angela had seen it only briefly while she haggled with Pedro on Wednesday. The Colonel and his wife would not be happy to learn there was another *unique* Yuri Gagarin stamp in Erfurt.

'I'm sure it's genuine. The problem seems to be that we have popped up on a Stasi agent's watch list.'

Helga reared back. 'You say *we*, as in *us*?' She gestured back and forth between the seats. 'Or your family?'

'At the moment I think it only involves my family.'

Helga looked relieved.

'I had a feeling that I was a followed from the Hauptbahnhof to Andreasstrasse.' Angela shrugged. 'I can't say I identified anyone, but I had a strange feeling. You must have heard of that sixth sense?'

The Colonel's wife nodded. 'It kept many of us alive during and after the war.'

'I felt it again yesterday while shopping. There was nobody obvious or out of place. There were a few different faces in the shops, but that has been the same everywhere this week. A few people seem to be stockpiling tins. You know, given the crisis in Cuba,'

'I understand. Old habits die hard – survival is about food.'

'The only slightly familiar character was a bearded worker. I'm sure I never saw anyone with facial hair at the train station.'

Helga sighed. 'You never would, if they were doing their job properly. They are trained to vary their disguises; they have a room full of clothes, hats and fake beards and moustaches.'

'I didn't say anything to Dieter. Then he came home last night and said he had been followed – the agent made it obvious – from his tailor shop to our front door.'

'Was it the same agent who followed you?'

'It sounded like it – the clothes were different; the beard was gone.' Angela waved an arm. 'But it sounds like it's easy for an agent to wear two or three faces in a day.'

Helga lowered her head to think.

'You've done nothing else to arouse suspicion?'

The question rankled, but Angela could not afford to lose this ally.

'No. We are law-abiding citizens. We've never experienced anything like this before.'

A comforting hand was offered and accepted.

'I'm sorry, Angela. You were helping us; it seems bad luck or timing has put you under the spotlight of one of Helmut's agents. We should have known that somebody would be following the Cuban trainees all the way to the train.'

Helga suddenly stood. 'Do you think you were followed here?'

'I checked – there was nobody obvious. Certainly no sign of the man I saw yesterday.'

'Come with me, Angela.'

They walked up a narrow staircase to a timber-panelled landing. They entered a bedroom with chintz curtains and matching bettdecke on a double bed. A dark schrankwand filled one wall. A window overlooked the street.

Helga guided her to the frame. 'Be as careful as you can. See if there is anyone down there you might have seen since leaving home.'

It was easy to eliminate suspicious agents; the Brechts lived in a residential part of the Altstadt and there were few people passing by. There was no sign of a Stasi man watching his superior's home.

'No. There's nobody I've seen before.'

Helga slumped onto the bed. 'That's going to make identifying the agent awkward. Helmut can't go into headquarters and ask who is following our dressmaker.'

'We know who it is.'

'You do?' Ingrid stood. 'How?'

'Because we believe the agent's son has been following our daughter at school. He's been very clumsy about it.'

Helga clapped, then rubbed her hands. 'That is very improper, and perfect for us. No agent should ever involve their family or share details of any cases. Helmut can nip this in the bud very discreetly. What is the agent's name?'

'Gunther Kist. His son is called Matthias.'

The names were committed to memory. No written record would exist inside the home of the Stasi boss.

'There is something else you should share with your husband,' Angela said.

'Involving this agent?'

'Yes. We think he was responsible for a break-in at a neighbour's apartment this morning.'

'Was it a burglary? I'm sure Stasi agents know there are laws they should never break. Theft is one of them. We are proud of our low crime rate in East Germany.'

'Nothing was taken. Things were moved or left out of place. My neighbour is one of the most fastidious housekeepers I know. It was obvious someone had deliberately disturbed the furnishings to mess with her mind.'

'Why do you think it was this Gunther Kist and not a random troublemaker?'

'Because their name is Richter, and they also live on the ground floor. We think Kist broke into the wrong apartment.'

Gunther Kist

The last paperwork of the day was almost complete. Kist was grateful for the empty office. He could finish in peace; his colleagues had adjourned to a nearby inn. The temptation had been strong to join them for a couple of beers. It had been a successful week from his point of view. Several dissidents had been convinced to pay more respect to the Party, the troublesome Cubans were out of the country, and he was methodically working on an important case – a corrupt colonel.

It was that potential coup that kept Kist from the warmth of the pub. Too much beer might be consumed. Kist was not normally garrulous, but his comrades were trained to listen for slips of the tongue. He could not afford the risk of tipping his hand before the evidence against Colonel Brecht had been gathered. That was a work in progress; the weekend would be devoted to planning.

Kist stood and stretched his arms and back; they seemed to cramp quicker in the office than on the street. His legs were strong; he could walk many kilometres in a day to keep track of subversives. He collected the documents to place in Carsten Hartwig's tray. The reports would be checked on Monday, as his supervisor rarely worked weekends.

He was surprised to find Hartwig's diary on the desk. Normally his supervisor locked it in a drawer, or took it home at night. It indicated that Hartwig was likely to return to the office before going home. Kist calculated quickly: they would be on to their second beers; there was time to read it.

There was no hesitation about reading a superior's notes. Nothing was private to the Stasi. Look at the case of Colonel Brecht – he was a black marketeer. How could you weed out that corruption if agents did not push boundaries? However, Kist did not pick up the black book immediately. It could be a trap.

He carefully looked around the edges of the diary. Kist was looking for a hair, a small piece of paper, some dust or powder: anything that would show the owner that the diary had been moved. An expert eye detected nothing out of the ordinary. Still, he would not lift or physically touch it. Kist returned to his desk, opened a drawer and pulled out two stamp tongs. They were perfect for dealing with delicate paper.

One set was used to open and fold back the hard cover. The other tongs slowly lifted the pages to reveal a record of Hartwig's meetings. Most were within the Stasi's Erfurt headquarters. A few were at pubs, perhaps after-hours chats with personal informants. The office appointments had the full names and ranks of agents and officers; the others merely listed a first name. Most likely they were fake, a separate file in Hartwig's locked cabinet holding the secret details.

Many pages had phone numbers. Hartwig spent much of his day lounging heavily in his seat with the handset to his ear. Those conversations were never much louder than a murmur. Any agents who tried to interrupt their supervisor were treated to a fierce glare. The contacts worthy of a public meeting at an inn must have been important, but there were no hints in the diary about their identities.

Kist finally reached the current date: October 26. He turned one more page, curious if Hartwig had arranged any weekend meetings. There was one entry, and it worried him. Hartwig was scheduled to meet Colonel Brecht at 11am. That was extremely unusual.

There were no important Stasi operations that might require weekend consultations. It was rare for a senior officer to be in the office on a Saturday. That was if the meeting was going to be at Andreasstrasse. There was nothing on the diary page to indicate where the Colonel and Hartwig were going to talk or what the topic might be.

An unexpected meeting between the corrupt colonel that Kist was secretly investigating and the ambitious supervisor who knew about it. Should he be worried? Yes, definitely. Kist understood that the Stasi was built on suspicion, power and taking advantage of both. He should have seriously considered the prospect that Hartwig would want to curry favour with a high-ranking officer.

The diary was carefully closed. There was no evidence it had been disturbed. He backed away to his own desk and sat. There was much to think about. Had the diary been planted? Kist was the only agent left in the office; Hartwig knew natural instincts would prompt a sly examination. Was it meant to make the investigator panic, to back off? It would be suicidal to pursue a colonel who had already been warned he was a target. Was Hartwig playing mind games or taking the next step up the Stasi hierarchy?

There was too much to consider. The inn with the other agents and Hartwig would not be the best place to clarify those thoughts. A beer was needed; it would be better enjoyed at Das Paridis on Semmelweisstrasse. The nuts would be free, and nobody would bother him. He could plan his next move. His back needed protecting as much as the Party.

Ingrid Richter

THE AIR ABOVE THE FEATHER BETTDECKE WAS CHILLY; INGRID SNUGGLED deeper into the bed. She was exhausted, a combination of four nights of traumatic dreams and fears about the future. Why should a 13-year-old have to worry if there would be a tomorrow? Ingrid's biggest concern should be whether her homework was correct, not thinking about nuclear annihilation.

It was hard to comprehend how often men resorted to war to settle their differences. Not just in the 20th Century; history classes had revealed men had been fighting for supremacy since they left the caves. They started with rocks and clubs, now they had bombs that could wipe out cities and nations in seconds. Any survivors would be back to Stone Age tools and weapons. Mankind was likely to repeat the same mistakes.

Ingrid's despair had plummeted since viewing her father's photo album. She had known he had been in the navy, but her impressions of Vati as a sailor had never extended to battle. There were no reminders – apart from the seldom seen album – of his war service. Erfurt was in the middle of the old Germany, far from the sea and former comrades. One petty officer had visited two years ago. Ingrid had sat quietly on the sofa as the guest talked about their lucky escape from a British air raid. Their ship had been ordered to change berths; the vessel that replaced theirs was sunk.

Vati was a gentle man, always ready to laugh and give her a cuddle when she skinned a knee while roller skating. He would tell her the names of the trees in the Steigerwald, always giving her the juiciest berries from the trails. She loved pottering around the Schrebergarten in summer as her father tended to the rows of carrots, cabbages and potatoes. Ingrid struggled to see that man as one of the hate-filled sailors and soldiers in the war movies.

There had been no conversation about the Stasi agent or his son during supper. Ingrid was too tired to pursue it after the plates had been washed. She briefly flirted with the idea of watching the West German television news; there might be progress in Moscow and Washington about the crisis in Cuba. The endless pictures of bombers, battleships and missiles might also inflame her vivid imagination; bed might be a better sanctuary.

There was a half day of school to get through in the morning. Mutti would have to get up at the usual time to ensure Ingrid had breakfast and made it out the door. She could go back to bed for more sleep as Vati did not have to work. He was looking forward to one of their final trips to their allotment before the first snow. She was struggling to find the same enthusiasm. Every time she looked at Vati that evening, she kept wondering about the swastika on his naval uniform. Had he chosen or been ordered to wear it?

Ingrid felt they were destined to have that conversation tomorrow. For three days the peace stick had done its job: keeping the world safe. She was certain it would still be in place; they would be guaranteed another 24 hours. Sleep came swiftly.

Tomas Schumann

A tatty towel was laid on the kitchen table for a maintenance procedure that had first been done 44 years previously. A small can of oil with a fine nozzle was retrieved from a cupboard. Next came the only tool required: a screwdriver. Finally, Schumann unlocked the cabinet that held the P08 Luger that had saved his life in World War I. It was placed in front of his chair, ready for cleaning.

The routine had slipped since he carried the Luger back to Germany in 1918. The mud and grit of the trenches had required daily attention to keep the mechanisms clear. A jammed gun would get you killed.

Life in Germany in the following years was turbulent, but weekly cleaning was enough to keep the Luger operational. The well-oiled pistol was close at hand when the Americans and Russians exchanged ownership of Erfurt in 1945. Relative calm and the formation of East Germany saw maintenance drift from fortnightly to monthly during the 1950s. The Luger had been touched once since the start of the new decade.

Schumann stared at the 9mm pistol. It always brought back memories of the first Tommy he killed with it, in Belgium. The Luger had not originally belonged to Schumann. An oberleutnant held it until a British bayonet drove him onto Schumann during a late-night trench raid. The young gefreiter was trapped underneath during the frenzied attack. The officer pin cushion saved the private from more severe injuries to his side. He could not raise his Mauser Gewehr 98 rifle, but the Luger was within reach. The Tommy was shot through the head, throat, chest, stomach. Schumann tried to shoot him in the head again, but the magazine was empty.

A bloodied Grau found him after the raid. They struggled to an aid station where Schumann refused to surrender the Luger. It had been in his possession ever since. The only regret was that he never went back to search the dead oberleutnant for the Luger's maintenance tool.

Schumann picked up the pistol and checked the safety. It looked in good condition despite the recent years of neglect. The magazine was ejected. It was empty; the bullets were kept in the same box in the locked cabinet. Old habits died hard. Not even Grau had known he still possessed it until Tuesday night.

Deftly, Schumann disassembled the Luger. He could have done it with his eyes closed. The only tricky part was removing the firing pin from the breech block. The tension on the spring could send it bouncing around the kitchen floor. Dabs of oil were applied and fingered over the crucial parts. Within a few minutes the Luger was in working order and back in the lined box inside the locked cabinet.

The Luger had always been a weapon for protection. It could not do much to fight off nuclear bombs and missiles, but it would be needed for the anarchy that was bound to follow.

He had seen how wild and crazy Berlin was in the years following the first defeat. The problem was that the anger did not dissipate with the Armistice. It was inflamed by the harsh penalties imposed by the Treaty of Versailles, creating the tinder box that Hitler was able to light. Millions who experienced those days did not survive the Third Reich. How many Germans understood the dangers ahead if the Soviets and Americans could not find a compromise? Despite his optimism earlier in the day with Class 7A, Schumann was not convinced the military commanders could be restrained.

The longer Khrushchev and Kennedy took to make a deal, the greater the risk for the world. The generals loved the power at their fingertips; they all wanted to strike first, foolishly believing they might survive in their bunkers to enjoy their victory.

Schumann carefully cleaned his hands in the basin. Would the pistol maintenance be required next week? Ironically, he hoped so; it meant the world was still turning. He turned on the kettle for herbal tea. That evening ritual had been introduced by his wife during their life in Berlin; it was another way of keeping her memory alive.

It was late. The American novel would keep him awake for another few hours. The satire in *Catch-22* was scathing but also entertaining. Perhaps old soldiers appreciated the ineptness of the military bureaucracy better than civilians.

Saturday, October 27, 1962

Ingrid Richter

It was inevitable that Ingrid's sleep would be filled with more drama. It was the third nightmare that involved her parents. Bizarrely she knew it was a dream from the start, yet her conscious self would not surface; she needed to let it unfold.

It started with Vati and his sailor comrades in the white uniforms she had seen in the album. They were smoking, lounging on a sandy beach under a sunny sky and palm trees. Vati was not much more than a boy. Then an officer ordered the crew to line up. Ingrid found herself floating above the formation as a new insignia was pinned to each chest. She could see the dreaded swastika.

One by one, the uniforms turned black. The carefree mood evaporated as military discipline took over. The officer ordered them to march. They tromped through the sand towards a timber pier; their battleship waited at anchor in a bay. The pace of the sailors intensified as they left the sand. The formation was trotting in unison as they thundered over the planks.

Ingrid could not see any tenders waiting to transport the crew to the mother ship. There was nothing but open water ahead. The officer's marching cadence had turned to a shriek. She looked closer; he was wearing a brown shirt, black tie, dark hair tumbling across his forehead. The clipped moustache mimicked the Führer, yet it wasn't Hitler. The officer urged the crew forward; line by line they plunged into the clear water. None surfaced. Ingrid could see them floundering on the seabed.

Vati was in the last line; he was going to follow his crewmates into the depths. It was time to save her father, the dream had to end. The surviving sailors surged forward; Ingrid struggled to escape the spectacle her mind had created. They were running. Could she wake before Vati jumped? She needed to warn him.

'No, no, no, no—don't jump!'

Vati did, but Ingrid never heard or saw the splash as the middle-room light snatched her back to reality.

'Another nightmare, Ingrid?' Her mother stood shivering in a nightgown.

'Yes, Mutti.' The warm bettdecke had not been lifted from the bed to hasten her school preparations.

'Was it about the missiles? Or the Stasi agent?'

Ingrid did not want to cause her parents any more worry.

'No. It was about a wolf chasing Sylvie and me through the forest.'

Her mother nodded, wrapped arms around herself. 'I left the breakfast table ready. Will you be okay to get yourself off to school?'

'Yes, Mutti. You deserve a sleep-in.'

That was usually part of their Saturday morning ritual. Once Ingrid was awake, Mutti could return to the warmth of her bed.

Ingrid dressed quickly, her breath steaming. At least the school radiators would be toasty by the time she arrived. Surprisingly, she felt reasonably refreshed; had the dream only occupied the last minute of her sleep? She understood the significance of the swastika. It had dominated her thoughts since finding it on Vati's naval uniform in the photo album. It was a topic that needed to be addressed – had he been a conscript or an eager participant in Hitler's war?

That would be best done at the Schrebergarten, just Ingrid and Vati together. Mutti never went in the colder months. Most autumn visitors stayed around their allotments and sheds; there were friendly greetings but none of the socialising enjoyed during spring, summer and early autumn.

Within 15 minutes Ingrid was quietly closing the door on her father's renewed snoring. Sylvie was already jiggling on the driveway. Ingrid handed over her spare gloves; the temperature was dropping each day.

'Oh! Thank you, Ingrid.' Sylvie quickly switched gloves. 'My hand-me-downs are so threadbare; I can barely feel my fingers.'

Ingrid checked the road, then the bakery.

'Have you seen that creepy Matthias?'

There were no smoky cars or bicycles to stop the first crossing.

'No. Perhaps he knows to keep away.'

'Or he might show up at the second bakery again on Tchaikowskistrasse.'

A golden leaf fluttered to the damp pavement; soon the trees would be bare. Ingrid wondered if they would see the first snowfalls. She looked to the grey skies; as usual, heavy clouds obscured any vapour trails for high-level airliners – or bombers. The whiff of brewing beer reminded her not to be so negative: life continued.

'It has been a strange week,' Sylvie said.

Ingrid wondered if her friend could read her mind.

'Yes. I wonder what Herr Schumann has in store for us today. Vati was still sleeping; there was no radio news. Did you hear anything?'

Sylvie snorted. 'Just grumpy siblings trying to eat and get ready for school. No updates about Cuba, Khrushchev or Kennedy. Do you think they might have solved their problems like sensible people?'

Ingrid looked at the few Saturday workers near Wenkell's bakery. The mood was much the same as it had been on Tuesday, the day East Germans learned they were trapped in a conflict between two superpowers.

'There's nobody dancing with joy that there's no planes over Erfurt.'

'Oh. That's something my brother told me last night. He said the Americans have so many nuclear bombers, they can fly around the clock. Whenever one lands to refuel and rest the crew, there is another taking off.' She looked to the clouds. 'They could be up there now and we would never know.'

Ingrid looped their arms.

'No need to worry, Sylvie; the peace stick has been working its magic. We'll know in a few minutes whether we have another day.'

Student numbers grew as they approached the school.

'It's funny how that stick can be reassuring,' Sylvie said. 'There's no reason to explain it, but it gives me hope. Do you think that's why Christians pray?'

Ingrid shrugged, not sure how religions worked.

'I've always wanted to talk to someone who goes to church,' Sylvie said. 'They make me curious. They never see their god; he never talks back to them. Yet they spend hours, against the Party's wishes, praying that he will make their lives better. Do they ever see the benefits of their faith?'

'Maybe it makes them feel better, like the peace stick works for us. That is something positive.'

The debate over the mysteries of religions petered out at the school entrance where there was a new obstruction in front of the peace stick – their Thälmann Pioneer leader, Hans Rathmann.

'Ingrid, Sylvie. Good morning.'

Rathmann was a formal, studious, dedicated young socialist, best avoided outside of school and Pioneer activities. Which they had done most of that week.

'You missed the Wednesday Pioneer meeting and two sports afternoons.'

Rathmann was dressed in the traditional blue shorts, his triangular necktie worn outside the jacket, an indication there was a Pioneer event after school.

'Do you know about our paper recycling drive this afternoon?'

'Yes, Hans.' Ingrid adjusted her ranzen, subtly nudging Sylvie to keep walking while she stopped to talk to him. 'I have another appointment.'

'What can be more important than doing your patriotic duty? We raise a lot of money for the Party – and save the environment.'

Ingrid knew how to trump the earnest Pioneer leader.

'I have a special Russian lesson this afternoon. My father understands the importance of learning the language from Russian speakers. He's arranged a session for me near the Thuringia Halle. You know the lazarett?'

'Of course.'

'The convalescing Russian soldiers generously provide lessons for fruit from our allotment.'

The Pioneer leader accepted the logic; feeding the Russians while learning from them would be a productive Saturday. Ingrid had not lied. There was a Russian hospital across from their Schrebergarten. She occasionally offered fruit to friendly soldiers who graciously thanked her in Russian. Her bluff would survive unless Rathmann asked to join in the Russian tuition. Fortunately, he thought of Sylvie, who had offered no excuse for dodging the drive.

'Where did Sylvie go? Does she know about the drive?'

'Perhaps. Maybe you should remind her before first bell.'

Rathmann jogged through the entrance, which allowed Ingrid to discreetly check the peace stick – it was still there; they had another 24 hours.

Two minutes later they were being led into their classroom by Rathmann, Sylvie grumpily at the end of the line.

'Why didn't you say we were both getting Russian lessons?' she said.

'Hans might have checked with you about the location of the classes. Did he say where the paper drive is happening?'

'No.'

'If you don't know where to go to collect paper, you can't join the group. My advice is to avoid Hans for the rest of the morning. There are only three classes. How hard can that be?'

Second bell sounded. Herr Schumann entered the room. Most of the class noticed their teacher's pace was not as brisk as on the previous two mornings. Raised eyebrows did the communicating between table mates.

Rathmann stood for his most important morning duty.

'Be ready!'

'Always ready!'

Hans turned to Herr Schumann. 'I report that 7A is ready for the class.' He saluted and sat.

Their teacher nodded, stood silently.

Herr Schumann looked troubled, like on Tuesday when he announced the world was on the edge of World War III. Ingrid felt Sylvie clasp her hand. The bad vibe was spreading throughout the class.

'I promised you that I would be honest and share what information I know about the crisis in Cuba.'

Several students murmured assent.

'I'm sorry to say that my optimism from the past couple of days might have been premature.'

Rathmann did not bother raising his hand. 'Is there going to be war?'

Herr Schuman started to shake his head, then stopped.

'A war is not certain, but it appears there is going to be military action in Cuba.'

'Why?'

'When?'

'No!'

It was impossible to separate the voices that had broken classroom etiquette.

Herr Schumann held up two hands, a signal for patience.

'The Americans claim the Soviets are continuing to build the missile sites in Cuba. In fact, they say the work has intensified – the Russians and Cubans are rushing to get the sites finished and ready for use.'

Thorsten raised his hand first.

'That doesn't mean the Russians will use the missiles. Surely, the whole purpose was to prevent the Americans from attacking Cuba. Once the bases are ready, the status quo should resume.'

Herr Schumann nodded approval for the logic.

'You might view it that way in East Germany. In Washington, the Americans see the missiles as a threat, and they won't allow them to stay. The newspapers have been highlighting comments from President Kennedy's television address on Monday. He said further action would be justified if military preparations continued. There is speculation that the next step is likely to be air raids against the Cuban sites. Possibly over the weekend.'

There was a mixture of gasps and howls.

Kurt's hand shot up. 'The Russians will have to retaliate – their honour demands it.'

'Yes. And if they do, what happens next? Will the Americans respond with greater firepower? The Russians will want to match that. Before we know it, an island dispute could escalate into a global conflict that could destroy us all.'

The sword that had been hanging over them since Tuesday was ready to fall. Ingrid was terrified, but not ready to give up hope. She raised her hand.

'Sir. The diplomats are still talking. What is happening at the United Nations?'

'Khrushchev has helped matters. He's told Soviet vessels heading for Cuba to temporarily stay away from the naval blockade zone. The Americans are showing no conciliation. They want work on the sites stopped, any missiles in Cuba removed and guarantees no more will be sent. There has to be give and take in negotiations – President Kennedy wants everything to go his way.'

Herr Schumann picked up a textbook; school life would go on until the missiles were launched.

Petra Stelzer had other ideas. 'Our problems all started in Cuba. They feel threatened by the Americans. Kennedy supported an invasion and has been trying to kill Castro. Khrushchev says Soviet missiles will stop those threats.'

'Yes, that is the issue in a nutshell,' Schumann said.

The book remained in hand; everyone knew Petra had more to say.

'If the Americans gave a guarantee to the United Nations that they would not attack Cuba or try to kill its leader, it would make sense for the Soviets to remove their missiles. No threat – no need for the weapons.'

Herr Schumann produced his first smile for the class.

'That makes perfect sense, Petra. We can only hope U Thant and everyone at the United Nations are trying to convince the Soviets and Americans that is the solution to the crisis.'

Gunther Kist

The meeting between Colonel Brecht and Carsten Hartwig was scheduled for 11. Gunther Kist was at a disadvantage: he did not know the location. Most likely it would be Stasi headquarters on Andreasstrasse. That was why he was sitting inside a café across the road at 10.41. He had been there for almost 20 minutes, in case either superior arrived early. A coffee, two pastries and half a dozen cigarettes had been consumed. Nobody had spoken to him. Kist knew the owner hated when Stasi men lingered in his café out of office hours: they were not good for casual weekend business.

Kist had considered waiting outside the Colonel's home and following him to the rendezvous. Brecht had never been a field man; there was no concern a veteran of the streets would be detected. However, there was a risk of being spotted by Hartwig at the destination. Kist would not be able to get close enough to eavesdrop on the conversation.

His best option was to hope they would meet at the office. The first arrival would initiate Kist's plan. He believed the tête-à-tête would occur in the Colonel's domain, not in the open space Hartwig shared with the agents.

Colonel Brecht was likely to be the only senior officer at headquarters. Many East Germans strived to keep the economy afloat with a six-day working week; those who ran the spies did not face such odious hours. The offices around Colonel Brecht would be empty. Kist knew the acoustics of the old building, especially when empty, would carry their voices. He was not likely to hear all of their conversation, but the gist would tell Kist whether he was in trouble or paranoid.

Kist checked his watch: 10 minutes to the meeting, no sign of either man. He resisted the urge to light another cigarette. Experience told him that always tempted fate; one puff and he would have to grind it into an ashtray or underfoot. His eyes were directed south along Andreasstrasse, the direction from which both men approached work each day. The Stasi entrance was in his peripheral vision; an opening door made him turn.

His fist clenched. Kist wanted to slam it on the table. He suppressed the rage as it would have upended the coffee cup. The smashing crockery would not have been heard across the road, but the tantrum would be reported; the café owner was a spitzel.

Colonel Brecht had exited first, setting off briskly towards the Domplatz. Carsten Hartwig was a few seconds behind. Kist watched him pause a metre from the entrance; a second later he was obscured by a passing tram.

Kist leaned back against the wall, angry and confused. Was the diary entry a bluff, or was there a crisis that had warranted an earlier meeting? Perhaps the events in Cuba had brought new orders from Berlin. Were there American sympathisers in Erfurt that had to be exposed? That would be a good thing; Kist enjoyed tracking traitors and spies. It also meant Hartwig had kept quiet about the corruption investigation.

The door opened. Hartwig offered a thin smile.

'Morning, Gunther.'

'Carsten. I ... I'm surprised to see you here on a Saturday.'

'Same here. I thought you were off duty for the weekend.' The big man gestured to the owner for a coffee and sat.

Both men had their backs against the wall.

'I had some paperwork to tidy up before Monday. I stopped for a pastry first.' Kist waved at the crumbs on his plate, a convenient prop.

'I checked my in-tray. All the required documents seemed to be there. Do you have other active cases that I don't know about?'

That was a loaded question. Kist had been told to forget about Colonel Brecht's private business. They both knew Kist was not going to drop the investigation; admitting that now could be a serious breach.

'No. Nothing that is not sanctioned by the Ministry.'

Kist swallowed. They were weasel words. The Colonel was corrupt. But Kist understood who held the balance of power – the two men who had snookered him with their secret meeting. Hartwig was toying with him; the diary had been left as bait; Kist had swallowed it too easily. Now his Stasi career was at risk. He swallowed his pride and let Hartwig play his hand.

'You are ready for new assignments on Monday?'

'Always ready.'

Both smiled at the Pioneer eagerness.

'Good. It has been brought to my attention that your enthusiasm might be best applied in other areas.'

Kist was worried. He was a field man; he loved the independence and adrenalin of the streets. There were few other palatable options.

'But I'm an expert in the field, Carsten. Why take me away from what I am good at? You know my arrest record — many have spent time inside our cells. I'm a good investigator.'

Hartwig nodded. 'I told the Colonel that. It would be a waste of your talent to search for Western food in East Germany's garbage.'

Kist paled. It was in the open; the Colonel had been told he was a target and acted first. There was a division assigned to find evidence of illegal Western items in piles of stinking rubbish. There was no worse job within the Stasi.

'Surely ...' Kist could only goldfish.

'Keep breathing, Gunther. I saved you from the trash. But you are off the streets — you'll be assigned to monitoring.'

It was a hammer blow; his days and nights would be spent listening to old men and women grumbling about the lack of fresh fruit in the shops. The occasional coup would be outweighed by the sheer drudgery of wasted hours with headphones and opening mail.

Kist was outranked and outplayed. He could not suppress a sudden burst of anger.

'Why did you betray me?'

Hartwig sipped his coffee. 'I didn't — you did it yourself.'

'How? I never went near him. I was gathering information from the Richter woman. She should be rattled, ready to talk about the illegal dealings with the Colonel.'

'That was your mistake.'

Kist wanted to smash the smugness from Hartwig's face and voice.

'Angela Richter was suspicious after meeting the Cubans. She thought she was followed when she went to *report* to the Colonel. Angela saw you again the next day while she was shopping.'

That annoyed Kist almost as much as the canning of his investigation. He prided himself on his field craft.

'But you went a step too far, Gunther. You went to the apartments at Friedrich-List Strasse.'

Kist shrugged. 'That was a new tactic I've heard about. Psychological harassment – let them know their homes aren't safe. Show the Stasi can get to them anywhere.'

'If you get the right apartment.'

'What do you mean?'

'You messed up the wrong home, Gunther.'

'No, I checked. The Richters live on the ground floor at number 10. The name was at the first door.'

Hartwig wiped his lips with a napkin. 'There are two families named Richter – Angela lives at the end of the corridor with her husband and daughter.'

Kist's head, shoulders and spirits sagged. He looked up when Hartwig's chair scraped. His superior was grim.

'You messed up in so many ways, Gunther. I warned you to back off – you didn't. The Colonel always had an ace up his sleeve – he could always claim Angela was his special informant. Think yourself lucky you're not out of a job. Report to your new post at seven o'clock Monday morning.'

Kist watched the chair be realigned with the table. One thing still puzzled him.

'Angela might have seen me, but how would she be able to identify me?'

'It was your son, Gunther. He was seen following Ingrid Richter to and from school. He made himself a pest between classes. Apparently, half the students know he's the son of a Stasi agent. It wasn't hard for the Richters to identify you and pass your name to the Colonel.'

Hartwig shook his head, put on his hat and left the café.

Ingrid Richter

Ingrid stood alone at the retaining wall that held their hopes of a life beyond the weekend. She had hustled Sylvie out of the corridor before Hans Rathmann could find her. The two class transitions were spent hiding in the girls' bathroom. Sylvie had not been told where to report for the Thälmann Pioneers' paper recycling run. The afternoon would be free if she could escape school without being pressganged by Rathmann.

Most of the students had cleared the courtyard and classrooms by the time Ingrid reached the wall. There was no sign of Sylvie; a frustrated Rathmann was probably preparing a written assessment of Sylvie's commitment to the cause for their next Pioneers meeting. After Herr Schumann's latest update, it might be more a question of whether there would be another meeting.

With no loitering sons of Stasi agents, enthusiastic Thälmann Pioneers, dippy boys with comics, or friends dribbling footballs, Ingrid had the peace stick to herself for the first time. That did not stop her glancing over both shoulders to confirm the isolation.

She bent down to check. Ingrid wanted to feel the symbol of hope that had sustained them. Her fingers scrabbled in the opening for a few seconds, then gently eased half of the peace stick clear. The buds she had noticed on Tuesday were still green; there was no evidence that curious fingers had tried to extract it.

It was odd to feel an overwhelming sense of relief each time they checked. Ingrid had declared their hopes for the future rested with a 15-centimetre twig hidden in a wall. It was a crazy idea, yet it was working; the world might still be teetering on the edge of a thermonuclear war, but it had not happened. People made wishes every day. Some were answered. Would Ingrid and Sylvie be among the few to tap into that intangible mystical luck?

Tensions were escalating in Washington. There would be no opportunity to check the peace stick tomorrow. Ingrid needed the glücksbringer to carry them through to first bell on Monday.

'You look like you are praying, Ingrid.'

Herr Schumann's satchel was bulging with essays as he stood in front of the covered walkway.

'I'm not religious, Herr Schumann.' She turned away from the wall, adjusted her ranzen. 'I was just thinking about the past week. I … I've never experienced anything like it.'

The teacher stopped, glanced at the wall, then back to his troubled student.

'I have contributed to much of your anxiety, I'm sure. I apologise if it has been too much to accept.'

Ingrid understood the apology went all the way back to the Buchenwald visit on Monday. 'That is alright, Herr Schumann.' She lifted her eyes. 'I prefer truth, as troubling or inconvenient as that might be. I would rather know the correct history and the dangers we face.'

Herr Schumann swallowed, nodded and walked towards the tram stop.

Ingrid Richter

INGRID LICKED HER LIPS AS THE TRAM RATTLED SOUTH ON *ARNSTÄDTER* Strasse. The taste of eggs in mustard sauce always lingered when served at lunch. Mutti had added extra butter to the boiled potatoes. It was a popular Saturday meal, fuelling Vati and Ingrid for an afternoon at the Schrebergarten.

The tram stopped for a passenger to exit at the Thüringenhalle; that left just five in the two carriages, including Ingrid and her father. Ingrid had the window seat, as usual in journeys with Vati. The massive stadium was empty; the football season had started but the team must have been playing away.

Vati went to some of the home games, but he sat beside her, lost in his own thoughts. Normally their tram rides or walks were chatty, Ingrid updating him on her week at school or Pioneer activities. Those trips seemed so ordinary compared to the week she had experienced.

'Everything okay, Ingrid?'

'Yes, Vati. Just thinking.'

He nodded as they exited and walked to the main road. They were in Löbervorstadt, one of the city's most historic and greenest suburbs; it held most of the Steigerwald. Their allotment was a few minutes walk. They crossed the road in front of the vast façade of the Thüringenhalle. No exhibitions were advertised; it was a quiet weekend for sport and culture in Erfurt. They crossed a lane that ran beside the hall.

On the other side was a tree-shrouded Jewish cemetery. Ingrid rarely paid attention to the large red building with arches and narrow pillars at the end of a long driveway. A sign indicated the cemetery had been operating since the 19th Century. Guilt welled; she realised many who should have been laid to rest in this peaceful woodland had been turned to ashes in ovens built by their fellow citizens. Headstones could be seen through the thinning autumn foliage. They were mostly old, although well-tended.

A tear was wiped without Vati noticing. He was striding half a step ahead, dressed in thick work trousers, jacket and stout boots. They turned right at Tannenstrasse; the cemetery and allotments further down were an oasis between the Thüringenhalle, stark government buildings and the Russian lazarett.

The southern suburbs were dotted with similar gardens. They were havens from brick apartments for up to nine months of the year. It had taken good connections to find one close to home and the tram line. Vati greeted the regulars as he entered; the family's allotment was closer to the lane on the other side. Ingrid smiled and waved at some of the older men. They were retired, spending most of the daylight hours mingling with friends from February until the snow came again. Even then, some enjoyed the solitude of their shed on the allotment over noisy apartments.

Ingrid had not spent much time at the Schrebergarten that summer. She and Mutti were at the camp on the Baltic for eight weeks. There had been a couple of dinners in the communal kitchen during September, and there would be no more family gatherings until the new year. Would there be a 1963? If there was, what new dramas would it hold? Could anything be worse than the Khrushchev-Kennedy conflict?

'You are very quiet today, Ingrid.' Vati unlocked their shed. It was big enough to hold a table, two chairs, a bed for when they stayed on hot summer nights, and gardening tools. Jars of preserves sat on shelves. They would be taken home in the bag Vati carried, along with the last of the cabbages. 'It has been a traumatic week – the missile crisis and interest from the Stasi. Would you like to talk as I weed?'

'Not at the moment, Vati. I might go for a wander.'

'Okay.' He picked up a hoe and attacked the greenery encroaching the soil in his share of the garden.

Ingrid wanted to talk to her father about his military service. Especially about the swastika – the most hated symbol of the Hitler years. She wanted to know if he had been a devoted follower or simply a follower of orders. Yet, she feared the answers. Vati was her hero, like Yuri Gagarin. The Russian's image had been tarnished; she didn't want that to happen again. Not so soon. She could not cope with another emotional upheaval. No wonder her head was spinning.

She picked up a branch from the next allotment. It had been pruned and left to rot. She trailed it through the dirt as she walked between the gardens. It was quieter on this side; most occupants had done their final autumn tidy. She looked towards the lazarett. The cabanas where Russian soldiers recovered from illness or injuries were quiet; it was too cold for the unhealthy to be outside. She had befriended a young soldier before the trip to the sea. Hans Rathmann would be impressed to know that Ingrid had practised her Russian language skills, even if she wasn't doing it today.

Fruit had been passed through the fence when it was in season. It was gratefully received by the soldier. They always looked thin; the aromas from the hospital kitchen never smelled appealing. Ingrid had viewed them as heroes until Herr Schumann's private history lesson at the concentration camp. The Russians were still allies, but something in the relationship had shifted for her. Their military leaders were part of the big lie, that they had been Erfurt and Buchenwald's liberators.

Ingrid drew a circle in the dirt with the stick. Should her attitude to Vati change, or even her adoration of Yuri Gagarin? Her parents had seemed sceptical the cosmonaut was a neo-Nazi. It was possible that Yuri was a victim of a cruel hoax. She did not know her father's affiliations – past or present – to the Führer. She had to be brave enough to confront the issue.

The stick trailed behind as Ingrid walked back to the family plot. Vati had rapidly worked through the weeds; a pile filled a bucket.

'Vati. Can I talk to you about a sensitive topic?'

Her father stopped hoeing. 'Certainly.' He wiped sweat from his brow. 'Is it something that we can discuss out here, or would you prefer to sit in the cabin?'

Ingrid looked at the nearest gardens: heads were down, spades were turning soil. But she suspected ears were always listening for gossip. She saw the communal kitchen was empty.

'Maybe I can make us some tea.'

'Okay. You get the water boiling and I'll haul these weeds to the compost.'

Ingrid gathered the essentials from a shelf. A kettle was on the gas ring by the time Vati arrived. He washed his hands in a basin and sat at a table. In a few minutes the tea was steaming at their fingertips.

'Vati. A lot of questions have been raised this week.'

Her father nodded, then sipped. His patience was admirable.

'I heard things about the Russians and Americans at Buchenwald on Monday. The next day, we learned that they could go to war over Cuba. At any minute. Because of the missiles the Russians were sneaking onto the island.'

'I don't know what you learned at Buchenwald, but certainly the missiles are enough to worry about.' He put the mug on the table. 'What is your main fear?'

Ingrid twirled her hot tea; she didn't have an asbestos tongue like Vati.

'Well, the idea of Americans dropping bombs on Erfurt scares me.' She lifted her eyes. 'But right now, I'm most worried about what you did in the war.'

Vati looked confused.

'I know you were in the navy. You were a sailor from the mid-'30s until the end of the war.'

'That's right. I was on the *Schlesien* most of that time.'

'Did you volunteer?'

'I did.' He picked up the tea. 'Does that concern you?'

Ingrid felt a knot in her stomach. She nodded.

'Why?'

'Did you join to fight for Hitler?'

Her father laughed. 'No, sweetheart. I joined the Reichsmarine to avoid being part of Hitler's war machine.'

'How can you join a battleship and not expect to fight in the war?'

Her father's eyes crinkled. 'It seems you have been doing some research on my naval days. Were you looking at the photo album?'

'Yes.'

He leaned back in his chair, sipped more tea, then nodded. 'I think I know what has upset you – the hoheitsabzeichen.'

'Don't you mean the hakenkreuz?'

Another nod. 'Yes, the swastika was part of the insignia, but it was compulsory. It was the national emblem – all enlisted men had to wear it. I was never a Nazi, Ingrid.'

Relieved, she finally drank some tea, and waited.

'I was a loyal German. When the war started, I had to fight for my country, but I was never doing it for Adolf Hitler. Very few of my crewmates agreed with the Führer or his mad plans. But it was dangerous to stand up to the Brown Shirts or the Nazis in the 1930s. That's why I joined the navy with my friends. Conscription was coming. If you weren't in the military already, you would be drafted into the army. The Reichsmarine seemed a better choice – fewer fanatics.'

Ingrid felt the pressure lifting.

'You saw photos of us in our white uniforms?'

A nod.

'The *Schlesien* was a relic from World War I. It was converted to a training ship the year I joined. We went to the Americas – North and South – in 1936 and '37. It gave us another perspective on the world. It opened many eyes to militarism and the extremism of Hitler and his cronies.'

'What happened when the war started?'

Her father returned his mug to the table and folded his arms.

'We were still a training ship; I was a petty officer third class. Towards the end of September, the *Schlesien* bombarded Polish artillery positions at Hel and Jastarnia. That was almost the extent of our offensive operations.'

He waved a hand waved aimlessly.

'Most of our heavy guns were removed to arm a newer vessel. We went back to training duties, ice breaking and escorting mine sweepers. Fuel became a problem as the war progressed – there was never enough for the frontline ships; we could barely do enough training to keep the *Schlesien* serviceable.'

The war history was stalled temporarily as another gardener entered the kitchen. Finding the kettle hot and the Richters reluctant to chat, he soon moved back to his garden with his tea.

'I saw photos of officers and sailors at a cemetery. What happened?'

Her father grimaced. 'Terrible luck. Our armaments were limited, but every vessel afloat was being pressed into service in 1945. We were operating south of Greifswalder Oie in the Baltic. Not far from your holiday camp at Glowe. The *Schlesien* struck a mine one morning, most likely dropped by a British plane.'

'You suffered casualties?'

Vati nodded. 'Two were killed. The flooding was bad, but our anti-aircraft guns were still working. They towed us closer to Swinemünde so we could help defend the city from the Russians.

'Once we got to shallow water, they changed their minds again. We were ordered to scuttle the *Schlesien*. The war ended a few days later. Hitler was dead, and my military service was over.'

Ingrid could see the pain the memories caused. His war had not been as brutal or confronting as many others. But all Germans suffered some loss. She saw it in her father's eyes. Did talking about the final days bring back memories of Katharina? Had he known that his fiancée had been killed in the February bomb raid, or were communications so bad he was not told until after the surrender? That was a question she did not need answered. Her curiosity was satisfied – her father had never been a Nazi.

A fresh wave of guilt washed over Ingrid. Her cheeks reddened; she had unintentionally caused Vati pain.

His hand clasped hers.

'You had a right to know about my time in the navy. Many survivors don't like to talk about those war days. I was always willing to share. I was never sure if you wanted to know. I can see the events of the past week have made you do a lot of thinking. These are the experiences that help us learn to be better people.'

He stood, took the cups to a tap and rinsed them. 'I had better get back to the weeding. Do you want to help?'

Tomas Schumann

THE WORRIES OF THE WORLD WEIGHED HEAVILY ON THE SHOULDERS OF drinkers at the rustic inn on Michaelisstrasse. There were seven men: five slouched communing with their beers at individual rough-hewn tables and two shared a corner booth. No drinker was under 60; a lifetime of wars, economic struggle, loss and more was etched on every face.

'Are any of them thinking about the showdown between the Russians and Americans?' Jürgen Grau gestured at the other clientele. 'Or do those men look permanently morose?'

Tomas Schuman slowly studied each drinker. One man was missing his left hand, another had a patch over his right eye, a third rocked gently, as if praying to the pilsner that was dulling his pain. The other two faced the wall. Schumann could not see if they shared the same ruddy complexions and noses held together by broken veins as the other three.

'I'm sure most are aware of the danger facing the world, but I think they are at the point where they don't care anymore.'

It was an unusual pub for the teachers. Their clothing marked them as respectable middle-class gentlemen, slumming it for a night or visiting from out of town, unaware Erfurt offered better inns. It had been an alternative to the Zum Goldenen Schwan. That was full of diners and drinkers, a band making the atmosphere too raucous for conversation.

This was the next quiet inn on the street, and neither of them had bothered to check the name as they entered. There was no chess board; beer and schnapps were their only requirements. They did not intend to get drunk, but neither would care if it happened. Grau rotated his beer glass a quarter turn, then drank.

'I've watched you do that for the past week,' Schumann said. 'Maybe I should ask why before I die.'

'My father used to do it. He said it activated the ingredients that had settled to the bottom of his ceramic mug.' Grau held up his glass.

'Probably a waste of time with a modern pilsner, but it helps me remember the old man.'

'I hope this is not going to be too maudlin, Jürgen.' Schumann smiled. 'You promised to brighten my Saturday night.'

Grau had arrived at Schumann's flat in Anger unexpectedly after the television news. There was little resistance to the late invitation; both saw that tension was on a knife edge in Moscow and Washington. They might not have many more opportunities to share a drink and conversation.

'I thought Khrushchev was smart enough to negotiate a face-saving solution,' Grau said. 'But now the shooting has started, who knows how they will stop it.'

Reports were coming through that American spy planes were being fired upon in Cuba. One of the U-2 reconnaissance aircraft was missing. That was a serious escalation. Add that to American claims work on the missile sites was continuing around the clock, and the world was in deeper trouble.

'Do you think it was the Russians or Cubans who fired on the Americans?' Schumann asked.

'Does it matter? I expect the American fighter jets and bombers are lining up to unload on any military they can find in Cuba.'

'Actually, I think identifying the shooter could be a way to scale things back.'

Grau turned his glass and drank. It was almost empty. He caught the barman's eye and held up two fingers. 'The Americans won't care if it was a Russian or Cuban gunner who blasted their plane out of the sky – they will destroy every military target they can find. Civilians will be unfortunate collateral damage.'

'I've been listening to the radio all afternoon. Castro's been ranting on television about shooting down intruders. If he ordered the anti-aircraft batteries to fire on the spy planes, that might give the Americans and Russians some breathing space. Khrushchev had already laid out his platform to the United Nations for negotiations. I can't see him spoiling that by shooting at the spy planes. The world knows nuclear missile sites are being constructed; firing at unarmed planes loaded with cameras is not going to help the Soviet cause.'

Grau mulled his friend's point of view as the fresh beers arrived. They toasted each other.

'I wonder what is happening in the Kremlin and the White House right now. These are weighty matters to consider. Both leaders are being bombarded with a variety of opinions. Whose advice do they take? The generals in both countries will be urging Khrushchev and Kennedy to attack – strike first and they might have a chance of survival.'

Schumann looked at his watch; it was after midnight in Moscow. 'I hope they are pouring coffee into Comrade Khrushchev rather than vodka. These are not matters that should be decided when drunk.'

Grau snorted. 'How would we tell the difference with the Russians? It was madness to sneak missiles under the nose of the Americans. Was that idea hatched after one bottle or five?'

A piece of pretzel was broken and chewed before Schumann replied. 'The more I think about it, the more I believe Khrushchev has underestimated Kennedy. The young president is learning from the humiliations of last year.' Schumann sipped beer to wash down the last crumbs. 'We know the Soviets are strategic thinkers; they plan 10, 20 years into the future. The Kremlin is not constrained by politicians or democratic elections. The most Kennedy can expect to spend in the Oval Office is eight years, if he's lucky. He could be gone by 1964 if he lets Khrushchev outwit him too many times. Kennedy's fighting for political survival every day while the Soviets are playing a long game.'

'I wish the Russians would stick to chess – at least nobody dies when they lose.'

They enjoyed the silence and their thoughts for a few minutes. The only movement came from the barman making regular trips from the beer tap to his clients.

'Did you hear the reports that the Americans have been testing their long-range ballistic missiles?'

Grau nodded. 'Provocative, but not unexpected. One had a range of 9,000 kilometres, the other 8,000. I wonder what impact that had on the Kremlin. There is so much we don't know about the diplomatic moves. Supposedly Khrushchev sent a communication last night offering to remove their weapons from Cuba under United Nations supervision. Then Moscow radio today says the deal is dependent upon the Americans taking their missiles out of Turkey. Now we hear that spy planes are being shot down. Who is in charge over there?'

Schumann paused with the glass to his lips. 'You could have a valid point there, Jürgen. I wonder if the Presidium is muscling in on Khrushchev. Dangling an offer one day, then putting more hooks on the line the next does not sound like the same person making the policy.'

'God help us then – they are all trying to make the plays.'

'That's the first time I've heard you say that for many years.'

Grau wrinkled his brow, recalling what he had said. 'Oh.'

'We used to pray all the time when the bombardments started in the trenches. We hoped there was a god who would listen – we begged for the bombs to fall elsewhere. On our friends, fellow Germans, we didn't care – we wanted to survive. Another day would put us closer to the end of the war.'

'I left my faith in the Belgian mud.' Grau wiped a finger through condensation on his glass. 'My family were Lutherans. They never understood why I would never go to church to thank God for saving my life.'

'I know. The same god who missed us with millions of bullets and shells was responsible for the carnage that cost millions of lives. If he is all powerful and merciful, why does he make mankind suffer so much? Two world wars and the threat of nuclear annihilation – at times I feel like a puppet on a string.'

The barman interrupted to say he was closing soon. East Germans had to follow the rules, end of the world or not. They ordered another glass and apple schnapps.

'It's the kinder I feel sorry for,' Schumann said. 'We are old men, we've had a chance to live our lives, although there are chapters I would never like to repeat.'

'How have your students coped with the stress this week, Tomas? Your class probably knows more about the dangers facing them than most. Mine are too young to comprehend the fate that awaits if two other grumpy old men can't find an agreement.'

Two glasses of schnapps arrived and were dispatched neatly in traditional fashion. Schumann regretted the decision; it would have been better to waddle home through the Altstadt without the taste of apple liqueur on his lips.

'7A has had a tougher week than most students anywhere. We

started in Buchenwald on Monday. The sins of our past are always confronting.' Schumann thought about Ingrid and the ovens. 'Only one student made the connection between the Topf & Söhne nameplate on the ovens. Most students hurry through that area; Ingrid Richter returned and questioned me about the company history in Erfurt. I told her, and I also revealed the Americans had liberated the camp.'

'That was the day before you told her the sky was about to fall in.' Schumann nodded.

'That's a lot for a young girl to cope with. Is she okay?'

The teacher thought back to his exit from school, finding Ingrid in front of the retaining wall. Ironically, it reminded him of a church scene: a child approaching the altar for their first communion or confirmation, Catholic traditions he had not considered for almost half a century.

'I believe she is handling it remarkably well. It might have caused her a few sleepless nights; you can't miss yawns from the front of the class. But the early anxiety is under control. She and her friends have been thinking deeply about the implications if Khrushchev and Kennedy can't settle their differences. Not just for them but for their family, friends and the world. They're not panicking – they are looking for solutions. Their answers might be simplistic, but they desperately hope for a future.'

The other patrons clambered from their seats as Grau surveyed the dregs in his glass. He held it towards his lifelong friend. 'Well, for the kinder – I wish their dreams come true.' They drank, then slowly wrapped themselves in scarves, gloves and hats. Grau held out an arm of his expensive coat. 'That's New Zealand wool. It cost me a fortune on the black market – I've only used it for one winter. The Soviets and the Americans can't end the world this week. I need another 10 Christmas snowfalls to make the cost worthwhile!'

Their laughter echoed through the empty cobbled streets of the Altstadt to their homes in Anger.

Sunday, October 29, 1962

Ingrid Richter

Planes featured in Ingrid's nightmare du jour on Saturday night. At first the steady drone reverberating around the middle room was her father's snoring. It segued to jet engines in the darkness. Ingrid heard, then saw, row upon row of American bombers from her bedroom window. Hundreds, possibly thousands, circling her home. Spotlights from the ground isolated silver wings as they lazily looped overhead.

In the movies, lines of tracer would arc into the sky as bombs dropped from bloated bellies. Not tonight over Erfurt. It was a standoff, neither the attackers nor defenders willing to take the first shot. The United States Air Force circled for hours as Ingrid watched and shivered. Finally, the jet whine grew distant; the spotlights on the clouds could not find any targets. The snoring from the master bedroom took precedence in Ingrid's semi-lucid mind.

Ingrid knew instantly where the inspiration for the latest dream came from: the television news. She and Vati had returned from the allotment in better spirits; some of the demons that had tormented her week had been buried. One of the most important people in her life was still a good and decent person. Vati had been part of Hitler's war machine, but he was not a Nazi. He had seen a way to navigate the growing militarism of Germany during the 1930s. The navy was the best way to avoid the extremists.

Mutti had fired up the boiler while they were gardening. The bath was steaming hot by the time they arrived home. The youngest always had first use, which was good and bad for Ingrid. It meant she had the cleanest and hottest water, but she had to be the quickest; the boiler could never heat enough for more than one bath.

There was no mention of swastikas, the Stasi or Cuba during supper. Her parents talked about the future. Everyone had enjoyed the holiday on the Baltic Sea; Mutti would talk to her friends early next year to see if she could work at the camp again. Ingrid should be able to join her in a tent; Vati could use his two-week annual holiday to explore more of the coast.

The reminder of the seaside adventures at Glowe were meant to boost Ingrid's spirits. She smiled dutifully, talked about the differences in ice creams between home and the seaside town. Secretly, she was thinking about the fate of Pedro Barios.

He had been gone three days; how much closer to home was he? Ingrid hoped that his passage might be stalled by the American blockade. If Pedro, Hector and Ermano could not get home to Cuba, they might have a better chance of surviving. Invading American soldiers could not kill the trio if they were floating in a ship at sea. If it escalated to a nuclear war, the fallout might never reach the middle of the Atlantic. Their ship could keep going, rounding South America to the Pacific. They could take their pick of beautiful islands to start anew: Fiji, Samoa, Tahiti. Not Hawaii. The tropical lushness and big waves looked inviting in the photos Ingrid had seen in the school library books, but it was part of America, an even closer target for the Soviets than the mainland.

An evening of mood swings held more twists; the West German television news put them back on the roller coaster. The news, initially, was positive: Khrushchev had offered an acceptable solution for the Americans, then pulled away from it. One step forward became two steps back when the Richters heard about the Cubans shooting at American spy planes. One was missing, most likely shot down, with no word on the fate of the pilot. Was he the first of many millions to die?

Her parents were stunned but tried to reassure their daughter. They said it might be the shock both leaders needed to come to their senses. It was one thing to shout angry words from across the oceans; spilling blood would make them confront the reality of their decisions. Their words had been intended to soothe Ingrid's troubled mind as she went to bed, but the taunting bombers proved they had failed.

Ingrid snuggled deeper under her bettdecke, every breath forming vapour in the chilly room. The snoring level from the next room had dipped. Mutti had probably pushed Vati onto his side. It was light beyond the curtains; rain pattered against the window. A few birds could be heard hunting for breakfast. There was no need to brave the cold on Sunday mornings; it was the one free day of the week. Ingrid closed her eyes, seeking happier thoughts than nuclear bombers. In a few weeks the skating rink would open; she could glide gracefully across the ice dreaming of representing her country in the Winter Olympics at Innsbruck in 1964. It was fanciful, but so much nicer than worrying about the world exploding around her at any moment.

'So much sleeping, Ingrid.' Her mother wriggled a toe through the feathers. 'Come on, I need you to help me in the kitchen this morning.'

The curtains were opened. The rain had stopped.

'What are we making?' Ingrid scratched at sleepy eyes.

Mutti was already wearing her apron.

'We're going to have Thüringer Klösse with breaded pork chops for lunch.'

Ingrid felt her saliva glands activate. Dumplings were traditional for mittagessen on Sundays, and Mutti's were mouth-wateringly delicious, especially with her brown gravy. There was a bit of preparation involved: peeling, grating, and squeezing the moisture from the potatoes. But it should not require such an early start.

Mutti read her mind.

'Oma and Opa are going to visit Tante Lisl and Onkel Stefan this afternoon. I'm sure they will welcome us too if I bake a butterkuchen for kaffeeklatsch.'

'Oh yes! Can I help you make that?'

'You can if you get out of bed now. We need to give the yeast time to rise.'

Ingrid dressed quickly in warm jersey, blouse and trousers; no dresses were required on non-school days. The eggs were boiling and Mutti was slicing bread by the time Ingrid reached the kitchen. She placed the honey and marmalade on the table. Vati would drag himself out of bed eventually, once everything was ready.

The afternoon family plan and food preparations were a welcome distraction. Baking knowledge was passed from mother to daughter, the recipes influenced by the years in East Prussia, Schleswig-Holstein and Thuringia. Vati was given a leave pass for fruehschoppen once he had squeezed all the water from the potatoes. Ingrid would fetch him from the pub a few minutes before lunch was on the table.

It was a happy morning for mother and daughter, sharing duties and learning family recipes. Generations of Germans had been doing this; Ingrid hoped she would get the chance to pass the knowledge to her own kinder. Mutti hauled two springform pans from a cupboard when the dough was ready.

'Are we taking two cakes, Mutti?'

'Just one, with butter, sugar and almond slices.' The mixture was poured into the first pan, then the second. 'I'll cover the top of this one with streusel. We don't want to leave crumbs all over the tram. We can eat it during the week!'

Tomas Schumann

THE PROPRIETOR OF TOMAS SCHUMANN'S FAVOURITE CAFÉ IN ANGER looked stunned as the teacher ambled by with a wave. Herr Vogel had already had the door open. For the past decade, the Sunday morning coffee and pastry had been as regular as the Gloriosa bell. Schumann enjoyed the ambience of the charming establishment, reading between chats with other weekend regulars of a similar vintage. The narrow façade – a small table and two seats either side of the entrance – made the café appear unusually claustrophobic that morning.

It was cold on Kaufmännerstrasse; there were occasional spits of rain, yet the quiet streets of the Altstadt held more appeal. Schumann was sure Herr Vogel would excuse his rudeness. Perhaps a quick cup on the return journey might reassure the owner that there was no betrayal; Schumann had not passed him by for another establishment.

Walks through the medieval heart of Erfurt declined in the colder months for Schumann. Icy streets after Christmas and New Year were no fun for a man over 60. The cobbles were already dangerous enough, slick from the dawn shower. They were better negotiated with a steady, shorter step; pride ruled out using a sturdy walking stick.

Schumann's heart was heavy; the beloved architecture of Erfurt that had endured more than half a millennium was under threat from new enemies. He stopped to admire timber hewn from trees that predated their most famous cleric; they were the web upon which the city was built. Homes and shops had suffered damage during the last war, but not to the same extent as bigger cities like Berlin and Hamburg. New render and paint would make a world of difference to the public appeal of Erfurt. Would residents ever get the chance to improve their national treasure?

Schumann chided himself: he should be enjoying the beauty of the Altstadt rather than worrying about the danger it faced in the days and weeks ahead. Erfurt had survived Swedish, French, Prussian, American, Russian and socialist administrations; maybe it was a charmed city.

He reached the empty Weningemarkt. The triangular square had been a hub of enterprise from the 11th Century. No traders could be found outdoors on a bleak Sunday morning in autumn. Schumann glanced around the three-to-four-storey homes that lined the perimeter. He had always harboured dreams of an apartment in this district, close to the river and the Krämerbrücke. It was beyond his teacher's salary and Party connections.

The dominant feature was the Aegidienkirche; the church spire towered over the little market; the ancient archway beneath was the eastern access to the bridge. He had never visited the chapel on the first floor; two years ago it had been restored as a place of worship by the Methodists.

He slipped a few Ostmarks to a shaking man in a tattered coat sheltering in a doorway. On another day the VoPos would hustle the Party embarrassment away from public view. Schumann could always recognise another survivor from the trenches.

Beyond the arch a narrow passage lured Schumann off the Krämerbrücke to the river. Ducks floated contentedly above the detritus of urban living. Most tourist cameras focused on the half-timbered homes and shops, but attention would soon be required to clean up the waterway.

Schumann enjoyed the view for five minutes then returned to the bridge. The aroma of roast meals cooking slowly in ancient ovens was tantalising. He presumed many were pork dinners, all accompanied by the cook's favourite Thuringia dumpling recipe. Perhaps the Gildehaus should be included on his city itinerary; he could afford to be a bit extravagant.

A few more pedestrians were striding across Fischmarkt. A trio of old men with canes stood in front of the Rathaus. Occasionally one glanced at the sky. It was almost a nervous tic in the city these days despite the few gaps in the cloud cover.

Schumann stopped briefly at the restaurant to assess how busy it was: fuller than normal, but enough spare tables for him to return for a treat. His weekend warm meals were usually taken at cheaper cafes closer to his apartment.

He could have invited Jürgen Grau for the Sunday walk; it might have warded off the melancholy that had built since the morning radio reports. Should the loss of one American life plunge the world into a nuclear conflict? The victim was an air force pilot, spying on another nation. A military man would have known the risk he was taking for his country. Schumann feared the dead man was symbolic of much more in the modern era.

Schumann's route took him along Marktstrasse. The good humour generated by the beer and schnapps with Jürgen Grau the previous evening was long gone. Perhaps that was why the streets were so empty; few could face their neighbours knowing it might be for the last time. Blood had been drawn; who knew when the shooting would stop?

An organ could be heard inside All Saints Church at the fork with Allerheiligenstrasse. It had been there since the 12th Century and now boasted the tallest tower in the Altstadt at 53 metres. He had attended two Catholic services there with his parents before the First World War, both baptisms for younger cousins. Neither had outlived Hitler. He presumed there had been no changes to the doctrine or interior since his last visit almost 50 years ago.

A tram rattled past as he reached the junction with the Domplatz. Few passengers were on board as it turned north. Schumann crossed to the square and hesitated; his hand reached into his jacket and sought reassurance. The metal was still cool to his fingers despite resting against his body for the past 20 minutes.

A few pedestrians entered the square from narrow streets and lanes from the east and south. They came in singles, pairs, a few families with school-age kinder. He didn't recognise any from the 31st Oberschule. Mostly, the pedestrians were older, like Schumann, born before dictators dreamed of world conquests.

An elderly lady smiled and nodded to Schumann as she tottered past the obelisk towards the stairway. The numbers gathered at the base of the Dom and Severikirche could never be compared to Martini. Yet, they were substantial, far more than the humble worshippers that might be seen ascending the steps most weekends for Mass. Schumann watched the line snake towards the top, then enter the cathedral on the left. Schumann checked his watch: five minutes to eleven. The previous Mass would have been in the Severikirche an hour or so earlier.

Schumann waited near the obelisk until the line thinned. A couple of familiar faces passed in the final minutes before the organ signalled the entrance of the priest. They ignored the reluctant pilgrim as they hustled up the stairway. The music was familiar, not that Schumann could put a name to it. His hand remained in his coat pocket as he steadily climbed the stairs. A Latin cadence could be heard through the Dom's open door. It was not enough to overcome the lingering scepticism.

Pigeons scattered as Schumann veered to the right. The Severikirche would serve his purpose just as well as the cathedral. He would feel too hypocritical to sit amongst a congregation and mouth responses by rote. All he needed was a pew and an altar at which to direct his plea for sanity and peace.

The Gothic grandeur was lost on Schumann. He kept his eyes downcast as he sought a row by himself. The seat was a momentary waystation as he eased old bones to a kneeling position. The metal crucifix was trailed from his pocket by 59 beads; the rosary had been left to him by his mother on her death in 1943.

Schumann had not had the linked wooden beads as he huddled in earth, timber and – occasionally – concrete bunkers during Allied bombardments in World War I. One hand had clutched his helmet, the other his rifle as a steady stream of soil was shaken loose. Prayers were uttered through gritted teeth. They could have been shouted, although there was no chance of them being heard by dying comrades over the thundering explosions.

There had been many traumatic experiences in Schumann's life. None had caused him to reach for the rosary beads for divine salvation. The rekindling of his faith had been prompted by a schoolgirl's ritual with a stick.

Schumann had watched Ingrid Richter at the school wall on Saturday morning. To a man who had nurtured young minds for more than 40 years, it appeared that Ingrid had turned the wall into a shrine. He saw her examine a stick, then reinsert it. To most people it might look like a game. Schumann instinctively felt it had much greater meaning to the child.

He looked at the crucifix and beads. The practice was ancient, dating back to the third or fourth century from what he could remember. The rosary was made of wood and metal; Ingrid's stick was rough wood – who could say which was the more practical or powerful symbol of hope?

That was the reason Schumann had swallowed his pride and doubts. He wanted a future for the kinder that he taught every day. Something had kept him safe during the heaviest bombardments in Belgium; perhaps he could find that magic again with an hour of prayer.

Schumann made the sign of the cross, then his thumb and fingers sought the first bead. The words were barely a whisper.

'Our Father, who art in heaven, hallowed be thy name; thy kingdom come; thy will be done on earth as it is in heaven ...'

Gunther Kist

Kist fingered the condensation on a pilsener glass as he sat by himself at Das Paridis. Fruehschoppen was traditionally a time to share a drink and a chat with neighbours, the wives at home preparing Thuringian dumplings. Conversations, on the rare occasions Kist allowed himself to join in, mostly revolved around grumpy wives, bullying bosses and sports results. It was boring.

A pretzel, courtesy of the manager, sat untouched on the table. The *hospitality* was a signal to the unaware that the lone drinker was either a Stasi agent or an informer. Political comments would be shelved until he departed.

There had been little sleep for the former field agent the night before. The restlessness was not caused by the Cuban crisis; Gunther Kist had barely glimpsed a news broadcast in the past two days. He was being treated badly by the Ministry for State Security, but an oath was a bond. Kist would stay loyal to the Party and trust the Stasi would soon realise their mistake and return him to frontline duties.

Kist was off the streets, but the habits of a field agent were ingrained. He raised the glass, using the movement to discreetly study the clientele. There were about 30 men, mostly in groups of three or four. The mood was more subdued than normal, the drinkers probably trying to guess when and where the first American missiles would land. An American spy plane had been shot down; some of the drinkers were knocking back the beers as if there would never be another Sunday pre-lunch session.

Kist saw no need to go beyond his normal two glasses. He would enjoy a roast pork meal with his family then plan his rehabilitation within the Stasi. Nobody was aware of the demotion, apart from Carsten Hartwig and the Colonel. It would be easy enough to hide the change in circumstances. The pay grade would not change. The work hours might be more regular than his wife was used to; she would never complain about that.

Another sip of beer was taken as Kist pondered what to do about

Matthias. His son had failed in the easy assignment of watching the Richter daughter. It was meant to be a discreet observation. Matthias had butchered it; now the parent who commissioned the junior agent would have to read tedious mail and listen to stupid conversations.

Matthias could not be punished for his transgression, lest it betray Kist's own change in status. Perhaps the training would be put on hold for six months. Kist expected to be back in the field by then. He would convince Hartwig that he was dependable or his private plan to skewer the Colonel in his own corruption would be successful.

The glass was raised for another sip and observation. Kist spluttered when he saw the lean man standing with two others near the entrance. It was Dieter Richter.

Ingrid Richter

Sylvie was standing on her driveway as Ingrid opened the entrance to her block.

'Hi, Sylvie. What are you doing?'

'I have to go to the park with my brother so he can kick his football. His friend who plays goalie has a cold.'

Ingrid tightened her jacket against the chill and looked at the sky. 'I think it's going to rain again.' She looked at her friend's only pair of trousers. 'It won't be fun diving around in the mud.'

'Wonderful.' She tugged at her warmest clothes. 'My mother won't wash these until Friday. I'll be lucky to have them dry for Saturday afternoon.' Sylvie shrugged. 'Where are you going?'

'I'm off to get Vati. He's having a beer at Das Paridis.'

'I can walk with you – Konrad wants to play just across the road at Beethovenplatz.'

'Okay, but I have to go now. Mutti said lunch will be ready in 15 minutes.'

'I'll tell Konrad that I'll meet him there.'

Sylvie ran to the entrance of Number 11. There was no need for a Stasi listening post in that block; the Witzenhause sibling conversations could be heard over half of Erfurt.

Thirty seconds later they were walking towards Semmelweisstrasse, the bar a few minutes around the corner.

'It's a pity you don't have longer until your lunch,' Sylvie said.

'Why?'

'We could have run to school to check on the peace stick.'

Ingrid's pace faltered. The thought had occurred to her, but the timing was unrealistic.

'Do you think we can do it?' Sylvie asked.

They stopped at the corner and looked back. Sylvie's brother was dribbling the football 60 metres behind.

'No. Your brother would go home and say you had run away.'

'Probably. Do you think the stick is okay – that we'll get another 24 hours?'

The pub was only a minute away. 'I think the luck will last the weekend. I stopped by the wall after you left yesterday and gave it an extra wish. Told it to keep us safe until Monday.'

They laughed; that's what it came down to in a nuclear showdown: wishes, magic, luck.

A few steps later they were outside the pub. They waited for Konrad to catch up before parting.

'See you in the morning, Ingrid.'

Ingrid usually found her father close to the door. He knew she hated weaving between tall, smelly men to find him. Vati had a sixth sense when Ingrid would arrive to announce lunch was almost ready.

She opened the door to an unusually quiet bar.

Gunther Kist

DIETER RICHTER HAD OBVIOUSLY SPOTTED HIM. HE STOOD HOLDING A nearly empty glass in his left hand, his eyes locked on Gunther Kist. The two drinkers with the tailor were wary of the sudden tension in their drinking companion. They turned towards Kist, immediately registering that he was Stasi. They sipped nervously as eyes swung back and forth between the two men. Kist watched as Richter put his right hand in his coat pocket. What did he have in there?

Kist squirmed in his seat. Standing would take this to a new level. The bar's subdued tone had dropped even further, heads turned in every direction to isolate the cause. Soon most gazes in the room were ping-ponging from the trio near the door to the man with his back against the wall. A few chairs scraped; they were not involved, but they wanted to see what happened next – or be able to run.

Richter took the initiative; every footstep on the timber floor as he approached Kist could be heard. He stopped a metre away, the glass in one hand, the other still in his pocket. Kist assessed him: six or seven years older, well-dressed, fit, a war veteran. He had not checked on Richter's military career. It might have been a wise move before stepping up the pressure on Thursday with his surveillance.

'Are you still following me and my family?'

The voice was firm, no sign of nerves. The question had not been shouted, but everyone in the pub heard.

Kist was annoyed and unnerved. Few people ever challenged the Stasi. He had every right to haul Richter to the prison and interrogate him for anti-social behaviour. The man's bluff would crumble on Stasi turf. But could he risk arresting him?

Richter raised the stakes. 'I thought you were told by your superiors to stay away from us.'

Kist watched Richter turn, letting the drinkers know this was a wounded lion.

'You know how important my family is to a certain *colonel*.' The hand in the right pocket jiggled; there was something in there: a gun, a knife? Surely not.

'I repeat … are you following me?'

One and a half beers, yet Kist felt his throat go dry. Never had he been confronted like this since joining the Ministry for State Security. Their reputation was more fearful amongst East Germans than that of the Gestapo during the Reich.

'No.' Kist had to break the stare down. He could not afford for this to get out of hand. If Richter attacked him, would the other drinkers join in? His colleagues would arrest them eventually. What value was that if Kist was left a vegetable? Most of these drinkers were former soldiers or sailors like Richter. They all had that look; Kist would never register as an unfortunate death on their conscience.

Too much was at stake on this battleground. Kist saw the right pocket twitch again. How could he escape without further humiliation?

'I live nearby,' Kist said. 'I often come here for fruehschoppen.' He waved at the bar. 'The manager will tell you that.'

That should have made Richter quake. The manager's shrug was not reassuring. Had someone at headquarters revealed Kist was being taken out of the field? Was undermining his Stasi status part of the Colonel's revenge?

'I had never seen you before Thursday – at my work and a few metres behind me all the way home. Now I find you at my pub. It seems like you are a Stasi man who works to his own rules. Perhaps I will have another talk with the Colonel – this afternoon.'

Kist felt sweat under his arms, an unusual reaction. Then came his salvation.

'Vati. Our lunch is almost ready.'

Both men turned to the door where Ingrid stood nervously.

Kist watched Dieter smile. 'Time we were going then.' Richter finished his pilsner, placed the glass on Kist's table and turned for the door. His hand left the pocket only to wave farewell to his companions.

Tomas Schumann

Tomas Schumann completed three rosaries, surprising himself with the desire to continue after his fingers completed each circuit of the 59 beads. He was aware of scuffing feet and creaking pews as worshipers old and new started and ended their vigils; he was content to remain in his own bubble.

The hypocrisy had evaporated as the cadence of the prayers swept him along. He could not calculate how long it had been since he recited a Hail Mary. The words returned to his lips without a stumble. A fourth rosary was aborted by aching knees and a sore back. Schumann hoped his efforts in the past hour would not be treated as too little too late by whatever deity was listening.

He paused at the top of the stairway between the Dom and Severikirche. The beads felt warm, comforting; it was almost 20 years since they had last accumulated prayers in the hands of his mother.

Voices from the entrance to the cathedral indicated the Mass was over. They sounded buoyant, ready for a new week of service to their god – and the Party. East Germany was a secular state that tolerated religion; Catholics were savvy enough to pay homage to religious and political masters.

Schumann turned to see small groups gathering near the doors. They were mostly aged over 40, a few families with school-age kinder. More people spilled from the Dom. Several women darted straight for the stairs, probably rushing home to check on roast meals that had been slow cooking during the service.

He stepped aside, unwilling to take his eyes off the growing congregation: 40 became 50, then 60. He was good at crowd calculations after four decades of wrangling students at school and on excursions. He stopped estimating when the numbers swelled beyond 100. The priest must have been giddy with excitement to preach to such numbers. Would he pray for the crisis to linger to retain his flock?

Schumann laughed at the cynicism that still lurked. Many of these churchgoers were like him: they dusted off the faith only in a crisis.

But if prayer could help find a solution, it had been worth his time. He set out to retrace his steps through the Altstadt; he fancied a hot meal at the Gildehaus. The rosary was returned to his pocket.

Ingrid Richter

Mutti laughed so hard, a piece of dumpling fell off her fork onto the plate.

'You were pretending to be what – a cowboy? Like a shootout in the dusty main street?'

Ingrid had never seen an American cowboy film, but her parents had before the barbed wire, minefields and border guards stopped their visits to family in the West. The dramas sounded exciting, although she wondered why every movie had to involve lots of shooting. Didn't enough people die in real life?

Vati smiled as he pushed some roast pork through thick gravy.

'I was playing with him.'

Mutti retrieved the dumpling. 'It was risky to humiliate a Stasi man in front of a pub full of drinkers, but I wish I had been there to see it.'

Her parents' laughter removed the fears that had accompanied Ingrid home from Das Paridis. She had pushed open the door to the bar, expecting to find Vati standing nearby, ready to finish his beer and hurry home for the delicious meal.

It had been as quiet as Buchenwald last Monday. Nobody noticed her arrival; all eyes were focused on two men across the room: one sitting, the other standing. The first shock was the man at the table: the Stasi agent who had been following her family. The next shock was the man standing over him: her father. He stood with a glass in one hand, the other in his jacket pocket. It was an odd stance.

They were the only people speaking. She heard Vati say he was going to talk to the Colonel that afternoon. Even a child could interpret that as a threat to a Stasi man. Ingrid intervened with her lunch message. The whole bar was surprised to find Ingrid in their midst. They had seemed almost disappointed when Vati removed his right hand to wave goodbye.

Ingrid had had to wait until the meal was on the table to hear the full story. Mutti's initial shock turned to delight when she learned that Gunther Kist had been put in his place.

'He thought you had a pistol in your coat pocket?'

Vati grinned and ate more dumpling.

'You were taking a chance. What if he called your bluff and tried to arrest you?'

'What would he charge me with? Scaring a tough Stasi agent with a loaded finger.'

A belly laugh was what the family needed after a week of stress and uncertainty.

Mutti spooned more dumplings onto their plates. 'Do you think he was disobeying orders to stay away from us, or was it a coincidence?'

'Klaus, one of the regulars at Das Paridis, says Gunther Kist drinks there occasionally. I've never seen him.' Her father sat back from the table and patted his stomach. 'Maybe I need to drink more beer.'

'I think it might be safer for you to find another inn for a few weeks,' Mutti said. 'You won't always be able to bluff the Stasi, even with our connection to the Colonel.'

Vati nodded as he chewed more pork and gravy.

Ingrid was enjoying the table banter. It was a distraction from the thoughts that had weighed upon her for six days. The radio had not been tuned to news broadcasts that morning. They all had wanted an escape for a few hours from the depressing stream of speculation and fear.

Mutti stood with her plate and the dumpling bowl. 'Hurry up, you two, we have to clean up and there are two trams to catch. We don't want to be late for kaffeeklatsch.'

Her father's sister and family lived in an outer suburb on the north side of the Altstadt. Tante Lisl was younger than Vati by five years; her twins, Jana and Anton, were only a class behind Ingrid, although they did not attend the same school.

Ingrid loved visiting their home; it had a large garden with fruit trees for climbing and hedges for hide and seek. In summer, Onkel Stefan would squirt them with a hose. Tante Lisl had been a talented gymnast; she taught them how to leap, roll, balance and form human pyramids.

The butterkuchen survived the tram journey and boisterous greetings at Johannesvorstadt inside a tin that once was part of a westpaket. Oma and Opa seemed especially happy about the unexpected family reunion. Ingrid had sat with her grandfather many times while he listened to radio broadcasts. His favourite shows and news services were from the West. The most recent visit to her grandparents' home in Braun Strasse had been the previous weekend. Opa's long hug indicated he held similar concerns about the fate of the world. Would there be many more family gatherings like this?

The children were soon free to roam the garden while the adults chatted inside.

'I have a new football, Ingrid,' Anton said. 'Do you want to play a game?'

The lawn was slick from an afternoon shower, and patches of mud discouraged the girls. Jana took charge.

'Ingrid and I have more important things to discuss.' Jana took her cousin by the hand and led her inside. Her brother booted the ball between two trees and raised an arm in the air to salute an imaginary crowd.

The home was a newer build, post war, with a second storey. Jana's room had a view over flat farmland to the east from a dormer window. It was only as they sat on the bed that Ingrid realised, she could see Buchenwald in the distance.

'You can see it?' Jana asked.

Ingrid turned to her cousin, then back to the concentration camp. 'Yes. I didn't know you could see it every morning when you opened the curtain.'

Jana went to stand by the window. 'I've tried to block it out. Now the school says we have to visit again this week.' She returned to the bed and sat with her back against the wall. 'I don't want to go.'

'When was the first visit?'

'Two years ago.'

'How much do you remember?'

'We rushed through as quickly as we could, but you couldn't avoid the ovens.'

Ingrid nodded. 'Did you know my class went last Monday?'

Jana shook her head. 'How was it? Horrible?'

'Worse – I saw more than I wanted to.'

Her cousin took her hand. 'Do they still have the hair and teeth displays? I don't want to see them again.'

'They're awful, but the most shocking thing I saw was a plaque on the ovens.'

Jana frowned.

'It was the name of the company that built, installed and maintained the ovens.'

The frown deepened.

'They were made here in Erfurt.' Ingrid looked across the lush fields. 'We're never going to be able to shake the guilt of what happened there.'

Tante Lisl called from the bottom of the stairs. 'Girls. Do you want some cake?'

The cousins grimaced. The anticipated treat had lost its appeal.

Tomas Schumann

Schumann stood in front of the three chess games on his sideboard at 7.40 on Sunday evening. He expected his Berlin friend would choose to remove a knight, a bishop and a pawn with his next moves. That would be when the mail arrived in a few days. The matches would reach a conclusion. He looked at the clock: 18 minutes until the Western television news service.

The teacher's mood had brightened throughout the day. He expected to feel guilt slowly overwhelm him after the hour on his knees with the rosary at Severikirche. It hadn't come. Perhaps a hearty lunch at the Gildehaus had helped. He had been drowsy by the time he returned to Anger; a snooze had refreshed him. The rest of the afternoon was spent finishing *Catch-22*. It was so apt: the individual had no power against a bureaucracy.

Schumann could not do anything directly to influence the Soviet leader and the American president. The larger congregation at the Dom that morning revealed lapsed Christians, like himself, still had a smidgen of faith in the power of prayer. Had it worked? Evidence had emerged in radio reports over the past hour. The source was Voice of America – Khrushchev and Kennedy had reached a deal about Cuba.

Monday, October 30, 1962

Ingrid Richter

The aroma from the brewery struck Ingrid as she opened the apartment block door. Perhaps extra hops, malt or yeast had been added to the mix. She looked up to see the grey blanket of the previous week broken by patches of blue. Maybe that helped the heady smell drift further. The temperature was in single digits, but the street lacked the biting chill of the previous week.

There was no sign of Sylvie; Ingrid was early. She wanted to ensure there was time to check the peace stick before the first class. Students tended to loiter around the entrance on Mondays, catching up with friends they had not seen for a day.

'Goodness. Fancy you arriving first.' Sylvie hauled on her ranzen as she rushed down the driveway. 'Did your mother drag you out of bed an hour early?'

Sylvie stopped suddenly and put a hand on Ingrid's arm.

'Oh. Sorry. Did you have another nightmare?'

Ingrid shook her head and they resumed walking.

'No. The opposite, in fact. I had the best sleep in a week – no dreams of guns, Stasi agents, gas ovens or swastikas.'

'Swastikas – when did they feature?'

Ingrid bit her lip. That was a slip – Sylvie had not been told about the controversial Yuri Gagarin stamp. That was one secret that would forever stay within the Richter family, unless Mutti sold it. But Sylvie had seen a swastika in the past few days – in Vati's military photos.

'You remember the hakenkreuz on my father's naval uniform?'

A nod. They waited for two Trabbis and a Wartburg to turn the corner.

'It upset me, so I spoke to him about it on Saturday at the Schrebergarten. He said it was part of the national emblem for the navy when they became the Kriegsmarine – they had to wear it.'

'That must have helped – you look bright-eyed this morning.'

Ingrid felt refreshed from almost 10 hours of sleep. They had all gone to bed early after returning from the family gathering. It had been a fun afternoon and evening, apart from the Buchenwald reminder from Jana's bedroom window. Mutti's butterkuchen had been demolished; when nobody wanted to go home, Tante Lisl had scrambled a supper of bread, cheese and the last of her Hungarian salami to feed nine. The television and radio were ignored; nobody wanted updates on a world they could not control.

The news silence continued on Monday morning during breakfast and school preparations. Mutti and Vati laughed frequently about yesterday's game of scharaden and did not want to spoil the good mood generated by Opa's antics. Waking for school without a nightmare renewed hope the diplomats at the United Nations were making headway with the Soviets and Americans. There was no sign of bombers or missiles – were Khrushchev and Kennedy listening?

They reached Herr Wenkell's bakery.

'We've got time for a pastry.' Sylvie jiggled some coins. 'I've got enough pfennigs for a pig's ear, how about you?'

'Why not?' Ingrid could afford an éclair but would never show up her friend.

They entered the shop to find the baker grinning.

'Good morning, young ladies.'

There seemed to be more chocolate and sugary treats on display than usual. Ingrid salivated but remained loyal. Two schweineohr were wrapped in paper and Herr Wenkell waved them away as he cheerfully greeted a new customer.

'He's back to his old self,' Sylvie said.

Ingrid chewed the flaky pastry and nodded. Should she take heart from the baker's change of attitude?

There was little chatter until they reached Am Schwemmbach. They were early, at least 10 minutes until first bell: ample time to stop by the peace wall. That thought made Ingrid smile; it was the first time she had thought of the location for their symbol of hope in that way. It was appropriate.

Sylvie was licking sticky fingers as they reached the wall. They both looked around; no students were paying them any attention. Even better, there was no sign of Matthias Kist; the message from the Colonel to his father might have resulted in a boot in the backside for the clumsy amateur.

They stood shoulder to shoulder and checked.

'It's still there,' Sylvie said. 'That's almost a week of protection.'

'Another week would be nice. And a month. Would a year be too much to hope for?' Ingrid whispered those dreams lest a passing student become curious. She wanted to touch the peace stick again but held back. It was their secret, just Sylvie and hers; to remove it totally from the hole in the bricks might destroy the luck that held the world together.

'You two look like you're praying.'

Gerard Mueller was standing beside Sylvie. He looked at the wall, saw nothing of interest, and turned back to the girls.

Sylvie found an answer.

'I was waiting for a fifth grader.' She gestured at the bricks. 'We saw him reading the new *Mosaik* comic on the wall last week. I want to borrow it.'

Gerard flicked his head. 'If that was Jonas, you're out of luck. He's already given it to Thorsten and I'm next in line.'

'Oh, that's a shame. I guess I'll have to buy it.'

Gerard had lost interest. He waved Sylvie off as he entered the school.

Ingrid was impressed.

'You amaze me with your quick thinking, Sylvie. I would still be here gold fishing, trying to think of an answer that wouldn't make Gerard curious.'

The giggles continued until their class line and first bell. They then silently followed Hans Rathmann through the corridor.

It had been a 24-hour news vacuum for Ingrid. Life in Erfurt had continued as Soviet and American leaders decided the fate of the world. The peace stick had offered comfort and reassurance of another day for Khrushchev and Kennedy to settle their differences. She found herself waiting for Herr Schumann's arrival without the trepidation of the previous four school days.

Second bell rang; Herr Schumann appeared in the arch to the classroom. He paused, which caused a flutter in Ingrid's chest. That's what he had done last Tuesday before dropping his bombshell. Ingrid looked at his eyes; they were downcast. She looked at Sylvie; had the peace stick failed?

Herr Schumann licked his lips, then marched to the front of the class. He turned, squared his shoulders. To Ingrid, that was a contrast from his browbeaten demeanour of the previous week.

Rathmann jumped to his feet to complete their ritual of obedience.

Herr Schumann smiled and waited for the Pioneers leader to resume his seat.

'Good morning, 7A.' He stood with hands behind his back. 'Last week I had to deliver some of the most shocking news that any of you could ever expect.'

There were murmurs of assent from many tables.

'I know it was distressing, but I thought it was important for you to understand the dire consequences of what was happening in Cuba.'

Schumann paused.

Ingrid found herself on the edge of her seat. What had happened on Sunday?

'I'm pleased with the way you all coped. In fact, I was proud of the analytical thinking that many applied – ways to survive a nuclear attack, solutions for the United Nations diplomats. You were all focused on the future and survival. That is commendable.'

Ingrid found Sylvie's hand sliding into hers yet again. The contact was reassuring for both.

'You will be extremely pleased to know that, after a dark week, I can share better news this morning. The Soviet leader, Nikita Khrushchev, has been in constant communication with the American president, John Kennedy, during the weekend. They have found a solution to the problem in Cuba.

'The United States has promised it will not invade Cuba and the naval blockade will be lifted. With no threat to Fidel Castro and his people, the Soviets say they can remove their missiles and dismantle the launch sites. That is a practical solution to the problem.'

Herr Schumann smiled.

'You don't have to worry about B-52 bombers or nuclear missiles. The threat of World War III has passed – for the moment.'

The cheering from Class 7A could be heard around the 31st Oberschule.

Tuesday, November 8, 2016

Erfurt, GERMANY

'Did you know the American generals wanted to bomb the Cuban missile sites and then invade *after* they reached an agreement with the Russians on the Sunday?'

Kurt Neubert looked at the stunned faces of his dining companions and the late arrival, Sylvie Fuchs, née Witzenhause.

The slender, ash-blonde woman had aged gracefully in Ingrid's opinion; Sylvie's personality had not lost its sparkle.

Kurt continued.

'Herr Schumann was too optimistic when he told us the threat was finished on the Monday. The American military didn't trust the Soviets. We were celebrating that a nuclear apocalypse was averted but the generals wanted to load up the planes with enough bombs to wipe Cuba off the planet.'

'How do you know that?' Sylvie had arrived part way through Ingrid's peace stick story. Professionally, Sylvie had never ventured far from Erfurt after graduating as a teacher. She balanced that career with being a doctor's wife, mother to three kinder and Oma to four. Much of Sylvie's teaching life had been spent at what was the 31st Oberschule before the fall of the Berlin Wall. She had never made it to Fiji.

Ingrid wanted some private time with her old friend to learn more about the years since leaving Erfurt for Berlin and, eventually, New Zealand. That would have to wait; the group was still focused on one of the most momentous events in their lives – indeed, of the past half century. Had the world avoided returning to the nuclear precipice because of the fear generated in 1962?

Kurt focused on Sylvie as she had missed his early insights.

'Robert Kennedy wrote a book about the crisis. He was one of the

President's confidantes inside the White House decision bubble long before they told the world the danger we were facing.'

Kurt emptied his red wine and held the glass towards Gerard.

'The book reveals so much that we never knew at the time. We had every right to be worried about nuclear annihilation — the men who had to find a solution were terrified they could not control events.'

Gerard Mueller topped up the men's wine glasses. The women had ordered more tea. The restaurant was almost empty, but the schoolfriends were not ready to leave.

'What didn't they tell us?' Thorsten asked.

'It took a long time to learn the contents of the letters between Khrushchev and Kennedy. The Americans were embarrassed they were being outflanked by the Russians.

'The CIA didn't cover itself in glory with the Bay of Pigs invasion in 1961. Their perspective on Cuba was still flawed when Khrushchev was ready to outwit them again the following year. They believed there had been about 10,000 Soviet troops in Cuba. There were 43,000! A second invasion would have been another catastrophic failure.'

Ingrid could see Kurt loved sharing this knowledge. The anxiety generated by the Cuban Crisis always returned whenever the world reached a new flashpoint. It showed how quickly confrontations could spill out of control; there were implications for every nation, not just the antagonists.

Common sense in Moscow and Washington had finally prevailed. The world moved on after the sites were dismantled and the missiles removed. A permanent hotline between Moscow and Washington was established to streamline communications in emergencies. Berlin remained the longest-running source of irritation in the East-West power struggle until the wall was breached in 1989.

Kurt's assessment on how close they were to disaster brought reminders of the angst that had been dormant in Ingrid for many years.

'The missiles the Soviets sneaked into Cuba had nuclear warheads. The Americans thought they were being shipped when the sites were completed. They also didn't know Soviet commanders in Cuba had authorisation to launch the missiles if they lost communications with Moscow during an attack.'

Kurt looked at each face in turn. 'For 13 days Kennedy was pressured by his military commanders to bomb the missile sites and then invade. If he had followed their advice and attacked, we would not be here at the Gildehaus tonight.'

Nobody talked for almost a minute.

Gerard tried to lighten the mood. 'Would someone have opened a cave restaurant by now? Roast bear du jour?'

Thorsten Koehler laughed. 'We'd probably still be living in the tunnels under the citadel.'

'You were listening to my story,' Ingrid said.

'Of course.'

Petra shifted in her seat. 'I'm impressed you and Sylvie were so proactive. The rest of us did nothing but worry – you two worked out a survival plan. And created a glücksbringer.'

'A peace stick.' Gerard smiled.

'What happened to it?' Petra asked.

Ingrid looked at Sylvie and shrugged.

'We left it there,' Ingrid said. 'It gave us hope and comfort during a terrible time. We believed that whatever luck it created might keep the world safe.'

Kurt sniffed. 'A stick in a school wall – as much value as prayer. In my opinion.'

Sylvie said, 'Have there been any nuclear attacks between the Russians and Americans since 1962, Kurt?'

Ingrid could still tell when Sylvie was indignant, even after more than 40 years of separation.

'No. But the nuclear arsenals have expanded massively. Nine countries have them now. They're all still on a hair trigger. We're still only moments away from destruction. The Doomsday Clock was set at 12 minutes in 1963. Now we're down to three minutes until the apocalypse.'

'But nobody has launched a nuclear attack since Japan in 1945.'

'No,' Kurt said.

'Well, who can say the peace stick hasn't done its job?'

Kurt raised a hand to question the logic. 'It's nonsense. You have no evidence.'

'And you can't prove that it didn't work.'

Gerard, Thorsten and Petra smiled. Ingrid recalled similar feisty encounters between Kurt and Sylvie in their senior classes. Herr Schumann would have enjoyed the renewed debate. Gerard said he had died in the south of France in 1979.

'Let's call it a draw, Kurt and Sylvie.' Gerard waved for the bill. 'I've got a surgery full of teeth to fill in the morning.'

A few minutes later they were hugging and kissing farewell in the Fischmarkt. Ingrid's hotel was within walking distance; it would take her past Sylvie's home on the Krämerbrücke. They looped arms, just like their school days, as they waved their friends away in a taxi. Another slowed; Sylvie signalled for the driver to stop.

'I thought you lived just up the street.' Ingrid gestured towards the bride, which, like the Altstadt, had undergone major gentrification since she had left the city. She was looking forward to peering in boutique and auction room windows as they chatted on the walk home.

'I do, but we can go there a bit later. I want to take you back to our old school.'

'Now? In the middle of the night? Has it changed that much since we were students in Herr Schumann's class?'

'No. Very little has changed. I taught there for 25 years. And that's why I think we should go now. Come on.'

Sylvie opened the rear door of the taxi and ushered her friend inside. Ingrid complied with a laugh.

'The elementary school on Schwemmbach, please.'

Ingrid settled into the comfortable leather seat. 'Was it different being a teacher at a place where you were a student?'

'Yes – after 1989. We weren't restrained by the policies of the Socialist Unity Party or fear of the Stasi.'

Ingrid enjoyed the swift tour of the old town. Most buildings had undergone some renovation or refurbishment. Erfurt retained its medieval character yet sat comfortably in the 21st Century. Tourists were taking pictures of the ancient architecture as they strolled the late-night streets.

'If I had a euro for every photo that has been taken of our home on the river, we could have retired 20 years ago,' Sylvie said.

'Who would ever have dreamed that you would end up living on the Merchants' Bridge. Does it get too busy for you?'

'Only in June, July, August … and September. Sometimes October.

Occasionally after a heavy Christmas snowfall. Tourists can never get enough photos.' Sylvie laughed.

The taxi crossed Yuri Gagarin Ring, seeking wider boulevards to the south.

'You never told me about your mother's Yuri Gagarin stamp and the swastika. What happened to it?'

'I've still got it, back in New Zealand.'

'Did you get anybody to assess whether it was real or valuable?'

'An Auckland philatelist was dubious – he offered me $10.'

Sylvie giggled. It sounded the same as their school days. 'I bet he would have sold it again on the international market for a fortune.'

'Probably. I never believed Yuri Gagarin was a Nazi sympathiser. He's the most famous person I ever met. Remember, I shook his hand during his visit to Erfurt in 1963? I'll never forget that day. He made me feel so special.'

Soon the taxi was stopping outside the entrance to their old school. The wall was still there.

Sylvie spoke to the driver. 'Can you please wait? We won't be long.'

Ingrid was grateful they would not have to find another taxi in the suburbs at that hour.

'Come on. I'm sure you're curious why I've dragged you back here.'

The November chill reminded Ingrid that Martini was just a couple of days away. She had timed her visit to coincide. She tightened the belt on her woollen jacket.

They stood side by side in front of what had been the 31st Oberschule. The utilitarian grey concrete had been brightened with a new render or paint; it was hard to tell in the darkness. There was enough light from a streetlamp to see the bricks that hid their peace stick 54 years previously. The wall had been treated to a paint job, possibly several since their school days. Ingrid looked closer; the hole was still there. She turned to Sylvie, who had turned on the flashlight on her mobile phone.

'Would we have ever dreamed of cordless phones with cameras, computers and lights?'

'The most I wanted was something to do my mathematics homework.'

Sylvie illuminated the wall. 'Check the hole.'

'Why? Do you think the peace stick is still there after all these years?'

'Go on. Have a look.'

Ingrid bent over; there was something about a centimetre inside. Her heart fluttered as she tried to extract it. Was it possible their symbol of hope had endured? It was difficult to get a grip; her fingers were not as nimble as a 13-year-old's.

'Here. Try these tweezers.'

Ingrid grasped the object. Within a few seconds it was being slowly withdrawn. The sudden elation that it might be the peace stick plummeted. It was not anything like the glücksbringer they had employed to save the world from nuclear destruction. It was wooden, like something used in a craft workshop. And it was longer than the original.

Ingrid held it up, disappointed. 'It's not the peace stick.'

'No. It's a modern version.'

'It looks like a piece of dowel.'

'You have been in New Zealand a long time. We call it dübel.' Sylvie shone the torch. 'What do you see now?'

Ingrid saw a fine print along the shaft. There was another flutter when she read the words at the top.

Ingrid & Sylvie's Peace Stick. Cuba 1962.

'Did you do this after I left Erfurt?'

'Not quite. Turn the dübel and read on.'

Below Cuba was 'Doomsday Clock 1974 – 9 minutes'. Beside it was 'DC 1980 – 7 minutes'. Then 'DC 1981 – 4 minutes'. The final entry on the same line was 'DC 1984 – 3 minutes'. Ingrid turned the wood; the entries continued up to the present year, recording the advance and retreat of the minute hand towards the feared apocalypse at midnight. The 2016 Doomsday Clock was at a perilous three minutes.

'I don't understand,' Ingrid said.

'You know the Doomsday Clock is a universal indicator of our vulnerability to catastrophe?'

'Yes.'

'And that, these days, the clock includes all global existential threats, such as climate change.'

'Yes.' Ingrid waved the stick like a wand. 'I understand all that. What I don't understand is what this stick is doing in our wall. Who did it?'

'I did. And some students. Young Germans terrified about world events beyond their control. They wanted a future – the same as we did in 1962.' Sylvie took the modern peace stick from her friend's hand. 'You started it. I ensured the legacy survived.'

'How?'

'I couldn't forget how close we were to a catastrophe. When it was confirmed that the last missiles were removed in November, I came back to check if it was still in place.'

'Was it?'

'Yes. It looked almost as fresh as the day it became the peace stick. I removed it – temporarily.'

The taxi driver tooted. Sylvie held up one finger.

'There was something magical about it. I felt it should be a permanent glücksbringer. I wrapped a small message around it – "Ingrid & Sylvie's Peace Stick. Cuba 1962".'

'Just like what's written on that replacement.'

Sylvie nodded.

'So ... other students found our peace stick over the years and understood the significance.'

'Yes. I came to teach here in 1974. You had left Erfurt; I hadn't been near the school for years. Imagine my surprise when I checked the wall and found the peace stick.'

'My goodness. What condition was it in – had students found it by then?'

'It was still in remarkable shape. Drier, and with three new notations.'

'Students had been using it as a glücksbringer, just like us? What did they put on the peace stick?'

'The first one was Israel 1967.'

Ingrid had to think hard – armed conflicts around the world sprang up like mushrooms.

'Wasn't the Six-Day War in '67 – Israel against Egypt, Syria, Jordan, Iraq, Lebanon?'

'Israel was believed to have nuclear weapons, so we all held our breath.'

'The Arab-Israeli war was over in less than a week. I wonder why a student thought it was as serious as the Cuba Crisis.'

'Because the Soviets were allies of Egypt and the Americans have always backed the Israelis. I guess the students were worried it might escalate if either intervened.'

Ingrid nodded. 'What was the next war?'

'India-Pakistan 1971. Bangladesh was formed out of the ashes. Again, the world wondered what the Soviets and Americans would do.'

'What was the third notation?'

'India 1974. They became the latest official nuclear power a few months before I arrived here as a teacher.'

Ingrid took back the peace stick and rolled it under the light. More years, the minute hand advancing and retreating according to the Bulletin of Atomic Scientists' assessment of new conflicts and the growing list of nuclear powers.

Ingrid thought of the most prominent conflicts that had impacted on the clock's movements. Iraq's invasion of Kuwait in 1990. The attacks on New York's Twin Towers in 2001 that led to the continuing war in Afghanistan. The US-led invasion of Iraq in 2003 on spurious claims that Saddam Hussein had weapons of mass destruction. The civil war in Syria in 2011 that spurred the growth of the ISIS caliphate. History repeating itself, many deaths, cities destroyed, the superpowers involved, the nuclear club expanding – but no use of nuclear weapons.

'Why did you change from recording the crises to the Doomsday Clock?'

'To simplify matters. There were too many conflicts to fit on the peace stick. I moved to the clock in 1984 when it was three minutes to 12. My last entry was in 1998 – Pakistan had joined the nuclear club and the clock was at nine minutes.'

'Did you change it to this?' Ingrid held the dübel.

'No. I worried I might destroy the good luck. Our peace stick was deteriorating by the mid-'90s. I guess someone changed it after 2002 when the clock moved to seven minutes. I like that they created a permanent homage to young hopes.'

Ingrid was delighted the peace stick had endured, that the following generations from their school had taken a chance on childish faith. 'How often do you come back to check?'

'A few weeks after the atomic scientists shift the clock.'

'Has the movement always been noted?'

'Every time.'

Ingrid laughed. 'I bet you tried to find a student here at the wall updating the peace stick; no junior Stasi agents or kinder reading comics to worry about.'

A shake of the head. 'It would have been interesting to talk to one. Why they removed the Israeli, India and Pakistan notes, but not Cuba. Maybe they thought the tribute should belong to you and me, Ingrid, for being the first.'

Another toot came from the taxi. The engine started.

'That driver has no appreciation for history,' Sylvie said. 'I think we had better replace the peace stick. The Americans are still embroiled in Afghanistan, the Syrian war shows no sign of ending. The world needs all the help it can get.'

Ingrid thought about the date as the peace stick was slotted into place. 'You know what day it is, Sylvie?'

'November 8 – Martini is in two days. It's so much bigger than when you lived in Erfurt. The Domplatz is filled with markets all day. Thousands still walk to the square with their candles. You have to stay to hear the Gloriosa ring out again at six o'clock.'

Ingrid waved off the enthusiasm. 'Of course I'll be here. But I meant today.' They turned for the taxi, in step like their schooldays. 'You know they will be counting the votes soon in the American presidential election.'

'I haven't paid it much attention. A former president's wife against a real estate mogul and television presenter. Hilary Clinton directed Barack Obama's foreign policy as US secretary of state. She spent eight years with her husband in the White House. What political experience does Donald Trump have?'

'None. But he's tapped into a lot of bitterness in the American heartland. They don't like what politicians are doing in Washington. Trump is a real chance to be win the White House.'

Sylvie and Ingrid stopped, looked back to where the peace stick was doing silent and secret service for the fate of mankind.

'I'm glad the peace stick has survived.' Ingrid said. 'There have been dozens of conflicts, yet somehow the world has avoided a thermonuclear war. Can you imagine the dangers ahead should Trump win the election?'

THE END

About The Author

Stephen Johnson is an Australian-born writer, TV producer, kayaker and traveller who now plots crime fiction from his garret overlooking the Tamaki River in Auckland.

His debut novel *Tugga's Mob* was inspired by three seasons working as a tour guide and driver on double decker buses around Europe in the '80s. It was a finalist in the 2020 Ngaio Marsh Awards for Best First Novel.

The second crime fiction novel, *Boxed,* was published in November 2021and is set in the world of greyhound racing and the Melbourne media. Both books are published by Clan Destine Press.

www.stephenjohnsonauthor.com

www.clandestinepress.net

Manufactured by Amazon.ca
Bolton, ON

29532345R00152